KRYMZYN

by

BC Powell

book one
The Journals of Krymzyn

Text copyright 2014 © BC Powell
All Rights Reserved

Published by BC Powell
bcpowellauthor.com

Cover design and artwork by Ravven
ravven.com

First Edition

ISBN 13: 978-0990500711
ISBN 10: 0990500713

Library of Congress Control Number: 2014910640

For my sons,

Quinn, Evan, and Ryan.

I love you guys.

Special Acknowledgments

To Amy, for reading and supporting my efforts, even through the horrible first drafts. To Pat Thomas, whose initial critique and notes helped me find the path to story balance. To Mickey Reed, for the comprehensive edit, encouragement, and dedication to help make this project the best it can be. To Amanda Krause, for the tedious final proofread. And to Ravven, your cover design is truly beautiful.

The Infinite Plane of Krymzyn

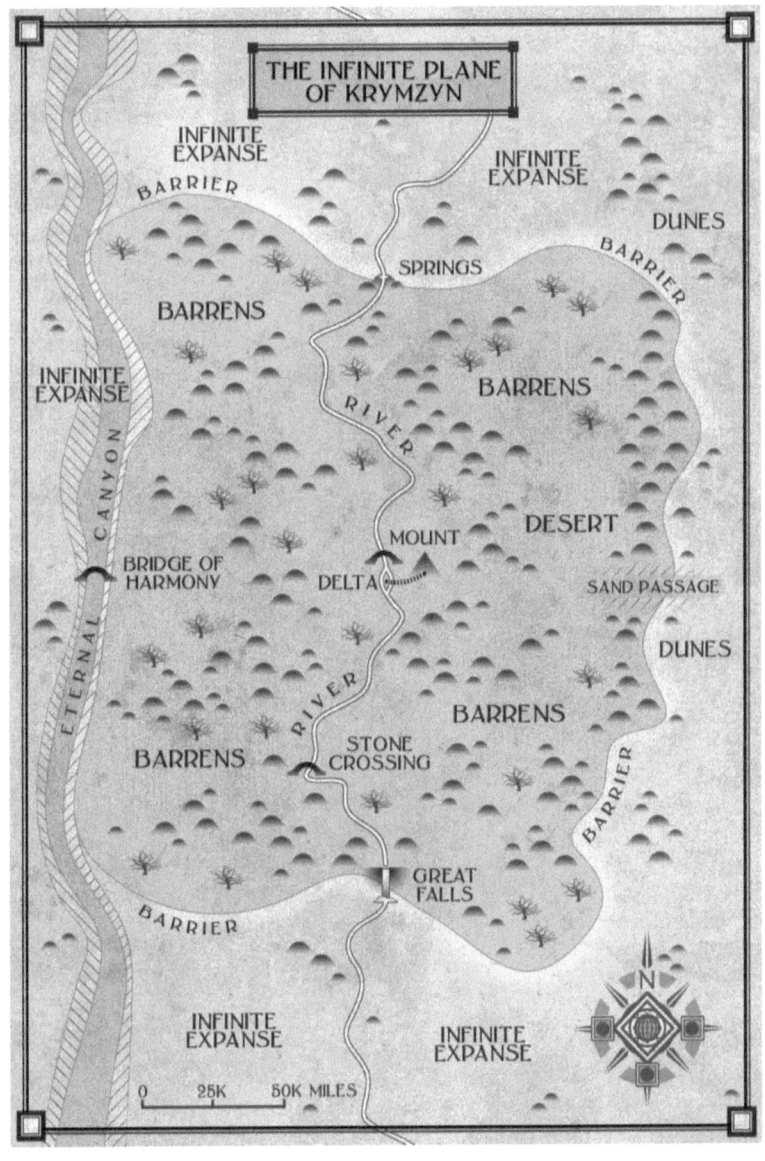

The Delta of Krymzyn

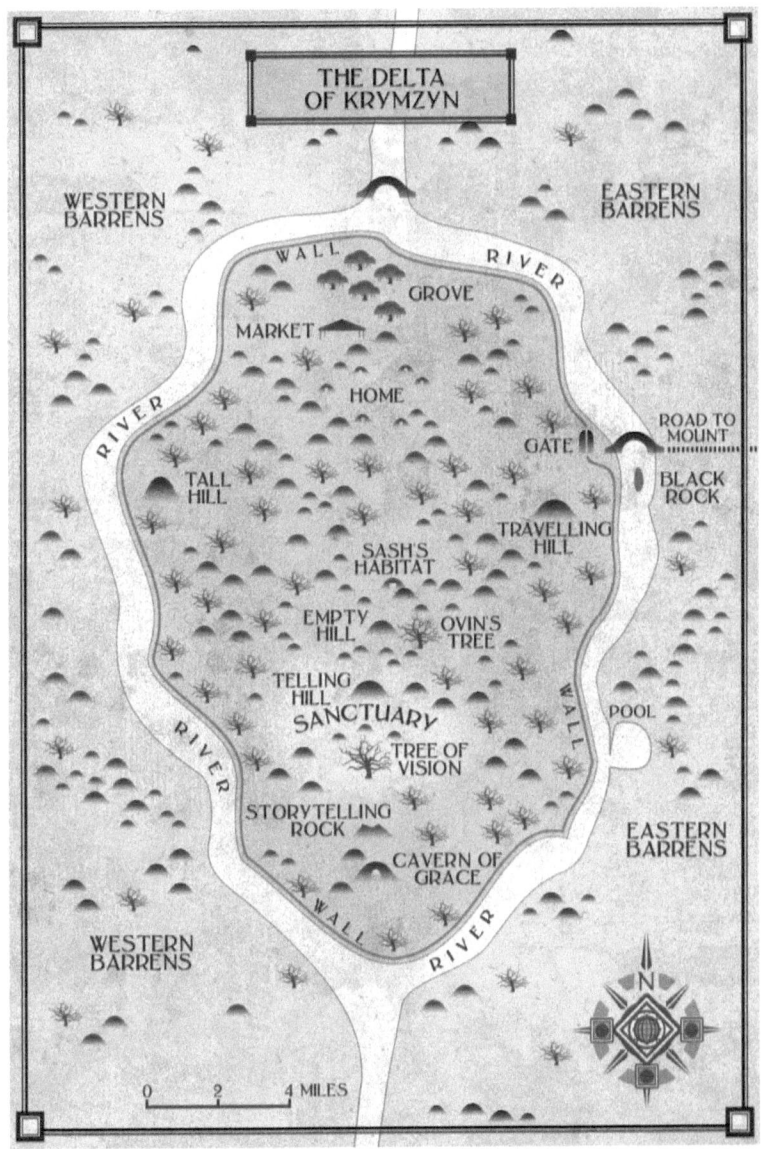

KRYMZYN

Prologue

The girl's eyes rise to static gray billows overhead. The solemn expression on her face never changes as she studies rays of scarlet and orange that cut through the clouds. Darkness isn't near, she immediately senses. Her Ritual won't be interrupted, but the Tree already knew that when it summoned her to Sanctuary.

Standing at the meadow's edge, she watches vibrant yellow leaves pass through her vision. Although there's no breeze, outstretched branches calmly sway in front of her. She lowers her eyes to the monstrous, ancient Tree centered in the crimson field. Unlike the sustaining trees that sleep when it's light, the Tree of Vision is always alert, forever in motion.

She turns her back to the Tree, contemplative as she scans hundreds of amber eyes focused on her. Statuesque as they stand on the red hills surrounding the meadow, clad in the same black pants that she wears, sleeveless, black shirts hugging their bodies; all in the grace of Krymzyn are here to witness her Ritual.

Black hair laced with shining color drapes the stoic faces that gaze upon her. Her color, her purpose, will be revealed in her own dark waves when the Ritual is complete.

The girl's eyes stop when they reach the other thirteen children of the Delta, each standing beside a Keeper. One boy scowls at her with a noticeably different expression than any other face in the crowd. His anger, she knows, is the result of his not being chosen for the Ritual.

Despite being taller than she, his body more mature and developed than her own, he wasn't given the sign. The muscles in her lean frame, hints of pubescent curves just beginning to show, sharpen in reaction to his glare. It's wrong of him to express anger, an extreme emotion. He should feel honor from attending the Ritual. But he's always been strange, distant. She knows he'll prove to have a purpose soon—she's been shown the vision—but his struggle with the Tree will be fierce.

A branch of the Tree rears back, sails across the meadow, and slams into an enormous bell. As a deafening clang reverberates through the hills, the girl glances up at light gleaming from silvery metallic curves. The bell, taller than any person in Krymzyn, swings from the arm of a towering steel pole.

"Why do you stand before us?" a woman's voice bellows.

The girl turns to face the seven Disciples. The woman who spoke, the tallest of the Disciples, steps forward from the center of the row. All seven stand erect, bright orange strands flaming against black hair, focused on her with reverent faces.

"To seek my purpose in Krymzyn," the girl quietly replies.

"Have you been given the sign?" the tallest Disciple

asks.

The girl holds her fists out in front her, opens both hands, and turns them up to the sky. Brilliant golden light radiates from her palms.

"Show Krymzyn the sign," the Disciple commands.

Raising her hands high over her head, the girl displays the luminous glow for all to see.

"Never has one so small been chosen," the Disciple whispers just loud enough for the girl to hear.

The girl respectfully bows her head in response while lowering her hands to her sides. Beside the row of Disciples waits her Keeper. She crosses the grass to the tall, muscular man with streaks of flaxen gold in his short hair. As he crouches in front of her, she looks thoughtfully into his eyes.

"Remember, the Tree only reveals what's inside you," the Keeper softly counsels the girl, "but you already know what's inside you, don't you? You already know what your Ritual will reveal."

"I'm grateful to you and the other Keepers for your guidance," she says with heartfelt sincerity.

The girl steps away from the Keeper and slowly walks around the perimeter of the Tree's limbs. Branches now slash violently through the air, her path just out of their reach. The last child to be called for the Ritual of Purpose met death. The girl watched from a hilltop, standing with the other children, as one branch clutched him tightly in its grasp. Another limb hammered against the side of his head, crushing his skull.

That boy had no purpose. The girl, unlike anyone else in Krymzyn, had known that before he was ever called to the

Tree. Just as she knows from a vision only she was shown that her jet-black mane will soon glimmer with scarlet. Her purpose as a Hunter of Krymzyn will be revealed in her hair. For the girl, the only unknown is what she'll be shown of the future.

The girl stops walking and stares at the Tree. She could climb to the top of the hill behind her, run back down, and blend her light. She's mastered the ability that only the seven Travelers possess, each of them immensely faster than all others who dwell in the Delta. Curling her toes in the red blades of grass, she looks down at her bare feet and decides that blending her light would be an arrogant display.

She lifts her face to the Tree and marches directly towards the massive trunk. As soon as she's in reach of the branches, a mighty limb coils high in the air, takes aim, and whips in her direction. In an instant, she visualizes every move she'll need to make to reach the trunk unharmed.

I dive under the first limb. As a second smashes to the ground beside me, I roll across the grass. After jumping to my feet, I break into a sprint and leap high over a limb swinging at my legs. I tuck into a flip past another branch. When my feet touch the ground, I charge to the trunk.

The girl sees it, understands each action as though it's already happened, but instead, she stops and stands perfectly still.

The lashing branch carves the air in front of her, but the girl doesn't flinch. As yellow leaves whisk across her face and arms, the limb freezes just inches from her body. Gasps of shock cascade from the hilltops to the meadow. No one, the people know, has ever consumed the sap of this Tree without first facing a brutal, often bloody challenge from the muscular branches.

The girl reaches her arms around the chiseled bark and cradles the branch to her chest. With an ethereal passion in her eyes, she lays a gentle cheek on the limb.

"I pledge my life to protect all that sustains and nurtures our balance," she whispers.

Silently, she stands motionless, clutching the branch to her beating heart, face pressed to lustrous carmine bark.

The branch slowly pulls away from her grasp. Her slender fingers caress the wood as it slips from her touch. Every limb of the Tree rises into the air and peacefully waves back and forth. With her head bowed, the girl strides to the center of the meadow.

When she reaches the base of the Tree, she drops to her knees, eternal roots dug into the ground beneath her. After extending both hands outward, the girl rests her palms against the trunk. She leans her face forward, opens her mouth, and presses her lips to the bark. Sap flows onto her tongue, freely offered by the Tree, until she swallows.

A burst of light surrounds her, the spectrum of color blinding to those who watch. As the rays engulf the girl, she's taken to the Vision of the Future meant only for her.

I see my own body, more mature than I am now. I lie on a steep slab of black stone in the middle of the river. Rain pours from the sky. Rapids surge by my sides. Huge waves crash against the edges of the rock and splash high above me. I'm unconscious. No, I've met death.

A young man kneels over me. His hair is strange—not black, no color of purpose to define him, just murky brown.

Eyes a color different than any in Krymzyn gaze down at my face. Dark-blue eyes, the same color as the needles of steel trees that grow on the Mount, focused on me with intense caring.

He touches the fingers of one hand to a gash in his wrist, bathes them in his own blood, and rubs them inside my mouth. Leaning over my face, he covers my lips with his. After bolting upright, he presses both of his hands on the center of my chest. He frantically pumps them against my body while I lie dead. Why is he doing this?

"You have to come back!" he shouts.

The desperate pleading in his voice stings me. I don't see the way he looks at me. I feel him inside. Strange emotions overwhelm me, feelings I've never known—feelings foreign to Krymzyn. I have no words to define these feelings. They drift away as my Vision of the Future fades, but something new has awakened inside me.

Chapter 1

"Chase," my mother said to me, "the nurse wants to ask you about your headaches and what happened in school today."

Sitting at the kitchen table, I took the phone from her outstretched hand. As I held it to my ear, Mom hovered over me with worry lines wrinkling her forehead and obvious concern in her brown eyes.

"Hi," I said.

"Hi, Chase," the nurse replied. "I just want to get a little more detail about the headaches you're having, especially the one today."

"Sure."

"How long have you been having the headaches?" she asked.

"Almost two weeks," I answered, "but they've been really bad the last few days."

I heard the faint sound of pencil writing on paper before she spoke again. "Do you feel nauseated during them?"

"Sometimes," I said. "More in the last day or two."

"Can you describe what happened in school this afternoon?"

"I was just sitting at my desk when the headache started. This one spread really fast, like from the back of my neck to my temples. I started shaking a little. Then it was like a strobe light went off in my brain."

"Did you lose consciousness?" the nurse asked with a much greater sense of urgency.

"No, I didn't pass out. I just heard kind of faraway sounds and saw weird things."

"What do you mean 'weird things'?"

"Storm clouds, a field of red grass, and then just really bright light."

I didn't say, "And a girl about my age, twelve, kneeling in front of a huge tree and surrounded by streams of light." It just sounded too crazy.

"How long did you see those things?" she asked.

"Just a few seconds," I answered. "As soon they ended, I went to the school nurse. I told her my head hurt so bad I felt like I was going to throw up. She gave me an ice pack and called my mom."

"How are you feeling now?"

"Better," I said. "Kind of a dull pain, but nothing like earlier."

"Thank you, Chase. I'm sorry you're going through this. Can you put your mom back on?"

I handed the phone back to my mother.

"So you don't think I should take him to the emergency room," Mom said after listening to the nurse for several seconds. She nodded her head in response to something the nurse said. "Thank you. We'll be there first thing in the morning."

Mom hung up the phone and let out a long sigh of relief. As she turned to me, she tucked strands of blondish-brown hair behind her ears.

"What did she say?" I asked.

"Probably adolescent migraines," Mom replied. "She said they're not uncommon in boys close to puberty."

"What about the things I saw?"

"She said we'll talk to the doctor about what you saw, but brief hallucinations can be part of migraines. Don't worry, Chase. We'll get this figured out." She leaned down and wrapped her arms around me. "I called your dad to tell him you wouldn't be at practice. He said he'd keep it short and get home as soon as he can."

Dad had coached my little league team since I started T-ball at the age of five. Even though it meant staying up late to finish work he'd brought home with him, not to mention fighting Los Angeles traffic in a mad dash to reach practices on time, he treasured the time he spent with his children. On the afternoons we didn't have baseball, he helped out with my little sister's soccer team.

After a long embrace with Mom, I walked to the family room. I had to navigate through dolls and miniature clothing scattered across the floor. As was often the case, my little sister Ally sat in the middle of the mess. I made my way through the clutter and flopped down on the sofa.

My phone had beeped several times since I'd left school. I quickly read the text messages from friends asking how I was feeling. Although I wanted to answer them, the headache was gradually coming back. I decided to reply later, set my phone on the coffee table, and mindlessly tried to watch a game show on television.

"How's your head?" Ally asked.

"Better, thanks," I answered.

"I saw Connor when Mom was getting you from the nurse's office. He told me you were so pale in class you looked like a ghost."

Connor had been my best friend since preschool.

"I was kind of freaked out," I replied.

"I'm glad you're feeling better now," she grinned.

"Thanks, Ally. I am too."

We all attended a small K–8 private school located in the San Fernando Valley, not far from our home in Sherman Oaks. News and gossip always spread fast in our school, even something as trivial as me spacing out in the middle of social studies and getting the shakes. I was sure by the time school let out that the story had been exaggerated into me crawling across the ceiling of my classroom like a demon in a horror film.

A handful of smooth, golden blond fur sprouted between my fingers when Casey shoved his head under my hand. With his nose pressed against my leg, he encouraged me to scratch the back of his neck with a wonderful, goofy smile that golden retrievers always seemed to have on their faces.

"Casey! Bad dog!" Ally griped after his tail swished into a blond-haired plastic figure.

He ignored her condemnation while I tried to ignore the rubber mallets gradually pounding harder inside my head. Some guy was spinning a wheel on the TV screen, and I was amazed he'd wasted money on a *U*. I mean, my sister could probably figure out what the board said, and she was only nine.

Without warning, the headache exploded. Pressure in the back of my head swelled, stabbing pain ripped through my skull, and my temples throbbed from within. Uncontrollable shaking spread through my arms and legs. When images on the TV screen burst into flashes of light, I tried to scream for my mom. The sound was strangled in my throat, only a hoarse whisper coming out.

*   *   *

I stand on a hill. The air around me is perfectly still. No warmth, no cold, no temperature at all, and no movement anywhere. Absolute silence encompasses me, except for the sound of my own sharp breath. My mind races, implodes trying to figure out where I am and how I got here.

My eyes widen as they rise to the sky. Enormous storm clouds, huge billows of dark gray, go on and on as far as I can see. It's exactly like the sky before a thunderstorm, except none of the clouds are moving. Orange and red rays slicing through the edges of the clouds cast a scarlet aura over the countryside.

Low, rolling hills blanketed by rich, crimson grass stretch to the horizon. I don't see buildings anywhere, no bushes or flowers, and nothing moving in the air. A few trees are scattered across the landscape, but there's nothing else to obstruct the expanse of hills. Even though I feel like I'm standing inside a surreal fluorescent painting under an ultraviolet light, I know this is real. Too real.

A huge old oak tree grows in the center of a meadow in front of me. Sculpted bark on the massive trunk, dark brown with a hint of red, seems to shine with an almost metallic luster. Not a single branch or twig on the weathered and worn monstrosity moves. Blazing red leaves, not fading from age or brittle like autumn leaves, but fresh and alive, hang in the stagnant air.

Several of the giant branches spread out so far that their ends droop to the ground. They look like they're reaching across the field in search of something. The smooth lines that crease the limbs remind me of muscles in an arm, flexed and tense.

A creature leaps over a ridge at the bottom of the hill—a girl, I'm stunned to see when I focus on her. Sleek and graceful, she lands in a crouch with her back facing me. Long, wavy black hair with dazzling streaks of red falls from the air around her, floats over her shoulders, and flows down her back. I know the color is real, not dyed like some of the girls in my school with temporary strands of purple or blue or green.

As she stands upright, I realize she's my height. Lean with toned muscles, she wears tight black pants, a sleeveless black shirt, and nothing else—not even shoes. A long, metallic spear with sharp points on both ends is tightly clutched in one of her hands. Her smooth, porcelain skin seems to reflect the light from around her.

She spins to face me. Like a startled animal in the wild, fierce and alert, the girl locks her huge amber eyes on mine.

Thick black lines trace her eyelids, instantly reminding me of a tiger or cheetah. The nostrils in her small, straight nose flare out from her diamond-shaped face when she breathes, and her blood red lips tighten.

I'm mesmerized by her face as she glares at me. She's beautiful and terrifying and sad and ferocious all at the same time, and it hurts like a gut-wrenching blow to my stomach to look at her. Or maybe it's not pain, but awe.

"Hey!" I timidly call out. "Where am I?"

"On the Empty Hill," the girl answers.

"No, I mean, like, what is this place?" I ask.

Our words delay after we speak them, momentarily pausing in the air before evaporating into my ears. My words are in English when they leave my mouth but transform into new, strange sounds I can still understand.

"Krymzyn," she replies.

When I hear the word "Krymzyn," I think of the color crimson, but I know it's spelled differently—K-r-y-m-z-y-n. That's the spelling I see in my mind after symbols, archaic runes of some kind, are separated, translated in the air, and then reassembled for me as a word I can comprehend.

"Do you know how I got here?" I yell down the hill.

She slowly walks to me without answering my question, mystifying amber eyes never leaving mine. There's no threat in her stride and her arms are relaxed, so I don't feel scared even though a spear is still dangling from her hand. When she stops in front of me, she squints at my eyes with a puzzled expression on her face.

"Why are you looking at me that way?" I ask.

"I've never seen blue eyes," she answers, "except in my

Vision . . ." She shakes her head and looks down at the ground.

"Except in your what?"

Her eyes spring back to mine. "I shouldn't speak with you," she says sternly. "Only Disciples speak with Tellers when they're here."

"Am I a Teller?" I ask.

"You must be if you're in Krymzyn, although it's odd you arrived on the Empty Hill instead of the Telling Hill. You also look too young to be a Teller."

"What's a Teller?"

"A visitor from another plane," she explains. "Tellers come to Krymzyn to share stories of their worlds with the Disciples."

I don't understand her answer, but something tickles my feet, so I glance down. My face scrunches with confusion when I realize I'm barefoot, blades of red grass between my toes, the shoes I was wearing at home gone. Black leathery pants are in place of my jeans, exactly like the ones the girl has on. Instead of my polo, I'm wearing a sleeveless black shirt made of the same material as the pants.

"Do you know how I got these clothes on?" I ask, returning my attention to the girl.

"Krymzyn dressed you in our manner when you arrived."

Although she's answering my questions, the answers don't make sense to me. Her answers really just confuse me. But the pain that was blasting through my head is gone, I'm not shaking anymore, and I feel alert, like my senses are heightened in some way.

"My name's Chase." At this point, I'm not sure what else to say or ask.

"I'm called Sash."

"I like your name," I remark honestly. "It seems to fit you."

"Thank you," she says, but she doesn't smile. "Yours is nice as well, although it's odd to have a verb as a name."

"You'll have to take that one up with my _parents_."

The word "parents" stays in the air longer than the other words. Instead of transforming into a foreign sound I can still understand, the word dissipates into the atmosphere without translating.

"I'm sorry, but your word has no meaning here," she says.

"Don't you have _parents_?" I ask, realizing that she just heard the word for the first time.

Ignoring my question, she tilts her head to the side and peers into my eyes. Like beams of light passing through my vision and traveling deep to my core, I feel her inside me.

"You're in great pain in your world," she murmurs.

"Yeah, I am, but I don't feel it here. How do you know that?"

"You're not frightened being here," she says in a monotone voice, again not answering my question.

"No, I'm not," I reply, thinking that I should be scared, but I'm actually fascinated more than anything else. Confused, but fascinated. "Where I come from, they'll say this is just a hallucination."

"Do you think you're hallucinating?" she asks.

"No," I answer, shaking my head. "This seems real to

me."

Her eyes drift away from mine and focus on something behind me. When I turn my head to see what she's looking at, I jump backwards from shock.

Chapter 2

The freakiest-looking person I've ever seen races towards us from the next hill. I can't believe how fast the incredibly tall man is sprinting across the grass. His strides are long and fluid, black pants and sleeveless shirt clinging to the flow of his lean, muscular body. Long, ebony hair shimmering with orange flies in the air behind his head and bounces off his shoulders. One hand holds a long metal spear with glints of red flashing from the scratchy surface.

"Who is that?" A shiver runs through me, and now I feel scared.

"A Disciple," she replies evenly.

"What's he going to do to me?" I frantically ask, turning my face to her.

"You have nothing to fear," she says, a look of sympathetic reassurance in her eyes. "No one in the grace of Krymzyn will ever harm you."

I don't know why, but I believe her more than anything I've ever believed in my life. Her presence seems to surround and comfort me. It's not a conscious thought, not a calculated decision on my part. Just an overwhelming truth from deep inside—I'm safe with her.

I look forward to see where the Disciple is and jolt off the ground because his face is right in front of mine.

"You've come to Krymzyn to tell us stories of your plane," he announces, his words translating in the air before reaching my ears.

His long, thin face is blank and emotionless, but his eyes bore into my mind. I stare at infinite black pupils, the amber circles around them smoldering like hot coals in a fire.

"I don't . . . I don't know what you're talking about," I stammer, trembling even though I still feel like I'm safe with the girl beside me.

"Why do you shake?" he asks with a slight scowl.

His cheekbones, nose, and chin are chiseled and sharp, while dark red lips seem almost painted on his face.

"I-I'm nervous," I stutter.

When he stands upright, I have to look almost straight up to see his eyes. He's so tall and fit, with well-defined muscles lining his bare arms, that he could have stepped off the court at a Lakers game.

"Do you know why you've arrived on the Empty Hill instead of the Telling Hill?" he asks me.

"I have no idea how I got here or anything you're talking about," I say, trying to keep my voice steady. "What is this place?"

"An infinite plane of existence."

"I don't know what that means. What's a plane of existence?"

"Exactly what the words imply," he answers with mild irritation in his voice. "Krymzyn is an infinite plane where all things exist in perfect balance."

"Your answer isn't really an answer," I complain, feeling somewhat emboldened by his lack of hostility. "That's like you asking me my name and I say, 'My name is what my name is.'"

He glares at me for several seconds before speaking. "While that answer would certainly be valid to an extent, *Chase*, it's not the most specific answer you could provide."

Goose bumps spread across my flesh. I never told him my name, and he wasn't anywhere near us when I said it to the girl.

"How do you know my name?" I demand.

He continues to stare at me, his face expressionless, but his eyes speak loudly, saying, *"Don't challenge me again, boy. I know things you can't imagine in your wildest fantasies—or conceive of in your worst nightmares."*

"The atmosphere announces your name to the Disciples when you arrive," he finally says, "just as it allows us to communicate with one another despite our different languages."

I nod, deciding that his response is actually the first thing I've heard here that makes sense to me, considering the way our words delay in the air.

"Do you have any idea how I got here?" I ask.

"Tellers arrive from all other planes of existence," he answers. "We don't question how but simply accept that they do."

"I don't live on a plane," I say. "I live on a planet called Earth that's in a universe."

"Any world outside Krymzyn, a universe you may call it, is another plane of existence."

"Why am I here?" I ask.

The Disciple shakes his head, glances at Sash, and then frowns when he returns his eyes to me. "You appear too small to be a Teller," he grumbles. "When you depart, you shouldn't return unless you've grown much taller."

"Darkness is near," Sash interrupts, carefully studying the sky through narrowed eyes.

"That can't be," the Disciple insists. "Darkness won't fall with a Teller in our presence."

"Darkness is almost upon us," she says. "I must find my Mentor."

Sash quickly nods to me before sprinting down the hill in a powerful, sleek stride. As she races across the meadow, her breathtaking speed is more captivating than a wild cheetah in full pursuit of its prey.

The light begins to flicker, so I look up at the sky. Like a time-lapse nature film, the clouds start to move, but not across the sky. Tumultuous churning within the outline of each billow animates the darkening clouds. The red and orange rays recede until it's so dark that I can barely see. My entire body flinches when the Disciple grabs the back of my shirt and snaps his face in front of mine.

"We can't leave this hill during Darkness," he says sternly. "We're safely out of reach here."

A drop of rain splatters on top of my head. Several more splash onto my face and arms, but they don't feel wet. Silvery beads of water race down my skin and fall to the ground, just like mercury sliding across a sheet of angled glass. Then the raindrops fall harder until they sting my skin.

I jerk my head to a loud creaking sound in the meadow.

The bark on the tree begins to glow red. One of the branches on the ground whips high into the air and coils like the head of a snake ready to strike. I try to pull away from the Disciple, but he tightens his grasp on the back of my shirt.

"Stand still!" he orders.

As gusts of wind shrill through the valleys around us, the glaring limbs of the tree lash back and forth across the meadow at the foot of the hill. Peering through the dark, the Disciple scans the countryside. When he stops on something behind us, I twist my neck to look over my shoulder.

On top of the next hill, a hulking silhouette of a man rumbles through the storm. The Disciple releases my shirt, sinks to his knees, and jams his fingertips into the grass.

"All of Krymzyn," he growls, "a Murkovin is west of the Empty Hill." He rises from the ground and shoves me behind his back. "Stay behind me, boy!"

Lowering to a crouch, the Disciple swings his weapon up in front of him. I peek around his side at the crest of the other hill. The shadowy figure, huge and muscular with a spear in his hands, grinds to a stop on the crest. The creature aims his face in our direction.

I jump to my side when something bristles against my arm. Like a sudden blast of wind, a luminescent specter gleams past my side and streaks towards the ghoulish man. Before another beat of my heart pounds inside my chest, wisps of light dissipate from the air on the slope of the other hill. They form the body of a girl with a spear in the clutch of both hands and red glistening from long, dark hair.

Even though she's half the size of the beast, she charges up the hill at him. As she closes in, the brutish creature coils and cocks his weapon by his side. He lunges his spear at her, but she dips under the tip and drops to the slick grass. After sliding feet-first past his legs, she skids to a stop behind him.

She leaps to her feet, thrusts her weapon into his back, and drives the creature forward. Vaulting into the air, she uses her weight to help power him down to the ground. The moment her feet hit the grass, she rips her spear out of his back and viciously plunges it into his skull. A momentary burst of murky light shoots out of the beast's head and surrounds the shaft of the girl's weapon.

With her fingers still wrapped around the spear, the girl looks up from the corpse. As though they're a pair of flaming embers, her eyes sear through the dark.

"Sash," I whisper.

My brain suddenly pulses against the inside of my skull. As the world around me spins faster and faster, I close my eyes to fight the dizziness. Clamping my hands to the sides of my head, I topple to the ground.

*   *   *

"Mommy, Mommy, Mommy!" Ally shrieked over Casey's steady barking.

Footsteps pounded through the hall until my mother appeared in the doorway. Her eyes gaped open with terror when she saw me.

Drool fell from my lips, my body shook uncontrollably, and excruciating pain stabbed through my head. A bitter taste spread from my throat to my mouth. When my stomach convulsed, I launched bile all over my lap, hearing the same guy on TV spinning the wheel.

Chapter 3

My mother rushed me to a hospital emergency room. A doctor asked where my headaches started, how they spread through my head, and what I'd felt during my seizure. After several X-rays of my skull, I was kept in the hospital overnight.

I started the next day encased in a hollow metal tube for thirty minutes for an MRI. They took blood samples from me twice. Finally, they pumped me full of blue fluid to record a CT scan.

At the end of the day, I told a neurosurgeon what I'd seen and heard during the seizure. I told him how real everything had seemed while I was in Krymzyn. The doctor's diagnosis was a "hypnagogic hallucination."

"It was real," I said firmly to Dr. Baskin. "I know it wasn't a dream or a hallucination or anything like that."

I'd dreamt about the place during the night in the hospital, and being there had been nothing like the dream. When that tree had sprung to life and the man had grabbed me, it had felt as real as if my hand were just resting on a table and someone stabbed a knife through it. The dream had felt nothing like that.

"Tell me something, Chase," Dr. Baskin said. "Did you smell anything during the hallucination?"

"I don't know," I answered after a few seconds of thought. "Not that I remember."

"Was there any kind of flavor in your mouth that you noticed?" he asked.

I had to think again before answering. "Just vomit when I got back."

He held up a diagram of the human brain showing the stem attached to the upper spinal cord. "Touch the bump on the back of your skull," he said.

I placed my fingers on the back of my head and rubbed the small lump.

"That's your occipital bone," the doctor explained. "Just underneath that"—he pointed to the spot in the picture—"is where your brain stem attaches to your spinal cord. Impulses are sent from that area to your sensory nerves, and that's exactly where your tumor is.

"The tumor," he continued, "applies pressure to your optic and auditory nerves. That pressure is what caused your seizure. The pressure sometimes results in hallucinations that can seem very real. Patients have described them as vivid, lucid dreams, similar to a hypnotic state. Smell and taste are never present in this type of hallucination because those sensory nerves aren't affected."

"But I felt it all inside me," I argued.

"Your brain transmits corresponding sensations to many nerves throughout your body, even to your sense of touch. Those sensations become part of the hallucination. I'm sure it felt very real to you at the time."

I was immediately put on anti-seizure medication to prevent any more episodes. A week later, my head was shaved, drugs were injected into me, and I counted backwards from ten until I passed out. The benign primitive neuroectodermal tumor was successfully cut out of the back of my skull. I pretty much just slept the first few days after surgery.

On the fourth day of my recovery in the hospital, I woke up early in the morning. My mother didn't stir until a nurse's footsteps crossed the floor of my room. Mom hadn't left my side since the operation, sleeping in the reclining chair beside my bed every night.

One of the day nurses, Amy, walked to the side of my bed and gazed at the sketch pad lying on my lap. Colored drawing pencils were scattered across the blanket and partially covered the tubes snaking into my arm. My mom's eyes opened and she drowsily sat up in her chair.

"How long have you been awake?" Mom asked me.

"About an hour," I answered.

"That drawing is awesome," Amy said genuinely, admiring the sketch on my lap.

"Thanks," I replied, smiling at her.

"Her eyes look like a tiger or something," Amy commented.

"Cheetah," I said. "That's what I want them to look like."

"It's cool the way you get her to look so beautiful and fierce at the same time." Amy turned to my mom. "He has quite a talent."

"It's a real gift," my mom said. "He's taken art classes for years, but what he has can't be taught."

"I'll say," Amy agreed, returning her eyes to the drawing. "Who is she?"

"Just a girl from"— I paused—"from my imagination."

Striking an exaggerated movie star pose, Amy swung a hand behind her head and pressed it against her curly, reddish-brown hair. "Maybe you'll draw me before you leave."

"Sure," I said with a big grin on my face. "I'd like that."

"I'm going to hold you to it," she said, smiling back at me. "But right now, we need to take a look at how you're healing." She leaned me forward, gently removed the bandages, and examined the back of my head. "That's doing nicely. You'll be ready for radiation in no time."

"Great," I replied sarcastically. "I can't wait."

"Chemo's a lot worse," Amy said. "You're lucky you don't have to go through that."

"Yeah, I guess so," I mumbled.

*   *   *

The radiation burns healed over the summer, my hair grew back, and follow-up scans didn't show any new growth. The neurosurgeon said that I couldn't risk head trauma, so any sports with potential contact were ruled out—even baseball and soccer, sports I'd played since I was a small child. To fill that void in my life, I took up running.

When I first started jogging on the streets around my house, I tried to imitate the long, sleek gait of the girl in

Krymzyn. I eventually found my own stride, developed my leg muscles, and increased the distances I ran.

On weekends, my dad drove us to trails located in the canyons between the San Fernando Valley and Los Angeles Basin. Side by side, we'd run together on the arid dirt paths. Dad provided constant encouragement, especially when I felt nerve pain related to the surgery. After the brain stem has been tampered with, pain is transmitted throughout the entire body for several months that follow. At times while I ran, the burning sensation in my arms and legs erupted into a raging inferno.

My best friend Connor was already a star on our junior high school track team. He competed in sprints ranging from the one hundred to four hundred meters, winning most races he entered. Tall, thin, and gangly with white-blond hair that flopped around his face when he ran, he didn't have what many would consider a sprinter's body. But his bursts of speed often dropped the jaws of those who watched. Even though he loathed long distances, he often ran with me after school and joined Dad and me for weekend treks through the hills.

Early during my freshman year of high school, a year and a half after my surgery, I'd sometimes run on the school track after classes were finished for the day. One afternoon, I noticed a track coach timing my laps with a stopwatch. When I finished running, he walked over to me and asked my name. He said that I had a natural long-distance runner's body since I was taller than average with a lean, athletic build and long legs. By the time our conversation ended, he'd convinced me to join the cross-country team.

To my surprise, I made varsity my freshman year. As a sophomore, I qualified for the Southern California regional meet. I finished in second place at the autumn state championship of my junior year. Hearing my name on the loudspeaker during morning announcements helped me feel normal and proud. I became Chase the cross-country runner, not the pathetic kid who had a tumor cut out of his skull in seventh grade.

I did well enough in school to know that I should write "well enough" as opposed to "good enough." My legs logged countless miles. Hours and hours each week were spent drawing and painting, moving to computer-based digital art programs as I grew older.

I kissed a girl for the first time when I was fourteen, made it to second base when I was sixteen, and also passed my driver's license test that year. Summer days were spent at Zuma Beach with friends, body boarding, running on the hard, wet sand at ocean's edge, and trying to forget about the fascinating girl and a place called Krymzyn. I was just like any other kid in a middle-class San Fernando Valley family— except for one thing.

"Preventative" was a word I'd learned to know well over those years. Every three months during the first year after my surgery, and every six months after that, I went to the hospital for a checkup, blood tests, and a brain scan. Because of the seizure, my parents insisted that our entire family take CPR classes. Any time I had a headache, I couldn't help but worry that it might have been caused by a new tumor.

The problem was, between running and the hours I worked at my computer on art projects, overexertion and eye-strain headaches were unavoidable. If I suffered from a headache two days in a row, my parents rushed me to the doctor just to be safe. One positive that came out of the experience was an honest, open communication between my parents and me that I'd always thought was rare for a kid my age. I could talk with them about anything.

After the fall cross-country championship my junior year, over Thanksgiving break, we had an unseasonably warm day that almost felt like summer. We quickly packed the car for our favorite family activity—a day at the beach.

Bodies thermally warmed in wetsuits, Dad and I spent an hour body-boarding together in the frigid Pacific water. We were about to paddle to shore when a new swell rose, shaping a set of majestic waves. I let the first few pass, but then gripped my board tightly and furiously kicked my finned-feet to get in position for a ride.

As the wave began to break, I flew across the sheer face of blue. I planned on riding it all the way to the beach, but the entire crest collapsed on top of me. The force of the wave flipped me, ripped the board leash from my wrist, and slammed me into the turbulent depths.

I spun to glints of scarlet that flashed into my eyes. Deep under the surface, a limp, unconscious body undulated in the frothing water. Streaks of red shone from black hair that thrashed in the current around a young woman's face—a face I'd seen before. I instantly recognized the girl from Krymzyn.

With my heart racing, I frantically stroked my arms in her direction. When I was less than three feet from her body, I reached out to grab her in my hands. My fingers clenched empty water and she vanished in a backwash of bubbles from a wave. I turned in circles, desperately trying to spot her, but she was gone. Unable to hold my breath any longer, I shot up to the surface.

I gasped for air several times while looking around me. The set of waves had ended and the sea was calm. The girl's body wasn't anywhere to be seen, my body-board the only thing floating in the water near me.

"Are you okay, Chase?" my father's voice called out from thirty yards away.

"I'm fine, thanks!" I shouted. "Bad wipeout. I'll meet you on shore."

Aiming towards my board, I dove under the surface again. The sand that had been churned up by the waves had all settled and the water was crystal-clear. I scoured the ocean around me in every direction, but it was empty. If she'd been real, my hands couldn't have missed catching her in their grasp. It had to have been a hallucination of some kind, but I couldn't figure out why the apparition had appeared out of nowhere. I hadn't thought about Krymzyn in several months.

After retrieving my board, I swam to shore. Once my fins, wetsuit, and board were stashed on the sand by my family, I went for a two-mile run at ocean's edge. I needed to be alone with my thoughts to try and figure out why I'd seen that image of Sash. A flurry of memories from when I was twelve flooded my mind, all of them as vivid as though they'd happened earlier that day.

When I finished my run, I plopped down on an empty part of the beach. Warm, late afternoon sunlight bathed my skin while I watched the break of aqua waves on golden sand. My mom strolled down the beach to me and sat by my side.

"You've seemed a little distant the last few days," Mom said, smiling. "Is everything okay?"

"I'm kind of bummed cross-country is over," I replied. "It always leaves me feeling a little empty."

"You've had a few more headaches recently. Is that bothering you?" The calm expression on her face tried to hide the concern that was evident in her tone.

"Not really," I answered. "I've been spending a lot of time painting, so I think it's just eye strain. No need to worry."

"I know you're on top of it, but it's also a lot for you to think about."

"It's not like I worry about it coming back that much anymore. It's really hard to explain."

"Try me," Mom implored.

I scooped a handful of dry fine sand and tightly clamped it in my fist. After holding my hand out in front of me, I relaxed my grip and let the sand slowly pour to the beach. Watching the grains catch sparks of sunlight as they fell, I searched for words that could accurately express the intangible emotions I'd so often felt since I was twelve.

"When I had the tumor," I finally said, "I felt like it opened my mind to possibilities that I'd never considered before. Like there's so much more in the universe than just what's in front of us every day. I know it sounds stupid, but I feel like I'm waiting for something to happen. Something amazing to happen, and I don't necessarily mean wonderful amazing. It might be horrible, I don't know, but something that will amaze me one way or the other. Does that make sense?"

Mom's eyes filled with sympathy. "Do you feel like life owes you something because of what you had to go through?"

"No, it's not that," I said, shaking my head. "It's more like, when they took out the tumor, it left an empty space in my brain that's waiting to be filled by something more than what I've experienced so far."

Mom looked at the ocean. She didn't answer for a few seconds while contemplating her response.

"You had to face the reality that your existence is finite at a very young age." She turned her face back to mine. "Most kids your age don't think much about death. I know I didn't when I was a teenager, so I think you want as much as possible out of life at a younger age than most people. Maybe because you know how fragile life is. You felt it firsthand."

I let her words soak in before replying, scrutinizing the sunset colors reflected in her eyes. "Yeah, something like that. I just wish I knew what it is I'm waiting for."

"Don't worry, Chase," she said. "You'll find it. Give it time."

Mom reached an arm around my shoulder and we silently listened to the waves crash on the beach. As the sun sank to the horizon, amber light danced across white foam crests.

Chapter 4

She slips the tip of her spear from the skull of a dead creature at her feet. Streams of black blood mixed with rain drip to the grass below. Veins that once bulged from the muscular body are now empty, fading lines of charcoal against pale, white skin. Despite being almost twice her size, the Murkovin had little defense against her wrath.

The girl steps over the body, rain spattering on her head, and walks to the other two corpses in the field. She ignores the second Murkovin but stops over the body of her Mentor, her guide in the ways of her purpose. She stares at the fading scarlet in his short black hair, wondering how one so experienced, so strong, could have been taken by surprise.

She wasn't shown a vision of her Mentor's death, or she never would have left his side. While spending Communal with the children, she'd sensed that Darkness was near. She'd traveled to their usual meeting place, but he'd never arrived.

Sounds of clashing steel had steered her to the battle. Two creatures from the Barrens had scaled the walls and secretly entered the Delta. Her Mentor had already been slain by the time she reached him, but the two Murkovin still lurked nearby. A fury had ignited inside the girl, was unleashed upon the intruders, and they'd quickly met death at the tip of her spear.

The girl looks up at the sky as the swirling clouds slow. The rainfall ends and fresh beams of light sever the edges of the clouds. Darkness has departed.

"Watchers will remove the Murkovin bodies," a woman, the tallest of the Disciples, says from behind her. "I'll summon a Traveler to take your Mentor's body to the Bed of Light."

"No," the girl objects. She lowers her face to the corpse of her Mentor. "I'll take him to the Mount."

"You know that isn't the duty of a Hunter," the Disciple reprimands.

The girl turns to face the woman and bows her head in a show of respect. When she speaks, her voice is quiet but firm with conviction.

"*I'll* take his body to the Bed of Light."

Clenching her jaw, the girl focuses her eyes on the Disciple. The two silently stare at one another.

"I'll have a Traveler accompany you," the Disciple finally responds.

"Thank you," the girl says.

The Disciple kneels, sinks the fingertips of one hand into the black dirt beneath the grass, and whispers a few words before standing again.

"Even with all your gifts," the Disciple says quietly, "you can't blame yourself for events out of your control."

"I know I shouldn't blame myself," the girl replies. "If I'd been shown his death before it occurred, I could have protected him, but I wasn't shown. I don't understand why I'm shown some things and not others."

The Disciple takes a step forward and towers over the girl. "The things you're shown, the purposes of the children or when Darkness is near, are events you can't alter. If a path has already been defined, you may not be able to change it."

The girl shakes her head. "It's difficult to accept when I know I could have saved him."

"You weren't meant to save him. You were meant to learn from him while he was alive. With his death, you'll no longer be an Apprentice. Even though you're still young, you're now asked to fulfill your purpose as a Hunter of Krymzyn."

The girl solemnly bows. "I'm honored to serve our balance.

The Disciple silently admires the girl standing in front of her, realizing how quickly she's maturing into a young woman. Despite the girl's recent growth, she's still younger than any before her to end an Apprenticeship. Well aware of the girl's extraordinary abilities since they were first displayed as a small child, the Disciple knows how difficult it must be for the girl to understand her gifts.

"Why you're sometimes shown the future," the Disciple says, "feel the things you feel, and are able to do all you can, none of us can explain. I know it's confusing to you, but in time, I believe it will make sense."

"Do you remember my Ritual of Purpose?" the girl asks.

"Of course. I thought a first would occur and more than one color might be revealed in your hair."

"During Communal after my Ritual, a Teller arrived, but

on the Empty Hill, not the Telling Hill."

"I remember," the Disciple says. "I was told of his arrival, although there were many anomalies associated with his visit."

"I know I shouldn't have approached him," the girl tells the Disciple, "but I couldn't resist my curiosity. He was confused and didn't understand why he was here. When we spoke, I could feel what was inside him. Not only what he felt being in our world, but what he felt in his. The types of feelings I sensed in him are the same things I feel all the time now, emotions that don't exist here in others."

"Did you find it helpful to be aware of those emotions in another?" the Disciple asks.

Sliding the tip of her spear across the grass at her feet, the girl wipes black Murkovin blood from the steel. "It helped me understand them. Some of the emotions I feel are extreme, like anger as severe as what the Murkovin must feel. Those are difficult to control."

The Disciple ponders the girl's words for several moments before speaking again. "Much of your journey is one that, I fear, must be traveled alone. You'll gain understanding as you travel your path. Although I may not fully grasp all that's inside you, I'll always try to provide what insight I can."

"Thank you," the girl sincerely replies. "The things I feel will never interfere with fulfilling my purpose to Krymzyn."

"Your honor is never in question. We all know you give every part of your life to protect what's sacred to us in a way no one else can."

Both of their heads turn towards beams of light gliding

over a nearby hilltop. The brilliant rays recede into the shape of a man. Tall and slim with cobalt blue highlights in his wavy black hair, the Traveler sprints across the meadow. With his spear in one hand, he coasts to a stop in front of the Disciple.

"Please accompany her to the Mount," the Disciple says. "She'll take her Mentor's body to the Bed of Light."

With a somber expression, the Traveler surveys the three corpses on the ground. When he looks at the girl, his eyes fill with respect.

"It will be my honor," he says.

The girl hands her spear to the Traveler, leans down, and lifts the body of her Mentor from the ground. With very little effort, almost no strain in her muscles, she hoists the corpse over her shoulder as though he were nothing more than a small child.

"Have a safe journey," the Disciple says.

The girl and the Traveler both bow to the woman before running to the east. Even with the weight of the body over her shoulder, the girl races ahead of the Traveler across the first meadow. After brief streams of light over rolling crimson hills, the two arrive at the eastern wall of the Delta and slow to a walk.

A Watcher, strands of bright green in his black hair, descends a steel ladder attached to an enormous black marble wall. When he reaches the ground, the man nods to the girl and the Traveler. He walks to the arched metallic doors in the wall, releases large, steel bolts that secure them, and swings one door open. The sound of raging water bursts through the gate.

The Traveler steps to a rack of soft black boots beside the wall. He slips one pair onto his bare feet before handing another pair to the girl. She gently lays the body of her Mentor on the ground while the Watcher bows his head to the corpse. After sliding the boots on her feet and tightly tying the straps around her ankles, the girl lifts the dead body onto her shoulder again.

The Traveler and the girl pass through the gate and step onto a steel bridge that spans the immense river. The colorless Barrens stretch out in front of them on the far side. Leading to the Mount of Krymzyn in the distance, a narrow road weaves through the wasteland.

The girl glances over her shoulder at the top of the wall where a female Watcher stands with her Apprentice. The Apprentice glares at the girl with anger in his eyes, just as he did during her Ritual of Purpose long ago.

He must be wondering why she would transport the body of her Mentor to the Mount instead of a Traveler, the girl concludes. She ignores his stare by turning away, but she senses the sting of his eyes on her back.

As the girl climbs the arc in the center of the bridge, the sound of churning rapids below, she looks down the violent river. Soaring silvery blue waves rise high in the air and crash down on the furious water. She stops walking when her attention is captured by a hulking slab of black rock in the middle of the river—the one she recognizes from her Vision of the Future.

When I spoke to him on the Empty Hill long ago, he was much younger than in my Vision of the Future, but there's no doubt it was the same face. When we talked, his blue eyes were brave even though he was in a world he didn't know. His eyes filled with wonder at all around him, were intelligent and kind. It was odd that he arrived on the Empty Hill just as I passed by, not the Telling Hill as he should have.

The last time I slept, I saw him in my dream. He looked the same age as I am now, but not yet as mature as in my Vision of the Future. In my dream, he again stood on the Empty Hill, but Darkness surrounded him. Tellers are never here during Darkness, yet Darkness fell the first time he was here, as well as in my dream.

That dream must have been a warning. Now that I'm no longer an Apprentice, I can choose where I hunt. I need to remain near the Empty Hill when the trees are awake. He won't know how to protect himself during Darkness.

Chapter 5

To get a used car for Christmas during my junior year of high school, I had to make a deal with my parents. I agreed to help drive my little sister to and from school, which I didn't mind.

My Christmas present to them was a family portrait I'd secretly been painting for many months. A tranquil sunset behind rolling blue waves was the background. In the foreground, Mom and Dad stood on the beach with Ally and me crouching on the sand at their sides.

Blowing in the ocean breeze, my mom's sandy brown hair was streaked with summer blond in the painting. Her round face with big, chocolate brown eyes and smiling cheeks expressed the serenity we always felt on family days at the beach. My dad, tall and lean, with wavy dark brown hair, sparkling blue eyes, and a long, straight nose on his slender face, stood with one arm around my mom's waist.

Studying the finished oil on canvas, I debated about a little more detail in the curl of the wave behind us. I also couldn't help but wonder if it was only in my perception that Ally looked exactly like my mom and I looked exactly like my dad or if that's how everyone saw us.

After I turned seventeen in January, track practice began. I was training to run the mile during the upcoming spring season. Ally played for the freshmen soccer team, and our practices ended at roughly the same time every day.

She sat beside me in the front seat as we drove home one afternoon on a busy four-lane boulevard through Sherman Oaks. I had a slight headache from the mixture of a strenuous track workout and battling heavy traffic during the drive.

The throbbing in my head abruptly seared into greater pain than I'd felt in many years. I immediately knew this headache hadn't been caused by tension or overexertion at track practice. The tremors were spreading way too fast through my skull, exactly like the headaches from five years earlier.

My hands began to tremble and cramped out of control around the steering wheel. When halos of red from the brake lights in front of us blinded me, I slammed my foot on the brake pedal, pushed with all my might, and heard the loud screech of rubber against asphalt.

"Chase!" my sister screamed from far away.

*   *   *

"Murkovin!" a roaring male voice echoes through the hills.

Rain plummets from the sky, blackened storm clouds churn in place, and my eyes try to adjust to Darkness. I spin to the shout behind me, immediately knowing I'm on the same hill as I'd been on when I was twelve. There's not a doubt in my mind.

Needles race up my spine when I see the shirtless creature crouched at the base of the hill. Tall with black veins bulging from ghostly white skin, the beast of a man scans the terrain. Wearing only black leathery pants, firm ridges of muscle lining his bare stomach and chest, he wildly swings a metal spear in one hand.

He snaps his head in my direction. Stringy black hair twined with white whips across his face, and his empty hand slashes the air in front of him. When his eyes hit mine, shadowy sockets flare blood red. The brute charges up the hill at me.

I lurch the other way and sprint down the slope to the meadow below. A torrent of rain bites at my skin as deafening creaks pierce the air. I see a flailing tree in front of me and try to stop, but my bare feet slip across the wet grass.

A glowing red limb lashes at me, pummels into my chest, and hurls me to the ground. As the branch hammers down again, I throw my hands up in defense. Blood instantly spurts from gashes torn into my face, neck, and arms. Rolling across the grass, I desperately try to get out of the tree's reach.

Stopping flat on my back, I stare straight up. A monstrous bough high above flexes into a fisted hand. I start to jump to my feet but a blur scoops me from the ground. As we speed away from the tree, silky wisps of black and scarlet brush across my face. A thunderous slam vibrates from behind us, the wooden fist pounding into the ground where, a moment earlier, my body would have been.

Into the valley we race until we're outside the range of groping limbs. After we slide to a stop, I'm gently set on the grass. I look up to see the girl I met when I was twelve standing over me—the girl called Sash.

Her thin arms barb with muscular detail when she swings her spear up in front of her. Steel spikes sticking out of a pack slung over her shoulder glint with dull light. She peers down at me through radiant amber eyes.

"Are you injured?" she growls, silver raindrops beading down her hair.

"A few cuts and bruises," I answer. "I'll be fine."

She jerks her head up, so I raise my head to look in the same direction. On top of the hill where I stood, a man in the black clothing of Krymzyn, vibrant green hair glittering in the dark, battles the creature I saw. After their spears clash, the green-haired man twists away. With a vicious lunge, he plunges the tip of his weapon into the muscular, white chest of the beast. A wail of agony tears through the hills while black blood gushes from the wound.

A woman leaps from behind the hill, a steel point leading her soar and trails of neon green behind her head. Rays of light burst around the shaft of her spear as she rams it through the creature's skull. The vile specter of man collapses to the ground.

"Are there more?" Sash shouts at them.

"Only this one!" the woman yells back.

"Stay here," Sash says calmly, returning her eyes to mine. "You're safe now."

I'm scared, shocked, fascinated . . . a barrage of

emotions race through me. I don't feel any physical effects from the seizure I know I'm in the middle of back on Earth, but I honestly can't assess my feelings at being here. Except for one overwhelming reaction—I'm finally amazed.

Sash charges through the rain towards the tree. Branches split the air around her as she sails off the ground. I sit up to watch, instantly hypnotized by her spectacular acrobatics.

A limb sweeps harmlessly below her feet. With the spear grasped tightly in both her hands, she blocks another branch at the apex of her leap. She lands, tucks into a roll under one more swinging limb, and finally launches off the grass to the trunk. Flexed arms of wood whip inward at her but have to stop as cracking sounds fill the meadow. Sash kneels safely by the base of the tree, the branches unable to reach her.

She pops a hand behind her head, snatches one of the stakes from the pack on her back, and forcefully stabs it into the tree. Twisting the metal point deep inside the bark, she locks the three-foot-long spike into the trunk.

In a flurry of motion, Sash stabs and twists again and again until all seven metallic stakes are anchored into the wood. Minutes pass while she protects the spikes from the boughs overhead, amber ferocity constantly burning in her eyes.

When a hint of orange pares the edges of the clouds, the rainfall thins. The limbs of the tree slowly reach outward, some up to the sky, and others drooping to the ground with their tips digging into the turf. The churning clouds slow until idle masses of dark gray return. Once the rain stops falling and it's fully light, the tree remains perfectly still.

Sash carefully removes one stake from the bark, twists the steel tip, and slips it into the cylinder on her back. After leaning her face to the trunk, she rests her forehead on the exact spot the spike punctured the tree. Both of her hands reach outward and she presses her palms to the bark. For a few seconds, she stands in reverence to the tree.

One by one, she removes the spikes. Each time she does, she repeats the moment of silence with her hands and forehead pressed to the bark. When the last metal stake is returned to her pack, Sash scoops her spear from the ground and crosses the meadow towards me.

She's grown taller—maybe five foot six now—slender and toned. Her face is my age with no lines or blemishes on her smooth, pale skin. Her fiery amber eyes, infinite black pupils, and rich burgundy lips look ageless and wise, like she's seventeen and twenty-seven and ninety-seven.

I try to stand but drop to my knees from a bolt of pain shooting down my back. Resting on the grass, I glance at my arms. Water may bead and run off me in Krymzyn, but my blood still scabs and stains my skin. I finally rise to my feet with a grimace. Sash stops in front of me.

"I'm sorry if the tree injured you," she says. "For your own safety, never be in reach of the branches."

"Thank you for helping me. I really appreciate it. You're a lot stronger than you look."

"I'm honored to provide aid to a visitor of Krymzyn," she humbly replies.

The man and woman who killed the creature walk down the hill towards us. The man drags the corpse by the hair. Even though I'm almost six feet tall now, they're both much taller than I am. A younger man walks by their side, also with black and green hair. Rugged and stocky, he looks no more than a year or two older than I am and he's about my height. Studying me intently, the three stop when they reach us.

"We'll escort the Teller to the Disciples," the woman says to Sash.

"No," Sash replies. "I'll attend to his needs. The Disciples will be busy because of the Murkovin."

"Tellers should only meet with Disciples!" the younger man hisses.

"He's injured and covered in blood," Sash says loudly, turning towards the young man.

"That's not your responsibility," he snarls.

"Balt!" the green-haired woman barks. "Never speak to another in that tone. She's only trying to help a visitor."

Sash doesn't respond, instead staring at the young man with an intensity and fury I've never seen in any creature anywhere. Her muscles flex until they're as tight as the band of a slingshot stretched almost to the breaking point, ready to release in an instant.

Even the eyes of the two older adults widen at the unbridled surge of energy that seems to surround her and the outrage flowing from her eyes. Balt tries to hold her glare but finally looks down at the ground.

"Sash," the green-haired woman says flatly, "you need to maintain control."

After another moment of tension, Sash relaxes her stance and turns to the woman. "I apologize. I'm upset by the intrusion of a Murkovin."

Sash kneels to the ground, sinks her fingertips into the

dirt beneath the grass, and whispers something. A few seconds later, she stands.

"Eval is aware of his presence," Sash says in a calm voice. "I told her that I'll tend to the Teller's needs until the Disciples finish trying to learn how a Murkovin entered the Delta. She'll summon me when they're ready for him at Sanctuary."

"Of course," the green-haired woman replies.

The three people with green hair nod farewell to Sash. As they walk away from us, the one named Balt looks over his shoulder. He fires a nasty glance at me, then at Sash, but quickly turns away. I lower my eyes to the muscular, hideous corpse the other man is dragging behind him.

"What do you call that thing?" I ask.

"Murkovin," Sash answers. "They dwell in the Barrens outside the Delta. Where we are now is inside the Delta of Krymzyn."

"What was it trying to do?"

"He wanted sap from the sustaining tree," she says with a hint of pain in her voice.

"Why sap?"

"Tree sap is our only sustenance in Krymzyn."

"Is that why you stabbed those things in the tree?"

She nods her head. "The stakes fill with sap."

"No offense, but why don't you do that when the tree isn't trying to kill you?" I ask.

"The sap only flows during Darkness, when the tree is awake," she explains. "The tree is only trying to protect itself."

"This whole place is really messed up," I remark.

She narrows her eyes slightly and I feel a teeming anger cast in my direction. For the second time in a few minutes, I sense the extraordinary power that resides inside her.

I immediately wish I'd bitten my tongue. But strangely, it's not from fear. After feeling so safe with her when I was younger, plus the fact that she just saved my life, I don't ever want to upset or hurt her in any way.

"Follow me," she says sharply. She spins to the valley and briskly walks away.

Chapter 6

"Sash," I call out to her.

She stops walking and turns to me.

"I'm sorry," I say, looking straight at her eyes. "I didn't mean to be rude or critical. I'm just a little *freaked* out right now . . . scared. I really appreciate you saving me. I'm sorry if I said anything wrong."

Her face softens with understanding at my apology. I'm sure she knows how frightened I must have felt arriving in the situation I did.

"You remember me from when you here before," she says as a statement of fact.

"Yes," I reply. "It's strange. I remember everything about being here. I'm Chase, by the way."

"I know who you are."

I start to walk towards her but wince from pain. Sash immediately steps to me.

"Are you able to walk?" she asks.

"Yeah, I'm *okay*," I answer.

"I can help heal your wounds. After that, you can rest until the Disciples call for you."

"Sounds like a good plan to me." I glance up at the light

in the sky. "Is it morning here?"

Sash shakes her head. "It's the middle of our night."

"But it was dark and now it's light."

"Most of the time, it's light in Krymzyn," she tells me. "We never know when Darkness will fall, nor do we know how long it will last. It could come at any time during the day or night."

Side by side, we slowly stroll into the valley.

"Where are we going?" I ask.

"To my habitat," she answers.

"Do you live with your _family_?"

"_Family_?" she questions.

"Your _mother_ and _father_," I say before remembering how "parents" never translated when I was younger. Apparently "mother" and "father" have no meaning here either.

"I don't understand," she replies.

"Who gave birth to you?"

"A woman who was chosen to carry me."

"How was she chosen?" My curiosity is soaring.

"After Darkness passes, if a new child is needed in Krymzyn, one man and one woman are given the sign of fertility. They know of their choice by amber sparkles in their veins. It's a great honor to be chosen."

"Your _parents_—sorry," I say, understanding now that any word that hangs in the air for a long time never translates, so I can quickly correct myself. "The man and woman who make you are just chosen randomly?"

"Nothing is random," she answers. "They're chosen because they have something inside them worthy of being passed on. As soon as they've been given the sign, the two meet at the Cavern of Grace and engage in the Ritual of Balance. The woman then carries the child until birth. Her only purpose while she's pregnant is to protect the child growing inside her. After she gives birth, she nurtures the child until another seventy periods of Darkness pass."

"What happens to the baby after that?"

"The child is then presented to the Keepers at the Naming Ritual. The woman's duty is finished. The Keepers raise and educate the child in the ways of Krymzyn until the height of purpose is reached. While the Keepers attend to the needs and education of the children, all of Krymzyn is responsible for their upbringing."

"Do you ever just spend time the woman who gave birth to you?" I ask.

"I don't know who she is," she answers.

Astonished by her answer, I stop walking. Sash stops in front me.

"You don't know who gave birth to you?"

"It's not necessary to know she is," she says. "None of the children know."

"What about the man who . . ." I pause to think of a word that might translate since I know "father" won't, but Sash speaks before I can come up with one.

"The man who provides the seed for growth. Again, there's no need to know who he is."

This time, I bite my tongue to hold in my response, one I'm certain she wouldn't appreciate.

"What happens when the child reaches the height of purpose?" I ask.

"The child is taken to the Tree of Vision for the Ritual of Purpose. Once the sap of that Tree is consumed, color is given to our hair and our purpose is revealed through that color. The child then becomes an Apprentice in the ways of their purpose.

"My hair streaked with scarlet, the color of a Hunter, and I served as an Apprentice with a Mentor named Yoni. While an Apprentice, I dwelled with the Keepers and other children. When Yoni met his death, I ended my Apprenticeship and was given my own habitat. I now serve my purpose to Krymzyn."

"Who are the green-haired people?"

"Watchers," she replies. "They protect the walls around the Delta. The youngest of the three, Balt, is an Apprentice."

When Sash starts walking up the valley again, I stroll beside her.

"Do you live your whole life alone after you leave the Keepers?" I ask.

"All of Krymzyn exists as one, but each dwells in solitude."

"What if someone's never chosen for the Ritual of Balance?"

She shrugs her shoulders. "Then their purpose is fulfilled until the height of death is reached. Hunters are never chosen because we need rest after Darkness and must always be available when Darkness falls."

"You never have, like, a _boyfriend_ or _husband_ or _partner_?"

"I don't know the meaning of those words," she says.

"You never have _sex_?" I blurt out, but again I wish I'd

bitten my tongue.

"I don't understand."

"Whatever goes on in the Ritual of Balance. Mating maybe?" I ask, happy that "mating" translates.

"Only if one is chosen for the Ritual."

She leads me around the base of a hill. I'm still confused and want to ask more about how hair color defines purpose but decide that I have enough information to absorb for now. What she told me explains why, in my mind, she often seems to have a sad, lonely expression on her face.

We walk into a narrow gorge of grass-lined ridges. An oval door constructed of black granite stone is tucked into the crease at the foot of the hill. She leads me to it, grasps a metal knob, and opens the door.

"Follow me inside," she says.

I crouch behind her as we enter a narrow tunnel of black crystalline stone. Darkness surrounds us when she closes the door.

"Awaken," Sash calls out.

At the end of the long tunnel, soft amber light slowly illuminates an opening. We slink towards the light, and I gasp when we enter the spacious cavern.

I raise my eyes to a high-domed ceiling, a sprawling crystal garden like the inside of a geode. Sharp spikes across the surface refract pinpoints of gold light from within. Tiny, bright orbs float like gravity-defying flakes of snow inside the fragmented crystal.

"Swirls," Sash says, seeing my curious expression. "Tiny creatures of light that dwell in the stone."

"How do they live in there?" I ask.

"They feed on minerals in the crystal. The proper sound from my voice causes them to illuminate or darken."

Sash walks across a smooth dark-blue quartz floor that dully reflects the light from overhead. The floor is polished but doesn't feel slippery beneath my bare feet as I follow her into the cavern. The walls are the same quartz as the floor, rich blue-gray with dull red and amber veins. A gentle rush of flowing water echoes through an opening at the far end of the cavern.

She slips the pack from her back and hangs it on a metallic rack fastened to the wall. Several more packs filled with the same kind of stakes hang beside it. She leans her spear against the wall and locks it into a clasp beside the rack.

I glance at the other side of the oval cavern. A large mattress-like pad lies on the ground by the wall across from us, longer than a king-sized bed but about the same width. It's covered by white fabric that looks like brushed cotton with two large, well-stuffed white pillows on top. I don't see any sheets or blankets for the bed.

"This is really incredible," I say.

"I hope you feel comfortable while you're here," she replies sincerely.

The air in the room feels exactly like the outside in Krymzyn, void of temperature. In this world, no one ever shivers from a winter chill, bundles in soft wool blankets, or warms themselves by a fire. In Krymzyn, the temperature just is.

"How old are you?" I ask.

"I've reached the height of purpose, completed my

Apprenticeship, and now fulfill my purpose."

"No, I just mean in _years_," I say, but "years" never translates.

"I don't understand," she says.

"How do you measure time here? Like a person's age?"

"A person's age is measured by their height, so one who is young is shorter, one who is old is taller. The greater passage of time is measured by the tenure of the same seven Disciples in service together, called an Era."

"What happens when someone stops growing?"

"Our growth in height begins at birth and ends at death," she says. "It slows as we grow older, but we always gain height."

I guess that explains why everyone I've seen here who's more than a few years older than I am looks so tall. I hold a hand up and snap my finger.

"The time that snap took is called a _second_ in my world. We have exact measurements of time, so sixty _seconds_ makes a _minute_, sixty _minutes_ an _hour_, twenty-four _hours_ are in a day, and three hundred sixty-five days make a _year_. We track it all with things called _clocks_ and _calendars_, time-measurement devices. I'm seventeen _years_ old."

She holds her hand up and snaps her finger. "You've lived five hundred thirty-six million, one hundred twelve thousand snaps," she says, "or _seconds_, as you call them. We don't need a device to measure time."

I stare at her, dumbfounded, and start to do the math in my head but get lost and start over. I quickly realize that I can't do it without a calculator and accept that the number she gave me is accurate.

"How do you know when it's time to do something?" I ask.

"We sleep when we tire, consume sap when we hunger, and perform our purpose as needed. We know what needs to be done and when to do it. Krymzyn lets us know when it's time for a Ritual or Communal."

It's strange to me the way she refers to Krymzyn as though it's a living entity, not just a place.

Sash walks to a simple four-legged table made of brushed metal. It stands against the wall opposite the bed. Shelves are carved into the glossy stone above the table, home to several pitchers and cups, a pair of scissors, and a sheathed knife, all made of the same type of steel. She points to a three-legged metallic stool by her side.

"Please sit," Sash says. "I know that now is the time to heal your wounds, although your measurement of time appears not to have alerted you."

I have to smile at what on Earth would have been a joke, even though her face is deadly serious.

Chapter 7

I walk to the stool and sit in front of the table. After Sash takes a steel pitcher and two cups from the shelves, she sets both cups in front of me. She pours thick liquid from the pitcher into each cup. The fluid looks like it should be scalding hot, but no steam rises from the mixture of red, orange, and yellow. The colors undulate inside the cups like slowly morphing molten globs inside a lava lamp.

"Take off your shirt," she says.

While pulling the sleeveless black shirt over my head, I pause to involuntarily flex at dull stabs of pain. Sash takes the shirt from me, crosses the room to the head of her bed, and hangs it on one of several metal hooks in the wall. After unbuckling the black rope around her waist, she loops it over one of the other hooks. The steel flask dangling from the end of the belt makes a few dull clangs against the quartz. Sash returns to me and pours liquid from the pitcher into her hand.

"Rest your arms on the table," she says.

After I do as she instructed, she slides her smooth, soft palm from the back of my wrist to my elbow, over my biceps, and up to my shoulder. I don't even feel the liquid on my skin. No slime or stick as I thought there would be—just pleasing tingles.

I blink firmly several times to make sure I see what I think I see. The scabs begin to slowly recede, and the smaller scrapes in my arm seem to heal before my eyes. She pours more of the liquid into her hands and gently rubs them up my arms, across my shoulders, and down my back. Every pain is instantly swept away, leaving my muscles alert and fresh.

"Drink," she says, tipping her head to the cup in front of me. She lifts the other cup and sips from it.

"What is this?" I ask, looking inside my cup.

"Sap of the sustaining trees," she answers.

Raising the cup to my lips, I stare at the swirling colors. When I take a sip, there's no taste, no smell, and the liquid is neither hot nor cold. It's the texture of honey but not at all sticky, and the fluid flows down my throat with each swallow.

Instantly, a feeling of pure, absolute energy surges through my muscles. Hunger feels satisfied and thirst quenched. With the strength I feel, I know that if I were crouched at the starting line of a three-mile cross-country course, I'd shatter the world record.

After I finish downing everything inside the cup, the swell of vitality gradually subsides into a serene and peaceful comfort. I feel content in every way.

"It's weird," I say to Sash. "I feel, like, really strong but also relaxed."

"The sap knows what you need and when you need it," she explains. "It strengthens your body but also calms your mind if you need rest."

We both set our cups on the table.

"Come with me," she says.

After standing from the stool, I follow Sash across the room to the opening of the second cavern. I'm spellbound by beauty when I enter.

At one end of the cave, a gentle fall of silvery blue water spills from a ledge ten feet over the ground. The floor of the cavern, a black pumice-like stone, is covered by a shallow stream of water from the fall. Translucent as it flows down a slight angle to the other side of the cave, the water disappears with a rushing sound through a narrow crevasse. The golden light from the crystal overhead glistens on the wet ground.

Sash leads me through the gentle flow of three-inch-deep water to the edge of the waterfall. I'm surprised that, once again, the water doesn't feel warm or cold, no temperature at all, but still soothing to my skin. The pumice stone isn't hard, doesn't scratch my feet, and feels like firm sponge where it's wet.

Standing with her back to me and her head down, Sash lets the water splash on the back of her neck. Using her hands, she scrubs dirt off her shirt and pants. When I step into the fall beside her, caressing beads wash over me and send invigorating electric sensations through my nerves.

I glance at Sash. With her eyes closed, she raises her face to the falling water. Her long black hair, scarlet aglow, cascades down her back almost to her waist. The water beads when it runs down her waves but doesn't seem to soak into her hair. I reach my hands up and run them over my own scalp. My hair feels clean and healthy, but not wet or damp against my head.

Sash steps out of the fall and walks towards the other room. Her hair bounces, flows behind her, as if she'd never been in the water. I'm struck by the realization that when we were outside, my clothes never felt wet, despite the pouring rain. Although water is dripping down my body, my pants don't feel like they're wet or clinging to my skin.

"When you finish cleansing," she says to me from the opening between caverns, "you need rest for the sap to finish healing you, and I need rest after Darkness. As I told you, it's the middle of our night. We can rest until the Disciples summon us."

Her expression, melancholy and distant, never changes. She seems tired, her eyes lacking the acute alertness I saw earlier. I'm not surprised after the mind-boggling physical display she put on whisking me to safety and fighting the tree.

I step out of the waterfall with my skin feeling refreshed and revitalized. It's the way it would feel if I'd just spent the entire day at a Beverly Hills spa—not that I'd know what that feels like. But in my mind, I imagine that this is how I'd feel.

When I enter the other room, Sash pulls her shirt over her head and hangs it on one of the hooks fastened to the wall. She doesn't try to hide her nudity from me. I'm momentarily captivated by the curves of her breasts. As she unfastens her pants, I finally tear my eyes away and turn my back to her.

I feel guilty for staring at her the way I did. Based on what she told me earlier, I can safely assume there's no sexual intent in her being unclothed in front me, so my conclusion is that nudity isn't a big deal in Krymzyn. But it seems wrong for me to look at her that way, especially with her not knowing. As I've already witnessed, she's so much more than just a gorgeous girl.

"Why are you looking at the wall?" she asks from behind me.

"I'm being polite," I answer, still focused on the quartz. "I'm waiting for you to finish changing your clothes."

"Why?"

"It's just how it is in my world. It's rude to watch the opposite _sex_ undress . . . the opposite gender . . . unless you're like, you know, _romantically_ involved."

"I don't know what that means," she says.

I squint my eyes in thought while figuring out how I can explain romance to her. "It's like what we were talking about earlier," I eventually say. "A man and a woman in my world can have a relationship that's more than just being friends. They can fall in _love_ . . . really care about each other and spend a lot of time together, even share their whole lives with one another. We call that _romance_ or being _romantic_."

"It seems like an odd custom," she comments. "I'm clothed now."

I turn around to face her. She's wearing simple white shorts, like gym shorts with a drawstring, and a white tank top.

"I think a lot of our customs will seem strange to each other," I say.

She nods her agreement. "I apologize, but I have no sleep clothes for you."

"It's _okay_. My pants already feel dry. I'll put my shirt

back on."

"Why do you keep saying '*okay*'?" she asks.

"It's something we say in my world, the same as 'alright,' like an affirmative."

"Okay," she says, although I'm not sure if she's ironically using the word to let me know that she understands the meaning or just repeating it. But the word translates now, so it must have been added to her vocabulary.

I step to the wall, take my shirt off its hook, and slip it on. After Sash walks to the bed, she climbs on the mattress and stretches out on her back with her head on a pillow.

"You may rest on my bed until the Disciples summon us," she says quietly. "If we haven't heard from them by the new morrow, I'll take you to them."

I walk to the bed and lie down beside her on my back. Staring straight up, I study the slowly moving points of light overhead. After a few moments, I look at Sash.

"Thank you again for saving me and everything you're doing for me," I say. "I'm sorry if I was rude earlier. I was just a little scared."

Her hand rests beside mine on the bed. I take it into my grasp and gently squeeze it. It's an innocent gesture of caring and thanks, nothing more. She yanks her hand away and clenches it into a fist on her chest.

"Why do you touch me?" she asks, still focused on the ceiling. There's no anger in her voice. It's soft and monotone, but there is a hint of curiosity.

"In my world, when we like someone, or care about them, or they've done something to help us, we touch. We shake or squeeze hands or put our arms around each other and _hug_."

"It seems unnecessary," she says.

"Don't you touch other people here?"

She turns her face to me, her amber eyes directly in front of mine. "There's no need other than in the Ritual of Balance or when providing assistance to someone who's injured."

"When you rested your face and hands against the tree earlier . . . why did you do that?"

"To nurture the tree because it provides sustenance for us," she says with warm devotion in her voice. "I want the tree to know I'm thankful."

"Where I come from," I say, "sometimes people need nurturing too."

She returns her eyes to the crystal ceiling.

"We should rest now," she says. "Peace."

Her word triggers the golden Swirls to slowly fade to blackness. I stare up through the dark with my eyes open and my arms limp by my sides. Sash's breathing slows to a steady, smooth pattern.

I try to analyze all I feel at finding myself in Krymzyn again. The catalyst for my being here, I know, has to be a new tumor. But that doesn't bother me at all while I'm here.

I finally admit to myself—even with the danger inherent to this world, I like being here. In a strange way, deep from inside me, I feel like I belong here. More importantly, considering everything that's happened, Sash and I seem to somehow be intertwined.

I start to feel tired and my eyelids begin to droop, but

every nerve in my body ignites when Sash gently rests her hand on mine.

Chapter 8

I opened my eyes and looked at the hand on top of mine. My fingers were tightly clamped to my car's steering wheel with Ally's hand wrapped around them. Her other hand was resting on my shoulder. My entire body shook, pain throbbed through my head, and drool covered my chin.

"Are you okay?" Ally frantically asked.

"I think so," I answered. "Did I hit anything?"

"No. The car behind us ran into us."

"Are you hurt?"

"I'm fine," she sighed.

"I'm really sorry, Ally. I blacked out."

"I was yelling at you to stop." Her eyes filled with tears and her voice cracked when she spoke again. "Then I realized you were having a seizure."

"It was just like before," I said quietly.

"Oh God, Chase," she said, shaking her head and starting to cry. "Not again. It's not fair."

"Are you sure you're okay?" I asked.

She pulled her hands away from me and sat back in her seat. Tears dripped down her cheeks. "I'm fine. The car barely bumped us."

"How long have we been sitting here?"

"Not long," she sobbed. "Less than a minute."

How can that be? I wondered. I'd been in Krymzyn for at least an hour, maybe two.

I released my seat belt and looked in the rearview mirror. With a scowl on his face, the driver of the car behind us was already standing by his hood. I felt a wave of relief that no one had been splattered all over a windshield.

As soon as I stepped out of the car, everything started spinning. My knees buckled and I tried to steady myself against the car. Like a marionette having all its strings sliced at once, my body went limp. I collapsed to the ground.

An ambulance drove me to the hospital. The x-rays clearly showed a new mass of growth on my brain stem—as if the seizure weren't evidence enough. The next day, blue fluid was back in my veins and a CT scan was run on my brain. The scan revealed a new tumor in the exact same area as five years earlier. Surgery was scheduled for the following week.

The only good news from the entire situation was that neither the driver of the other car nor my sister had any injuries. I felt horrible that Ally had been in the car with me when it had happened. Needless to say, I couldn't drive anymore, and I didn't want to after the wreck.

I didn't tell anyone about what I knew would be called a hallucination. I didn't tell anyone that while I'd been in Krymzyn, despite the initial fear, I'd felt like the void in my mind had finally been filled. For the first time since I was twelve, the sense of waiting for something had left me. It was a combination of feelings only I could understand—the amazement, the fascination, and the belief that there was a reason I'd gone there beyond just a random occurrence. And more than anything else, I knew Krymzyn was real.

Just like when I was twelve, I was immediately put on anti-seizure medication. Desperately wanting to return to Krymzyn before the tumor was taken out of me, I debated not taking the pills. I had to see Sash again, learn more about her and Krymzyn, and try to understand the connection I felt to her and that world.

Even with the medication, I had several mild seizures over the next week, but they only brought flashes of light and distant sounds. Two days before my surgery, I quit taking the anti-seizure meds. I needed to go back before it was too late. There was no argument in my mind.

The day of my surgery arrived. I dressed in a hospital gown and stretched out facedown on a surgical table. A nurse secured my head into padded braces, tubes were needled into my arms, and electronic sensors were adhered to my temples.

As I was wheeled into the operating room, bright lights from overhead cast reflections on the shiny floor. My head started throbbing despite the drugs flowing into me, and I felt pressure building in the back of my neck.

"I know you've been through this before," Dr. Baskin said after the anesthesiologist turned a few knobs, "but I want you to relax and count backwards from ten for us."

Dull circles of light began to pulse on the floor. They seemed to rise off the surface until they filled my vision.

"Ten, nine," I said, desperately trying to fight the effects of the anesthesia. Before I reached eight, every muscle in my body convulsed.

*   *   *

I immediately study the sky. Shafts of bright light dissect the edges of the motionless clouds. I let out a long sigh of relief that I didn't arrive during Darkness. No, the relief is because I returned to Krymzyn.

Red spreads out before my eyes, and nothing has changed except the position of the branches reaching outward from the dormant tree in the meadow. Everything is still, absent of any movement.

When I look down, I see that I'm barefoot and dressed in "the manner of Krymzyn." My muscles are relaxed, and my mind is alert. I don't feel any effects from the drugs invading my consciousness back in my world.

Before I have a chance to figure out what to do, the same tall man I spoke to when I was twelve races over a hill in the distance. Orange and black hair trails behind his head and a metal flask swings by his side. The long steel spear in his hand reminds me of how terrified I felt during my first encounter with him.

Long ago, Sash told me that no one in Krymzyn would harm me, and I believed her. More specifically, "No one in the grace of Krymzyn," which I'm guessing didn't include that Murkovin creature and definitely not the tree. So as I wait for him, I don't feel the need to run or defend myself.

The man sprints across a meadow, up the hill, and stops a few feet in front of me. He's not even breathing hard after running faster than anyone I've ever seen, except maybe Sash when we were younger. There's not a drop of sweat on his face.

"I welcome you on your return to Krymzyn, Teller Chase," he says, nodding his head to me.

Despite how much I've grown, he's still at least four inches taller than I am. There's neither happiness nor sadness in his expression. Not anger, not calm—just a blank stare. I decide that, despite the sharp angles in his face, nose, cheekbones, and chin, the simmering amber in his black-lined eyes, and the vibrant orange highlights in his black hair, he's a strangely good-looking man. He's a little on the freaky side to be sure, but he's handsome, kind of like a mid-forties European model in a luxury sports car commercial.

"I remember you," I say calmly. "What's your name?"

Seeming to ignore me, he drops to one knee and sinks the fingertips of a hand into the ground. He whispers something inaudible before standing again.

"I'm called Tork," he replies, studying me carefully. "I've been told you were here during Darkness."

"That tree over there"—I point to the meadow—"would have killed me if Sash hadn't saved me."

"That's unfortunate," he replies with true concern in his voice. "I must tell you, we Disciples are quite confused by your arrival during Darkness. No Teller other than you has ever been in Krymzyn when Darkness has descended."

"How do you know no other Teller has been here during Darkness?" I ask. "A Teller may have been killed before you even knew about it."

"As I told you when you were smaller," he says firmly,

"the atmosphere announces the arrival of Tellers to us. With the exception of you, Tellers always arrive on the Telling Hill in Sanctuary. We'd be quite aware of a strange corpse anywhere else in Krymzyn."

"I guess I'll have to take your word for it."

"If words are spoken in Krymzyn," he chastises with the same irritated look I remember from when I was younger, "they are the truth."

"Will Sash know I'm here?" I ask. "I'd like to thank her for saving me."

"Only the Disciples are told of a Teller's arrival, but I've summoned her to meet us."

"Thank you. It means a lot to me."

"Let's proceed to Sanctuary," he says, pointing one hand in the direction from which he came.

As I walk beside him, I glance over my shoulder at the valley behind us. I see that we're heading in the opposite direction from Sash's cavern—or habitat, as she called it.

"I apologize again if you were at risk during your previous visit," Tork says to me as we walk. "I trust you don't feel any threat upon your return."

"No, I feel fine. I'm actually _happy_—satisfied—I got to come back before they . . ." I correct the word that doesn't translate but stop talking before I finish my sentence. I don't want to mention that, in my world, I'm in the middle of having my head cut open.

"Before they what?" he asks.

"Nothing," I say. "I don't know why I said that."

He scrutinizes my face, and I know that he knows I'm lying. In a strange way, I feel guilty. It's the same way I felt after gawking at Sash with her shirt off. There's a sense of purity, honesty, to everyone I've seen here, excluding the Murkovin. It just seems to emanate from their being.

"What direction are we walking?" I ask, wanting to change the subject. After years of cross-country running, it's also a habit of mine, always wanting to have my bearings.

"We walk south," he replies. The word hangs a little while in the air but eventually translates.

"So, you have north, south, east, and west?"

"Of course," he says as though I've asked the dumbest question ever.

"How do you know which is which?"

"The light always points north in Krymzyn. Always to the north."

I look up at the sky and, for the first time, notice that all the rays of light are basically pointing in the same direction.

"Do these clouds ever go away?" I ask.

"Never," he says. "The light from behind would be blinding if not for the clouds."

"What makes the light?"

"Energy," Tork answers, but the word takes a long time to translate.

We silently walk side by side at a brisk pace, up and down a hill and around another weathered, red-leaved tree in the center of a meadow. Tork steers me on a path to avoid stepping on any of the branches on the ground, always keeping a buffer of a few feet between us, like a border collie guiding sheep while maintaining a safe distance.

"You must always be careful not to damage a sustaining tree while it sleeps," he warns, noticing that I'm staring at the tips of the branches sunk into the ground. "You don't want the tree to be angry when it awakens."

"That might make more sense to me than anything else I've heard here," I say.

He doesn't smile, laugh, or respond to my statement in any way. From talking to Sash, I learned that slang doesn't fly in Krymzyn. I guess I can add sarcasm to that list.

As we climb a slightly larger hill, six tall, lean figures appear on the crest, all dressed in black pants and sleeveless black shirts. They all stand with their bare feet immersed in the red blades of grass. Black hair intertwined with bright orange strands tops their heads, metallic spears are clutched in their hands, and they examine me with intense amber eyes.

When we reach the top of the hill, Tork steps to the end of the row of what I assume are the Disciples, and to my shock, all seven figures bow to me. The tallest of the seven, oldest from what Sash had told me about how they measure age here, is a woman in the center of the row. She's at least six foot four, a hair taller than Tork. She looks a little older than my parents, maybe fifty, but her sharp features can only be described as beautiful. With a spear clutched in one hand and a lean but muscular body, she's an imposing figure.

"Finally, we meet the Teller Chase," the tall woman declares, a commanding tone in her voice. "Although I'm beginning to wonder if your purpose here is actually something more than Telling."

Chapter 9

"I present Eval," Tork says to me, "tallest of the Disciples currently in Krymzyn."

I quickly recall every name I've heard in Krymzyn— Sash, Tork, Balt, Yoni, and now, Eval.

"It's nice to meet you," I say with my eyes glued to Eval. "Does everyone here have four letters in their name?"

"Quite astute of you to notice," Eval answers. "Our naming custom is one letter for each of the four primary directions in Krymzyn."

As she examines me, her eyes remind me of Sash. They look like Sash's eyes, although it's hard to tell since everyone here has catlike amber eyes lined in black. But their focus, the way I feel them as much as see them, all remind me of Sash.

"Can you tell me why I'm here?" I ask.

"The only beings to visit Krymzyn from other worlds are Tellers," she explains, "although the anomalies related to your visits raise many questions regarding your actual purpose here."

"What exactly is a Teller supposed to do?"

"Tellers arrive in Krymzyn from every other plane of

existence at various points during the life cycles of those worlds. They tell us, the Disciples, details of life on their plane so that we're confident balance properly exists there. If balance in one of those worlds is disturbed, Krymzyn may attempt to resolve the situation. In some situations, a plane may be allowed to self-destruct. Without this process, other planes couldn't exist."

"I've got news for you," I say. "My plane exists with or without you and me."

"Although you may believe all things everywhere to be as they are in your world," she says firmly, "that belief is simply not a truth of existence."

"Are you trying to tell me you're like God or something?"

"We're Disciples of Krymzyn. Nothing more, nothing less."

I scan the row of seven people, not really wanting to spend my entire visit in a religious or philosophical discussion. Neither of those topics is something I'm really interested in, whether I'm here or on Earth.

The two Disciples sandwiched between Tork and Eval—a man and a woman—are both a bit shorter than Tork. They seem like they're in their late thirties or early forties, and they're just as strangely attractive as everyone else I've seen in this world. Well, Sash isn't really all that strange—other than the amber eyes and glowing scarlet in her hair. But "attractive" can't begin to describe anything about Sash.

The woman and two men on the other side of Eval don't appear to be older than in their twenties. They range in height from five foot eleven to six foot two. Also good-looking in an unusual way, they look like they could have stepped off a billboard for the latest fashion fad—if that fad happened to be black leathery pants, a sleeveless black shirt, and stoic faces topped by Halloween wigs.

"What are all the anomalies with my visits?" I ask.

"Are you fully aware when you depart your plane?" Eval replies, ignoring my question. They sure do that to me a lot here.

"I guess you could say that," I answer, not wanting to get into the seizure, tumor scenario.

"Strange," she says. "When Tellers arrive from other planes, they're typically asleep or in a meditative state while in their own world."

"What are the other anomalies?" I ask, returning to my initial question.

"On your first visit, you appeared to be much younger than any Teller to arrive before you. Tellers always arrive on this hill, called the Telling Hill, yet you arrive in another location. Darkness has never fallen while a Teller has been in Krymzyn, yet it's happened twice with you here. And no Teller has ever witnessed a sustaining tree awake or has been exposed to those who dwell in the Barrens."

"You mean the Murkovin?"

"Yes," Eval answers. "The Murkovin."

"What exactly are they?"

"Murkovin are creatures who belong to the Barrens outside the Delta. They live on sap from trees in the Barrens. That sap is contaminated. It results in irrational, extreme emotions in those who drink it. The more they drink, the more they need the sap. Those of us living in the grace of

Krymzyn take only what we need for existence from the supply our Hunters provide from healthy trees in the Delta."

"So they're, like, _addicted_ . . . just live to drink sap?" I ask, explaining the word that doesn't translate.

"Exactly," Eval replies. "So much so that they destroy the limbs of trees in the Barrens during light so they may more freely drink the sap during Darkness. Many of the trees in the Barrens die at their hands. Some Murkovin attempt to enter the Delta during Darkness, seeking sap from our trees or even to drink it from the blood of those who dwell here."

"Why don't you just hunt them all down and kill them?"

"They serve a valuable purpose," she says thoughtfully. "The Murkovin are a constant reminder to us of how important balance with our world is in order to sustain life."

I shake my head. "Everyone talks about balance here, but it seems like a pretty dangerous place from what I've seen."

"Balance doesn't imply an absence of danger," she tells me. "In fact, danger may allow balance to properly exist. But I do apologize if you felt threatened."

"It's _okay_," I say. "The Watchers took care of the Murkovin, and Sash saved me from the tree."

"Following the Murkovin intrusion, we were busy with the Watchers at the wall. Otherwise, one of us would have found you. When we learned you were injured and with Sash, we knew you would be safe and well cared for."

"I was both," I comment.

"The strangest anomaly to me," Eval says, "is that we've yet to have an opportunity to hear of your plane from you, although there's really no need. A Teller from the planet

Earth has visited Krymzyn in the recent past. We learned what we needed to know of your plane from that Teller."

"How do you know I'm from Earth?"

"You told me on your first visit," Tork interjects.

I think back to my conversation with him when I was twelve, remembering that I did tell him.

"How long ago was this other Teller here?" I ask.

"When Tork and I were early in our service as Disciples," Eval answers, "but before any of the others standing here had been called to fulfill their purpose."

Based on Eval's answer, I conclude that Eval and Tork are the two senior Disciples.

They all shift their eyes to my side before I say anything else. I turn my head to see Sash walking to the top of the hill. She glances at me and nods with the usual somber look on her face. When she stops in front of the row of Disciples, they all drop to one knee and bow their heads.

"Hunter Sash," Eval declares, "you've honored Krymzyn by your actions to protect and heal the Teller Chase. In his presence, we humbly thank you for your service to our guest."

I look from the Disciples to Sash. Her expression doesn't change, but she sinks to one knee and speaks with a soft sincerity that melts my insides.

"If I've served Krymzyn, it is I who feels honor."

Sash and the Disciples all stand.

"Communal is upon us," Eval says, "although this is another event that shouldn't occur while a Teller is visiting."

"What goes on during Communal?" I ask.

"We're alone with our thoughts," Eval answers, "but as

one with Krymzyn."

"I'm just curious—how do you know it's time for Communal?"

"Krymzyn shows us," she says.

Eval holds out a hand and turns her palm up. Magenta rays rise from her skin—light that wasn't there moments ago. All of the Disciples, arms dangling by their sides, now have magenta light illuminating their hands. Sash extends a palm in my direction, showing me the same light pulsating from her skin.

"I would suggest," Eval says, "that, while it may break with our custom of spending Communal alone, Chase spend this time with Sash, if neither of you has an objection."

"It will be my honor," Sash replies.

As Eval and Sash silently gaze at one another, I glance back and forth between them. A look of knowing is exchanged, like some deep secret is being shared. Eval suddenly turns her head to me.

"Is this acceptable to you, Chase?" Eval asks.

"Absolutely," I answer.

"Perhaps," Eval says to Sash, "since Chase appears to be the curious type, you'll take him to the Tall Hill. He can see the Delta, the Barrens, and the beauty of Krymzyn."

Chapter 10

Based on the direction of light overhead, Sash and I walk northwest towards what's obviously the tallest hill on the Krymzyn Delta. Her pace is brisk, leaning forward into an incredibly long, graceful stride. Even with my longer legs and walking as fast as I can, I have to almost trot to keep up with her.

"Thanks again for helping me," I say. "I don't know what I would've done without you."

"It was my honor to help you," she replies.

"Honor's a big thing around here, isn't it?"

"Honor provides balance, and balance is the purpose of our existence," she says. "What's your purpose on your plane?"

"I'm a student," I answer, somewhat surprised that the word translates.

"What do you learn?"

"Lots of things. I'm not sure what I want to do yet. Maybe be a _graphic artist_."

"I don't know of that task," she says.

"I _draw_ things, _pictures_."

"_Pictures_?" she asks.

I realize that I've never seen a pen, pencil, or piece of paper in Krymzyn. Not a book or work of art anywhere.

"A _picture_ is a _drawing_ . . . or a _painting_ . . . an image a person creates of something else, like a mountain or a river or another person."

"For what purpose?"

"So people can see things they wouldn't get to see. Or see people who are interesting or _famous_—well-known—or an emotion that the _artist_ sees."

"I apologize, but I don't understand."

I stop walking. "Watch what I'm doing," I say.

She stands still and watches me. I clench my hand into a fist in front of me, extend my forefinger, and trace one side of a tree trunk in the air. As I return my hand to the base of the imaginary trunk, I pull in my forefinger, and extend it again each time I add something to the image. I gradually create branches spreading out from the trunk, most reaching up high but a few falling down to the ground.

"What do you see?" I ask when I finish my invisible painting in the air.

"A tree," she says with mild surprise.

"What kind of tree?"

"A sustaining tree."

"Was it a healthy tree, or was it damaged?"

"A healthy tree," she answers, nodding her head.

"In my world, we have things called _paper_ and _canvas_— thick white rectangular fabric—and _pencils_ and _paint_— things that make dark lines or colors. I _draw_ like I did with my finger using the _paint_, and the _paint_ leaves the shapes and colors on the _paper_ or _canvas_ that end up being what I _draw_."

"Why would you do that?" she asks as we start to walk again.

"Just to make people feel good when they look at it. Or to inspire an emotion. Like how you knew that was a healthy tree. I wanted you to see it that way."

"Or you could have made me see a damaged tree?" she asks.

"Yes," I say, "but the sustaining trees seem important to you, so I wanted you to see a healthy tree."

"They are important," she replies. "Thank you for showing it to me that way."

"You're welcome. Don't you have ways to record things that happen here or show what things look like?"

"All is recorded in our minds," she explains.

"What if you need to, like, solve a math problem or show somebody where something is?"

"We do so in our minds or with our words."

I remember the way she instantly told me my age in snaps.

"If you multiply twelve hundred and eleven by thirty-seven, divide that by seventy-three, then multiply again by one hundred and twenty-three, what do you get?"

"Seventy-five thousand, four hundred ninety-six, with a remainder of seven hundred and twenty-six one-thousandths," she answers without hesitation.

"I'll have to take your word for it," I chuckle. "In my world, we need to _write_ that all down on _paper_ or use a thing called a _calculator_ to do it for us."

"That seems inefficient," she says.

"We're not quite as quick in the mind as you are."

When we reach the base of the hill, Sash increases her walking pace. It takes us fifteen minutes to climb up the slope, and Sash never slows her pace.

I'm completely out of breath when we reach the top, though Sash never seems winded at all. Once on the crest, the constant silence I'm used to hearing in Krymzyn is replaced by the echo of rushing water. I marvel at the panoramic view surrounding me. All I've really seen of Krymzyn is a small area in the south-central portion of the Delta.

An enormous black marble wall lines the edges of the football-shaped Delta. Several green-haired Watchers walk along the top of the wall. Forking at the north, a broad river viciously flows down either side of the Delta and rejoins at the south. Furious raging rapids swell through the river. Silvery blue waves smash against a few giant, black granite rocks spiking out of the surface. The water churns like torrents of semitransparent liquid metal reflecting the scarlet and orange light from overhead.

Across the river, red grass gradually dissipates into an expanse of black dirt. Occasional sustaining trees with charcoal-black bark, gangly and old, are scattered across the rocky, hilly plains. Many are stripped bare of branches, just towering stumps of black rising from the ground. The few that have limbs are laced with sparse gray leaves. The light in the sky fades from red and orange over the Delta to tones of gray in the Barrens.

To the east, a narrow, gradually rising black road leads through the bleak hills. In the distance, a black mountain reaches up to the sky. It's as tall as any mountain I've ever seen, the peak hidden in the clouds. Rays of green light shine around the mountain, creating a verdant luster in the rocky black slopes.

I look from the northernmost point of the Delta down to the south, recognizing the hill I'm pretty sure is the Telling Hill we just came from. A broad, circular meadow slightly farther south, obviously the largest field in the Delta, is home to a gargantuan oak-like tree at least three times the size of any of the others. The bark glows deep red as the branches gently sway in the static air. Lemon-yellow leaves, not red like those of the sustaining trees, garnish the limbs.

"One tree is moving," I say with surprise. "The one with yellow leaves."

"The Tree of Vision is always aware," Sash says.

"That's the Tree that tells you your purpose?"

"It reveals our purpose," she answers.

"Where do I arrive?" I ask.

Sash points to a small hill in the center of the southern half of the Delta. In a meadow on one side of the hill sprouts the lone sustaining tree that almost killed me. The small hill—the Empty Hill, they call it—is surrounded by slightly taller hills and little else, explaining the name.

I'm pretty good at calculating distances from all the miles of cross-country training. I scan the length of the Delta again and estimate it to be twenty miles long by ten miles wide.

"This is really incredible," I say, turning to Sash. "The beauty is amazing."

"I often come to this hilltop to see the contrast between

the Barrens and the Delta," she replies. "It reminds me of what's important."

There's not the slightest hint of happiness on her face, but there's a look of deep appreciation in her eyes as they roam the crimson hills. When her eyes stop on me, I can't look away from her.

"Doesn't anyone ever _smile_ here?" I ask.

"What's _smile_?"

I curl the corners of my mouth up into a smile and point to my lips. "Something we do in my world when we're _happy_."

"_Happy_?"

"Satisfied. Just a good feeling inside. We call that _happiness_, or being _happy_."

"We don't need facial expressions to share our feelings of fulfillment," she says.

I nod, even though I don't really understand her response. I feel, as I often do here, that she could explain in more detail if she wanted to.

"Do you remember the first time we met?" I ask.

She nods her head. "On the Empty Hill, when we were much smaller. It was after my Ritual of Purpose."

"I was really confused that I was here, but I felt safe once we started talking."

"I remember," Sash says. "You were frightened when you saw Tork, but still brave."

"I saw you before that. Before we met. You were kneeling at the Tree."

"I know," she replies with her eyes locked on mine. "I felt you watching me during my Ritual."

"How did you know it was me?"

"I know the way your eyes feel."

Her answer actually makes sense to me. I know how her eyes feel when they peer inside me, as they do now.

"You're so beautiful," I whisper, almost under my breath.

"It's odd to define a person as beautiful," she says with a slightly more contemplative expression on her face.

"Where I come from, we do it all the time. How do you define someone here?"

"By their ability to fulfill their purpose with what's inside them. Beauty isn't a purpose."

"You should tell that to some of the girls where I live," I mumble.

"I don't understand your meaning," she says.

"Never mind. It's not important. When I said you're beautiful, I wasn't talking about just the way you look. I meant what's inside you."

"In Krymzyn, we always look to the inside," she replies.

Her eyes seem to reach even deeper to my core, the same way they did when we were twelve. For a split second, maybe in my imagination, I feel thousands of dull pinpricks inside me. My entire body feels like a leg that's waking up after falling asleep, and the feeling seems to be coming from her.

"You know, Sash, as strange as this place is to me in some ways, there's something really . . . I don't know—peaceful about it. Kind of logical and calming."

"Maybe you feel balance here," she says.

"Maybe I do."

Sash sits on the ground, lays her spear beside her, and rests her arms on her knees. "You should sit," she says, motioning her head to the ground at her side. "You seem tired from the climb."

I sit beside her with my legs stretched out in front of me. "I am a little. I want to ask you something kind of weird."

"You may ask what you will."

"Do you ever feel like . . . I don't know. This sounds so _lame_ . . . sorry, ignorant. Do you ever feel like you and I are connected somehow?"

"What do you mean by connected?" she asks.

I know she understands the meaning of the word because it translates, but she's unsure of the context.

"Like, the way I arrive on the hill close to where you live instead of the Telling Hill and always seem to see you when I get here. The way I saw you before we ever met, and you knew I saw you. The way you were there to rescue me the last time I was here.

"The Disciples told me that my visits are different than any other Teller before me. It's like we're meant to be sitting here together right now. Like part of our purpose is to know each other and share things together."

She stares into my eyes for several seconds while she deliberates how to respond. Before answering, she looks away to the bottom of the hill.

"When the Tree of Vision reveals our purpose, each of us is shown our own Vision of the Future. This Vision is something that will come to pass and is meant to guide us. We're to tell no one of this Vision. It's only for the mind of the one shown, so I shouldn't reveal my Vision to you or anyone else.

"Your face," she continues, returning her eyes to mine, "was in my Vision. I recognized you the first time I saw you on the Empty Hill, your blue eyes. I began to feel things from your world—emotions others here don't feel and would define as extreme. Some of them feel good. Some are painful and difficult to control. I feel them all the time but understand them better through you. I feel how you balance them. That's all I should say, but I believe it answers your question."

I'm surprised by what she tells me, but also relieved that I'm not imagining something more than random coincidence between us. I want to ask her more about what the emotions are she feels from my world, but my attention is drawn to movement over her shoulder.

Two golden-haired figures, a man and a woman with spears in their hands, walk up the hill towards us. Two children—one an adorable girl with straight jet-black hair framing her round face, maybe twelve or thirteen, and a handsome boy, ten or eleven, stocky, with curly black hair— suddenly dart past the adults. Sash turns to see what I'm looking at.

"Keepers," Sash says, "with two of our children."

The Keepers stop halfway up the hill, but the children keep sprinting towards us. The girl's stride is long and sleek, her speed stunning as she races up the hill. Her face reminds me of my sister at that age as I get a closer look. The boy is wilder, less control in his young gait, although it's steady and strong. Fierce determination flows from their amber eyes.

"I thought everyone spends Communal alone," I say.

"Not the children," Sash replies.

They stop a few feet in front of us and both quickly bow. Sash nods her head, and I smile to them. They stare at me with a mixture of curiosity and distrust.

"The Teller is well balanced," Sash says to the children. "There's no need for fear."

"In my world," I say, "I compete in something we call cross-country, a race of speed across hills. Both of you would be _champions_."

"_Champions_?" the girl asks after the word dissipates.

"Winners of the race," I answer. "Those who finish first."

"I believe Chase the Teller is praising your speed," Sash explains.

"Yes," I say, smiling. "That's exactly what Chase the Teller is doing."

Both kids bow to me in obvious gratitude, glance at one another, and suddenly fling their bodies to the ground. After they cross their arms over their chests and stiffen their legs, they roll away down the hill. I'm surprised by the lack of smiles on their faces or laughter filling the air, just the continued look of determination. It's a test to them, not a whimsy as it would be on Earth.

The girl is the first to reach a flat area partially down the side of the steep hill. She leaps to her feet and bolts towards the Keepers with no stagger at all from dizziness. The boy sprawls onto the flat ground and catches himself with his fingers dug into the grass just before sliding off the ledge to another steep part of the slope. He pulls himself forward, springs up, and sprints after the girl. When both children reach the Keepers, the four walk down the hill away from us.

"I believe Tela, the girl," Sash says to me, "will be a Traveler when her purpose is revealed. She has great speed and a strong mind."

"Traveler?" I ask.

"Travelers are the fastest of all in Krymzyn. They take things across the Delta and travel between the Delta and the Mount."

"What about the boy?"

"He's quite brave," she answers. "Cavu is a bit reckless, but he already demonstrates mature respect for our trees. He has a tremendous desire to protect the Delta. I believe he'll be a Watcher, although I don't know for certain yet."

I study Sash's face and eyes. "Do you know things before they happen?" I ask, certain that I already know the answer to that question.

"Some things," she says. When she looks down at the bottom of the hill again, a shadow of sadness falls over her face. "I'm shown visions. They're like glimpses from waking dreams. While Tela rolled down the hill, I saw streaks of blue in her hair—the color of a Traveler. I know when Darkness is near. I can feel it inside me. Sometimes, I see something directly in front of me that will soon happen as though it's happening in that instant, and I can change the outcome before it actually occurs."

"Do other people here see these things?"

"No," she says, shaking her head. "Only me."

"Is it hard on you?" I ask, reacting to the pain evident on her face.

Turning her face to me, she seems surprised by my

question. "You're the only person to ever ask me that."

"I don't mean to be _nosy_—too personal," I say.

"I don't mind," she replies. "It feels right to talk to you about these things. It's not what I'm shown that hurts me. It's what I'm not shown—things I could have changed. I don't always understand the emotions I feel from your world, and that's even more difficult. I don't even have names to go with some of those feelings. They can be overwhelming at times. No one here understands them, so it helps me when you're here."

We gaze at each other for several seconds. I suddenly feel closer to her than I've felt to anyone in my life. She's reaching inside me again. I want to take her in my arms and hold her, comfort her, and share the feelings I have for her. But she's already told me that physical contact doesn't exist here.

"I'd like to _kiss_ you," I say.

"What's _kiss_?" she asks.

I immediately decide that a verbal explanation can't begin to do justice to the meaning of the word or the way it feels. As I think about it, I decide that it may sound pointless to her. But I don't want to let this moment pass, so I slowly move my face to hers and gently kiss her lips. She doesn't return my kiss, but she also doesn't pull away. When I lean back, her face wrinkles with confusion.

"Why did you do that?" she asks.

"That's a _kiss_," I say.

"What's the purpose of a _kiss_?"

"It's like when I touched your hand. It's another way two people nurture one another where I come from, but it shows you like them more than just as a friend."

"It seems strange," she muses. "Is that to show how you feel about me?"

"It's to share how we feel about each other. But if you don't feel that way, I won't do it again."

Never taking her eyes off mine, she inches her face forward and closes half the distance between us. When she stops, I move my face the other half and softly press my lips against hers. Sash awkwardly returns a brief kiss this time, and then we kiss again. I open my mouth slightly and slide my tongue between her lips. She hesitates, unsure, but does the same, and our tongues gently intertwine.

After our kiss, I wrap my arms around her and hold her close to me. She hesitates again, obviously not knowing what a hug is, but then slips her hands around my waist. We clutch each other tightly until I feel a deep sorrow come over me. I pull away to look into her amber eyes.

"Sash," I say, shaking my head, "I don't think I'm coming back to Krymzyn again."

"Why do you say that?"

"The reason I come here is a growth inside my head. It's called a _tumor_." I point to the spot on the back of my head. "That's why you knew I was in pain when I was younger. Right now, in my world, some people are about to take the _tumor_ out of my head. When it's gone, I won't come back. I want to come back and see you and spend time with you, but I can't control that."

The amber from her eyes streams into mine. I feel her completely inside me, sharing my sadness. She leans to me and gently kisses my lips.

"Chase," she whispers when our kiss ends, "you will return."

Her lips touch mine again, but I feel dizzy. My head starts to spin, my hands tremble against her body, and I close my eyes. Darkness from inside consumes my vision.

Chapter 11

I must have drawn twenty pictures of Sash and twenty landscapes of the view from the Tall Hill while propped up in my hospital bed during the days of recovery. My mom never left my side, just like after the surgery when I was twelve. My dad and sister spent every minute they could with me. Connor and his family visited every day I stayed in the hospital.

Despite the biopsy revealing a benign tumor, my doctor recommended chemotherapy just in case there were undetectable traces of the growth left that could lead to cancer. After the surgical wounds healed, three weeks of radiation treatments were followed by the start of chemo.

When each of my chemo treatments ended, I stayed in the hospital for a few hours of monitoring prior to being released. I was wheeled into a common room filled with toys, video games, and DVDs in the children's cancer wing. After my second treatment, I saw a boy, maybe eleven years old, with sandy hair and green eyes, sitting alone in a wheelchair. The back of his head was shaved, and he stared despondently at the floor.

"Hey, I'm Chase," I said after getting out of my chair

94

and walking over to him.

"I'm Davis," he said quietly, looking up at me.

"Are you here alone?"

"My mom had to pick up my little brother," he replied.

"Me too," I said. "My mom had to get my sister. What are you here for?"

"I had a brain tumor," he answered, "and I have cancer." The despair in his voice betrayed the brave expression on his face.

"That sucks," I said, resting a hand on his shoulder. "I'm really sorry."

"You have it too?" he asked, sounding like he was afraid of my answer.

"I had a benign tumor in my head. My second one in five years."

"I'm really glad you don't have cancer," he told me.

"Thank you. Me too. Hey, feel like playing?" I asked, motioning my head to the video game box.

"Sure," he answered with a smile.

I wheeled him over to the monitor and set up the game. I'd planned on letting him win, but that strategy quickly proved to be unnecessary as he thoroughly kicked my ass over several rounds of a fantasy warrior battle. Little things like brain cancer and chemo couldn't stop the flurry of his fingers moving from button to button on the controller and his expert steering of the miniature joystick.

"Do you want to see something cool?" I asked when I'd had enough of his virtual thrashing.

"Sure," he replied.

I walked to where my backpack was lying on the

ground, took out my sketch pad, and returned to the seat beside his wheelchair.

"Did you ever have hallucinations before they removed your tumor?" I asked.

"No, not really."

"Did you have seizures?"

"Yeah," he said. "I'd get a really bad headache and see, like, bright lights."

"Did you have any other hallucinations?" I asked.

"No, why?"

I opened my drawing tablet and held it in front of him. "This is where I went and what I saw during my seizures."

His eyes widened and his mouth opened with amazement. A smile of wonder gradually took over his face as I turned the pages of my sketch pad. I explained each full-color drawing of the Krymzyn landscape, the Disciples, sustaining trees in motion, the waterfall inside a cavern, and pages and pages of Sash. He jerked backwards at one sketch and shivered slightly as the smile left his face—a reaction to the detailed depiction of a Murkovin.

"Those are incredible!" he exclaimed when we finished looking through the tablet. "That should be, like, a video game or something."

"Thanks," I said. "It's really cool when I go there."

"But it's just a hallucination?"

"No," I answered, shaking my head. "It's real. I know it's real."

I didn't show him one drawing that was buried on the last page. It felt too personal to me to show it to anyone else. I often looked at the close-up portrait of Sash when I was alone. Her facial expression was exactly the same one she'd had after disclosing she'd seen me in her Vision of the Future. At the bottom of the page, I didn't write the last three words she'd spoken to me before I'd left. Instead, I drew a question mark.

What I always wondered when I looked at that question mark, knowing that she knew things about the future, was *When would I return?* A week? A month? Ten years? I had no way of knowing and never had a chance to ask her. The only thing I knew was that a brain tumor was the trigger to send me there. Unless a new tumor developed, I didn't think I'd go back.

As clumps of our hair fell out in the weeks that followed, Davis and I shaved the rest of our heads together. The backs of our skulls were already bare from our surgeries. We spent hours playing video games after our treatments, and I taught him how to really draw.

I learned that he stayed in the hospital twenty-four hours a day while they tried to eradicate the aggressive cancer spreading through his brain. His parents and little brother spent as much time as they could with him, but he still had hours of solitude each day. I began going to the hospital to see him most afternoons when school let out, even after my round of chemo treatments were completed.

My driver's license had been suspended because of the seizures and surgery. On days my mom couldn't take me to the hospital to visit Davis, I walked to a bus stop, transferred to the subway, and then walked the rest of the way.

When weekends came, I'd sometimes spend an entire day with him, taking walks outside, tossing a ball around when he felt up to it, or just playing games. Even when his family was there, they didn't mind my presence. They knew that my own medical history, surviving a tumor when I was his age, created a sense of security in Davis.

Whenever we were alone, he asked me to tell him stories about Krymzyn. We'd look through my drawings while I shared most of what happened to me there. My short-term memory was sporadic at best, a frightening by-product of chemotherapy that lingered for many months. I started writing down every detail of my experiences in that world, starting with my first trip there when I was twelve. The journal served as my reminder, a way to refresh my mind, in case I ever did return.

*   *   *

"Hey, guys," I called out to a group of kids from my school. Connor and I were hanging out at the mall on the first Sunday after school had let out for the summer.

"Hi, Chase," a girl named Stephanie replied. "Hi, Connor."

Trim with blond hair and blue eyes, she was the consummate California girl. Stephanie was at the mall with a group of her friends, a mix of guys and girls from our school. We all stopped in front of each other and quickly said hello. I knew most of them pretty well, and while I'd describe them as friends, they weren't close friends.

"How are you feeling?" Stephanie asked me. The pity in

her eyes was obvious. Her reserved body language made her look uncomfortable standing beside me or, I don't know, maybe that was just my imagination.

"I'm doing great," I said enthusiastically.

She quickly scanned my body, her eyes starting at my feet and rising up to my face. Dressed in cargo shorts and a T-shirt, both baggy due to my weight loss, I know I looked like the walking dead. My healthy tan was gone, my muscles had suffered severe atrophy, and coarse, brown hair was just beginning to grow from my bald head. Like menacing racing stripes, two distinct surgical scars lined the back of my skull.

"I'm really glad to hear that," she replied. "You look like you're doing better." She didn't sound very convincing.

"What are you guys up to?" Connor asked the group.

"We just saw a movie," Stephanie said. "Now we're going to Justin's to go swimming. What about you?"

"We're headed to see a movie," Connor answered.

Another group of kids about our age weaved through the bag-laden shoppers strolling by us. They weren't from our school and we didn't know them. Out of the corner of my eye, I caught a few of them staring at me. When I snapped my head towards them, they looked away.

"We have to get going," Stephanie said. "We're kind of in a hurry. You guys have fun."

We all exchanged good-byes before Stephanie and her friends walked away through the crowded mall. Stephanie turned her head over her shoulder and looked straight at Connor's eyes.

"A few of us are going to the beach on Thursday. If you want to go, text me."

Connor didn't answer as she looked away. I clenched my jaw to keep my own face blank, but the sting of rejection burned my eyes.

"They're assholes," Connor said, resting his hand on my shoulder. "You don't need them."

"It's just so weird," I complained. "She used to flirt with me all the time. Now it's like she and her friends think if they're anywhere near me, they'll get cancer or something."

"You know who your real friends are," he said firmly.

He was right. The track team had all been incredibly supportive of me. I'd gone to every meet through the spring to cheer all of them on. It was the only real activity I'd felt up to, other than visiting Davis. The team never once distanced themselves from me or looked at me with pity in their eyes.

Connor and I had a small group of close friends that had been together for years. Many of them had gone to the same K–8 school we had attended and were now at the same high school. They did everything they could to support and encourage me, but they also tried to make sure I felt as normal as possible. The last thing I wanted was for people to feel sorry for me or make me feel different, and pity sure wouldn't help my psychological recovery. But I'd seen and felt plenty of the distant treatment that Stephanie and her friends threw my way.

"I guess I do," I said. "It just gets to me sometimes. Like I don't already have enough to deal with?"

"You can't let it bother you," he insisted. "Your real friends always have your back."

"Thanks, Connor."

We slapped our right hands together, gripped them

firmly, and pulled each other into a tight hug.

*   *   *

The next Saturday morning, exactly four months after my surgery, I was getting dressed in my room when I heard the phone ring. My mom was about to drive me to the hospital to spend the day with Davis and his parents. His prognosis hadn't changed much over the months that had passed since I'd first met him.

The door to my bedroom swung open a minute later, revealing my mom's face. Her eyes were red and tears stained her cheeks. I didn't need to hear the words that were going to come out of her mouth. I knew what she was about to say.

"Davis is gone," she said, trying to keep her voice steady. "Last night in his sleep."

She walked to me and reached out her arms. I sank into them as my stomach knotted and tears clouded my eyes. With my face buried in her neck, I was unable to contain the waves of excruciating sorrow and grief.

I carried a thin twelve-by-sixteen-inch brown cardboard box in my hand when we went to his funeral. I'd barely slept for the past four days, working on a painting of Davis well into the early morning hours. I'd had just enough time to dry mount, matte, and frame the picture before we left home for the service. The close-up portrait of Davis—a beaming smile on his face, sparkle of life in his green eyes, and a full head of sandy-blond hair—was exactly how I wanted to remember him.

At the cemetery, his mom, dad, and little brother stood across the grave from me and my family. The casket had already been lowered into a hole in the ground, a pyramid of flowers at the head. A large circle of people watched as a handful of dirt was tossed into the grave.

I raised my eyes from the ground to his mother. Light glistened on a single tear that fell off her face from the streams running down her cheeks. As though the world slammed into slow motion, my eyes followed the tear for what felt like thirty seconds, until it splashed on a blade of grass at her feet. A flash of crimson glowed around the green edges, but I knew that was just my imagination. I walked around the grave, slipped the frame from the box, and handed the painting to his father.

"I want you to have this," I said. "This is how he always looked to me."

The family all smiled at the painting while tears continued to fall from their eyes. After his mother reached her arms around me, her chest heaved against mine.

"I hope you know how much he cherished the time you spent with him," she whispered hoarsely in my ear.

"I did too," I said. "Every second."

I didn't tell her that I'd learned a lot about life from that really cool, incredibly brave little eleven-year-old. Like that sometimes, wonderful things happen to assholes who don't deserve it, while cruel, horrendous things happen to really good people. No matter how you want to spin it, no matter what God you do or don't believe in, the reality is that life isn't fair and never will be. That's just the way it is, and all you can do is suck it up and accept it and go on with your life. But that doesn't mean it won't hurt sometimes.

Chapter 12

With cloudless azure skies overhead and warm, dry air surrounding me, I spent the entire summer and fall doing nothing but running. Residual chemicals from chemotherapy were gradually sweated out of my body as I tried to make up for months and months of lost training.

Due to the brain surgery, every muscle in my body stung with constant torment when I ran. At times, the pain amplified beyond description, but I didn't care. The pain just made me run harder. I remembered Davis when I ran, the agony he and his family had suffered with no reward, and any pain I felt couldn't begin to compare.

As my feet and legs pounded across endless miles of hilly dirt trails, my thoughts inevitably drifted to Sash. The time we spent together on the Tall Hill was replayed over and over again in my mind. I tried to analyze and understand the undeniable connection I felt with her, the same connection she'd admitted to feeling with me. Running was my only real chance to be alone with those thoughts. So I ran . . . and ran . . . and ran.

At the last regular cross-country race during the fall season of my senior year, I qualified for the regional meet.

With a furious sprint to the finish line at regionals, I passed two other runners to earn the last spot in the high school state championship.

When I bounced up and down at the starting line of state finals, my physical condition was only at about eighty percent of where it had been before the surgery. What I lacked in muscle strength, I was determined to make up for with mental focus.

Just before the starter's gun fired, I glanced at Connor standing with my family and coach by the side of the course. Connor clenched a hand into a fist, pounded it against his chest several times, and mouthed one word to me.

It was the same word he had said to me before the start of my races for many years. The same word that, as he'd crouch in the starting blocks before a sprint, I'd yell at him from the side of the track. That word had become our private credo—not only for sports, but for life.

Believe.

Neither of us was religious. The only connotation was to always, beyond everything else in life, believe in ourselves. That word had never had more meaning than it did in the moments before that race.

Mom, Dad, Ally, and Connor were cheering and jumping up and down when I sprinted across the finish line of the three-mile course. Despite the November chill in the air, I was drenched in sweat. Everything I had inside me, physically and mentally, had been sacrificed to that course. I had nothing left when the race ended.

"You know, if it weren't for the tumor, I know you would've won this race," Dad said as he hugged my panting, sweat-soaked body at the finish line. "You should be really proud of fourth place, Chase. Awesome run."

I smiled when our embrace ended, leaned over, and rested my hands on my knees. "I didn't need to win," I said, looking up at him. "I just had to finish the race."

His smile beamed with approval, pride, and understanding.

The rest of my senior year was difficult. Since I was unable to drive, always being dependent on my parents and friends was a huge inconvenience. The feeling of separation, of being viewed as different, damaged, even pitied, was always with me.

I spent more and more time alone, running, painting, and thinking about everything that had happened to me in Krymzyn. I tried to understand how I knew beyond any doubt that Krymzyn was real. More than that, I believed that there was a reason for my visits there, but I had no idea what that reason was.

During my senior year, I went to the hospital every three months for preventative scans, not that a scan would prevent anything. The checkups always created apprehension and anxiety in both me and my family. I never wanted to be the source of agony for my parents again, to watch them suffer through another surgery and recovery because of me. Guilt couldn't begin to describe how I felt when I realized that a small part of me was always disappointed when the scans were negative. I longed to see Sash again, but only a tumor would take me to her.

I never mentioned Krymzyn to anyone other than Davis, but they all saw my paintings. I'd told them that the images were just from my imagination, but they also had to have realized they were the same things I'd drawn since I was twelve. I assumed they thought that my drawings were part of my own internal therapy. My family let me know that they were always there for me if I wanted to talk, and while we discussed my physical and emotional recovery, "hallucinations" never entered the conversation.

The mile wasn't my best race—longer distances were my strong suit—but I made it to the state semifinals in that event at the end of my senior year. I'd already decided not to run competitively in college despite a few partial scholarship offers from smaller schools. I was sure the larger schools feared my medical history, but none of that was important to me. When I was accepted to one of the most prestigious art schools in the country, The Art Center College of Design in Pasadena, nothing else really mattered.

My parents insisted that I live at home and commute for the entire four years of college. I was allowed to start driving again after being seizure-free for a year, but my parents and doctors still wanted me to live at home. The thirty-minute drive to school never bothered me. I often took running clothes with me so I could trek through the hills over Pasadena in the evenings.

Connor attended USC as a film major. Although both of our schedules were hectic, we remained as close as brothers and saw each other almost every weekend. But I drifted farther away from other friends and focused more and more on my art.

My father converted a room behind our garage into a studio for me. Whenever I was in the cozy, well-lit workspace, Casey slept at the side of my desk on a dog bed. He was getting older, much less active, and plenty of white had replaced the gold fur around his face. Instead of runs, I took him for long late-night walks.

When I wasn't working on a project for school, I sometimes sat at my computer and painted digital landscapes of Krymzyn or pictures of Sash. But as the four years of college passed, the memories of Krymzyn gradually faded and seemed much less real. The only reminder as I grew older was the soft feminine voice I'd sometimes hear out of nowhere, always whispering the same three words.

"You will return."

* * *

A Hollywood graphic design firm offered me an internship during my senior year of college that led to a job after graduation. The company worked on everything from movie posters to TV commercials, but my specialty was video game design. I also started dating a young woman named Jessica my last year of college.

I had a sketch pad full of drawings of Jess, her long raven hair, slender face, athletic body, and big almond-shaped eyes. One time, on top of a charcoal sketch of her, I mindlessly used colored pencils to add amber in her eyes and wavy red lines in her hair. As I stared at the drawing, I knew that her resemblance to Sash was what had really attracted me to her.

An apartment in the Los Feliz area of Los Angeles became my home after graduation. On the fringe of Hollywood, it was close to my job and the Hollywood Hills, with their miles and miles of trails for running.

At the age of twenty-two, I was living on my own for the first time. I missed my family and the security I felt being around them, so I'd stop by once or twice a week to visit my parents. I always had the excuse of visiting Casey, but I'm sure they knew it was really to console my own feelings of loneliness.

Ally was attending the University of California at Berkeley, majoring in environmental sciences. I might have received the artistic gifts in the family, but my sister had the intellectual aptitude.

Connor landed a job as a production assistant with a documentary film company. His hours were long, but it was the perfect entry-level position for him. His goal was to eventually make films that would do what they could to change the world—or at least open a few eyes. Despite our busy schedules, we always made time to go for a run together or grab a beer after work.

Jess accepted a job with an advertising agency in San Francisco. We did the long-distance thing for a few months but gradually drifted apart and argued more, until the dreaded and unavoidable phone call.

"I just don't feel like we're going anywhere," Jess said. "I mean, after a year together, you still won't even make love to me."

"I told you," I mumbled. "I just want to wait."

"Wait for what, Chase?" she asked. "I know it's not a

moral thing. So you tell me what it is."

"I don't know, Jess. I really don't."

"You're the only twenty-two-year-old virgin I know—guy or girl!" she yelled. "Don't I turn you on?"

"Jess, you know it's not that," I said, and it wasn't. She was way out of my league, I often thought.

"Then I guess you don't love me enough," she pouted.

How was I supposed to answer? That I was clinging to some whacked-out fantasy girl who might only exist due to hallucinations caused by a brain tumor? Tell Jess that I believed the voice I kept hearing over and over in my head that said, "You will return"? Tell her that I believed even more in the connection I felt with the girl who'd spoken those words, a connection that was stronger than anything I felt with anyone here on Earth?

And tell her that if Sash and I did ever make love, given that sex didn't exist there except in the Ritual of Balance—which, according to Sash, she'd never be chosen for—I wanted us to be on level ground? That I wanted us to be able to share the experience of our first time together so that it was new and exciting and perfect? Was that how I was supposed to answer? Because if I did answer that way, even if it was the truth, it would sound really insane—even to me—and I'd probably end up in a psych ward.

"I just want it to feel right," I answered, knowing that there was only one person it could ever feel right with.

"If it doesn't feel right by now," Jess said, "it never will."

And that was the end of that.

Chapter 13

"I'm sorry I can't be here to protect you," the young woman whispers to the tree.

Her forehead rests against charcoal bark while one hand gently caresses the trunk. An enormous branch, recently ripped from the tree, lies rotting at her feet.

After the young woman leans back from the decaying bark, her eyes roam the drab Barrens in front of her. She spots a pale figure skulking along the crest of a faraway hill. The sadness on her face flares into raging fury. She tightens the grasp on her spear, digs her feet against the ground, and launches into a sprint towards the creature.

"Stop!" a woman's voice, the tallest of the Disciples, shouts from the road behind her.

The young woman ignores the Disciple's command. Slivers of light bloom from her body until brilliant beams skim over the treacherous wasteland. She slides to a stop on the once-distant hill. With her eyes and ears alert, her spear at the ready, she studies the terrain in front of her.

A shallow, narrow gully cuts through the black dirt at the bottom of the low hill she stands on. Across the ravine, a steep rise ends in a jagged ridge. As her eyes sweep across the scraggly rocks, her ears twitch at the slightest sound. The Murkovin lurks behind, the young woman concludes. She charges forward but halts in her tracks just before reaching the gully.

I leap over the ravine, sprint up the hill, and soar over the ridge. The Murkovin I saw crouches below the edge. I thrust the tip of my spear through his skull as I land, but three more wait in hiding.

One charges from my left, two from my right. Spinning to my right, I block the attack of one, twist again, and impale the gut of the second on my spear. He grabs the steel shaft with both hands, strength still in his arms.

A spear tip gouges my shoulder and blood spills down my arm. My grasp on my spear weakens as I try to pull it from the wounded Murkovin. The one who stabbed me jabs again. I dodge the tip, but the last creature rams his spear straight into the back of my skull.

Crouching at the edge of the gully, the young woman quickly scans the ridge again. She slowly steps backwards until stopping on the top of the hill behind her. With tremendous force, she slams the point of her spear to the ground. Sparks fly off the tip as the steel shatters black crystals of dirt.

"If you enter the Delta," she taunts, "you will meet death!"

The young woman waits vigilantly, her muscles tense and spear in hand. If they attack her in the open, she's certain the result will be different than if she enters their trap.

She glances behind her. The female Disciple still stands

on the road near the edge of the bridge, two Watchers now at the Disciple's side. The young woman snaps her head back to the ridge, but the Murkovin never appear.

After turning away from the gully, the young woman sprints towards the road but doesn't blend her light. The Murkovin won't attack her so close to the bridge and with several Watchers nearby. When she nears the road, she slows to a walk, the thrashing river at her side. Her vision is drawn to a large black slab of stone in the center of the rapids.

Why am I protected from death with a vision now when I was shown my own dead body on that rock in my Vision of the Future? Why was I not shown the events that will lead to my death in the river so I can prevent them?

She looks at the road where a tall female Watcher stands on one side of the Disciple. A green-haired man who recently ended his Apprenticeship and is now a Watcher lingers on the other side. His scalding eyes bear down on the young woman as she walks to the road.

He stares at me as he often does. I don't like the way he looks at me—I never have. It makes me feel uncomfortable, as if he wants something from me, wants to possess or control me. It's the kind of expression no one should ever have when looking at another. There's no respect in his eyes.

The blue-eyed Teller looked at me in a strange way once, but his stare was different. His eyes filled with appreciation as he gazed upon me. There was shame in his eyes when I took my clothes off in front of him, as though it had some significance in his world. But there was also innocence and respect in his stare. I felt safe in his eyes.

"We crossed the bridge when we saw the Murkovin," the female Watcher says when the young woman reaches the road. "We would have come to your aid, but as you know, we can't match your speed."

The young woman bows to the Watcher in a show of thanks.

"Please leave us," the Disciple says, turning to the female Watcher. "Thank you for quickly coming to my side."

The two Watchers walk to the bridge and cross over the metal surface. The young woman glowers at the back of the green-haired man's head until he reaches the arch of the bridge. He never turns to look at her, but she knows that she feels the pierce of her glare.

"We don't kill Murkovin without cause, only in defense," the Disciple lectures. "You must remember, they too serve a purpose to our balance, and the Barrens belong to them."

"I could feel the tree's pain," the young woman argues. "I know it's wrong of me, but I wanted to inflict that same pain on those who caused it to the tree."

The Disciple stares silently at the young woman, admiring the incredibly strong, extraordinary adult she's grown into. The Disciple had asked the young woman to accompany her into the Barrens, although not the duty of a Hunter. She had thought that the young woman's perceptive abilities might help find clues as to how Murkovin had recently entered the Delta.

"You must never succumb to the same extreme emotions the Murkovin feel," the Disciple says. "I sometimes wonder how you survive with so much feeling inside you."

"I once told you," the young woman replies, "that when

the Teller who first came after my Ritual of Purpose was here, I could feel what he felt in his world as well as what he felt being in ours."

"I remember," the Disciple says. "That's why, when he was here long ago, I thought it might help you to spend Communal with him. It's unfortunate that his visits stopped."

"He was also in my Vision of the Future," the young woman confides.

"We're to share that Vision with no one else," the Disciple reminds her. "That Vision was for your eyes only."

"I was shown my death in my Vision," the young woman says, ignoring the Disciple's reproach. "I wasn't upset at the sight of my body. I don't fear death, although I don't want my life to end too soon. The Teller was by my side. I was overwhelmed by his emotions as he leaned over my body. That's when the things I feel opened inside me."

The Disciple gazes thoughtfully at the young woman, eventually making a decision to break with long-standing tradition, with the ways of Krymzyn.

"The Teller was in your Vision of the Future?" the Disciple asks.

"Yes," the young woman answers.

"Did you see your manner of death in your Vision?"

"No. Just my body on a rock in the river, but I knew my life had left me."

"What was the Teller doing?" the Disciple asks.

"I believe he was trying to revive me. I felt his desperation. It's as though his feelings are what opened me to the many extreme emotions that I still don't understand.

Sometimes, like when I saw the Murkovin moments ago, I find them difficult to control."

"It's possible," the Disciple says after a few moments of contemplation, "that the important part of your Vision wasn't you. To be shown one's death would alter the way a person lives their life and the decisions they make. I don't believe that would benefit you in any way, and the Tree knew that when it showed you the Vision. So it's possible, if you saw your body, it was only meant as a way to open you to these emotions that Krymzyn wants you to understand."

"Why would Krymzyn want me to feel these things?"

"As other planes have evolved," the Disciple explains, "Krymzyn has always been a constant. We've learned from recent Tellers that several planes have seen immense growth and change never experienced before. Evolution doesn't imply only positive change. Many negatives are inherent to the process, and many struggles. The necessity to maintain balance with one's world is even greater than before.

"In order for Krymzyn to provide the essence of balance needed for other planes to exist, it's obvious that, on some levels, we must experience change. A part of Krymzyn needs to better understand what's felt in those worlds, even if the emotions appear to be a regression from our own balance. Although the reasons why may be unclear to us now, they'll eventually be revealed. I fear that it's a burden you must often bear alone, but I know how strong you are."

The young woman lowers her eyes to the ground, weighing the Disciple's words. "I understand," she finally says. "It helped me when he was here. I could sense his reaction to the emotions and understand how he controls them."

"As I said, it's a shame his visits ceased."

The young woman turns away and steps onto the bridge. After examining her reflection in the steel below her feet, she looks back at the Disciple.

"He'll return soon," the young woman says.

"How do you know?" the Disciple asks.

"My Vision of the Future hasn't yet come to pass. In my Vision, my face looked as it does now."

The Disciple nods her head before walking to the young woman. Side by side, they cross silently over the bridge, the hostile river flowing beneath them. The young woman pauses and closes her eyes.

As much as I long to be with him again, to understand all I feel inside, I don't want him to feel pain in his world.

Chapter 14

I was sitting in my cubicle at the office building on Sunset Boulevard a few months after Jess and I had broken up. It was the beginning of spring after my twenty-third birthday. Hours had passed since I'd taken a break from painting character designs for a video game. The fantasy quest followed sexy, kind of mental, psychic mutants who gradually gained super-warrior powers as each level was passed.

Eyestrain resulted in a dull pain in my forehead. I rubbed my temples and glanced at a clock on the wall. Even though the work day was almost over, I wanted to finish a female character composite before I left for the night.

When I leaned back to look at my screen, warmth spread through my veins. Staring back at me, the digitally painted young woman in full action pose, slender muscles straining, amber eyes glowing into mine, was Sash.

I closed my eyes, suddenly feeling a familiar pain rip through the back of my head—a pain I hadn't felt in almost six years. The throbbing started in the nape of my neck, webbed through the curve of my skull, and riveted into my forehead. I opened my eyes as my muscles tightened and hands clenched. The light from my monitor spiraled around me, but my only reaction was to smile.

*   *   *

"Sash!" I shout as soon as I see that I'm standing on the Empty Hill. Valleys of infinite silence echo my voice. "Sash!" I yell again.

Not caring that I haven't been here in six years or that Darkness might fall, I run down the hill in the direction of her habitat. I pass the outstretched branches of the ancient sustaining tree, my bare feet feeling the soft, velvety texture of the red blades of grass beneath them.

"The Teller Chase has returned to Krymzyn," I hear a loud male voice say from behind me.

I spin to see Tork standing a few feet away. "Do you know where Sash is?" I ask.

"Another first has occurred with your arrival," he replies, ignoring my question. "A Teller has never been in Krymzyn during a child's Ritual of Purpose, but here you are, as all of Krymzyn will soon gather for this event."

"Will Sash be there?"

"Of course Sash will be there," Tork replies. "Where else would she be?"

I let out a sigh of relief that she's alive and safe. "Is it at all strange to you that you haven't seen me in six _years_—a long time—and I'm suddenly here?"

"I see you," he says, then slowly turns in a circle. When

his back is to me, he says, "I don't see you." He speaks again at the end of his rotation. "Now I see you again. You may have grown taller, your appearance may have changed slightly, but that's all."

"Well, I sure missed you," I say.

He tilts his head to the side and scrunches his eyebrows. I remind myself that sarcasm doesn't exist here.

"Did you aim something at me?"

"Nothing that would hurt you," I answer.

"Hmm," he replies. "The Ritual will soon begin. We must go."

"How do you know the Ritual's about to begin?"

"By the ringing of the bell, of course," he says as though I should know what that means. "Shall we make haste?"

We both take off running towards Sanctuary. As we cross the red hills and meadows, Tork occasionally slows for me to keep pace. When we reach what I remember is the Telling Hill, he continues to run over the hill, down through an empty narrow valley, and up to the top of a slightly taller hill. I gasp when we stop on the crest.

In the meadow below, the one I remember being the largest in Krymzyn when I saw it from the Tall Hill, sprouts the enormous, surreal Tree of Vision. It's larger than any tree I've ever seen on Earth, probably the size of the Angel Oak in South Carolina, with rich red-brown bark emitting a crimson luster. The branches, some almost the length of a football field, gently sway overhead as if in a breeze. I recognize the radiant, yellow leaves I saw when I was seventeen. I remember everything about being in Krymzyn, every detail, like it happened yesterday.

At the foot of the hill, a few feet past the outer edge of the branches, stand the other six Disciples. Beside them, a giant steel pole with an arm hooking towards the Tree reflects light from overhead. A brushed-steel bell, at least ten feet tall, hangs from the arm of the pole. When I look around the empty hills surrounding the meadow, my heart sinks from not seeing Sash. Eval turns away from the Tree, sees us, and walks up the hill to where we stand.

"Chase from the planet called Earth," Eval says when she reaches us, "your arrival presents yet another anomaly."

She looks a little older, still elegantly beautiful, and maybe an inch taller after six years, although it's hard to tell. I've peaked at about six foot one, but still have to tilt my head back a little to look at her eyes.

"You know, Eval," I say, "it sure seems like I don't have much time for telling when I'm here, even though I'm supposed to be a Teller."

"That's occurred to me as well, as we've discussed before. But there must be a purpose to your visits, even if we don't fully understand what that purpose is yet. I can only surmise that, since you're here now, you're meant to observe the Ritual."

"It will be my honor," I say, quickly remembering the vernacular of Krymzyn.

From behind Eval, one of the giant limbs suddenly whips through the air and slams into the bell. A blaring ring resounds through the countryside.

"The second bell," Tork says to me, "calling the people of Krymzyn to the Ritual. The first ring, just prior to your arrival, alerted us that a child had reached the height of purpose. The third ring will begin the Ritual."

People soon appear on the hilltops surrounding the meadow. Some have neon green hair mixed with black—I remember that those are Watchers. Others have scarlet in their hair like Sash, so I know they're Hunters. The people with cobalt blue strands are Travelers, Sash had explained to me. I also see a few with striking magenta and several with bright cyan, but I don't know what those colors signify.

Fourteen gold-haired Keepers soon walk to the top of the hill we stand on with fourteen black-haired children beside them. The age range of the children looks to be from two to eighteen. Everyone is wearing the exact same black pants and sleeveless shirts. Everyone is barefoot. The adults all have rope belts buckled around their waists with steel flasks hanging by their hips, and all carry long double-tipped spears in their hands.

One Keeper and one boy, the child who appears to be the oldest, continue down the hill to where the other Disciples stand. As I examine his face, I realize that it's one of the two kids from the day I sat on the Tall Hill with Sash. He's maybe five foot nine now, muscular and stocky with a ruggedly handsome face under his black curls. I assume he's the one to have reached the height of purpose since he's the only child to walk into the meadow.

Although I can't explain why, a familiar tingling spreads from my chest all the way to my hands and feet. It's the same way I felt on the Tall Hill when Sash reached inside me with her eyes. I spin to my rear.

Marching up the hill in a deliberate stride, almost directly towards me, is Sash. I inhale a sharp breath. My stomach flutters and my heart pounds so hard that it's booming inside my head.

She freezes when she sees me, stares into my eyes for a second, then looks down at the ground. She's grown two inches, about five foot eight now, still lean and toned. Sash slowly raises her eyes to mine, revealing only minute changes in her face. Her cheekbones are a little more pronounced, her lips are fuller—subtle hints that six years have passed.

Amber flares from her eyes and seems to surround me. I don't know if I'm imagining that the corners of her mouth curl up into an almost imperceptible smile. But as I watch, the unmistakable smile spreads from her dark red lips, up through her smooth cheeks, and into her eyes. Never has someone fallen so far, so fast, just from the sight of a smile. A fall that, for me, has no end.

I start to walk down the hill but suddenly break into a run. I can't control it, can't stop myself, and throw my arms around Sash. She drops her spear to the ground and slips her hands around my waist. She pushes her feet firmly against the ground to press her body harder against mine. I lean my head back and immerse myself in her eyes, seeing the trace of a smile still on her face.

"How did you know I'd return?" I ask.

She lifts a hand to my face and runs a fingertip along the curve of my cheekbone, down my jawline, and around my chin. "In my Vision of the Future, your face looked as it does now, not as it did when you were last here."

"I must have drawn a thousand _pictures_ of you," I say, "and not one can begin to compare with how incredible you look to me right now. I'd stare at those _pictures_ and _wish_ with everything inside me that I could see you and talk with you and be with you."

"Sometimes, before I'd sleep, I'd see your face," she replies, seeming to understand my meaning with the word "wish." "I longed to see you again, but you never arrived."

"I'm here now," I say, pulling her close to me.

We stand silently, our bodies pressed together, fitting perfectly in each other's arms. She eventually whispers in my ear.

"It feels so good to be with you, but we must attend the Ritual."

After we release our embrace, Sash picks her spear up from the ground. We turn and walk to the top of the hill side by side. Eval and Tork both study us with curious faces. PDA doesn't happen in Krymzyn. In fact, the "A" of PDA doesn't even seem to exist here, so I'm sure they're more confused than anything.

"I was just greeting Sash in the manner of my plane," I say to Eval when we reach her. "It's called a _hug_. Do you want one too?"

I extend my arms out, genuinely wanting to share a physical greeting from my world with her, but she cocks her head to the side and squints at me.

"Since you and Sash are familiar with one another," Eval says, ignoring my gesture, "perhaps she'll be able to explain the events of the Ritual to you as they occur."

"I'd really like that," I say.

"It will be my honor," Sash adds, the soft sound of her voice floating into me and starting the flutters in my stomach all over again.

"How do you measure the height of purpose?" I ask Eval.

"You show a keen interest in the ways of Krymzyn," she remarks, a note of approval in her tone.

"I'm fascinated by everything here."

"So it seems," she says. "In answer to your question, the height of purpose varies from child to child. Some reach it when they're still short, others not until they're almost your height."

I assume the age range she refers to is roughly sixteen to twenty-one, based on the boy I saw and Eval's vague description. Vague in the way so many explanations are in Krymzyn, I remember.

"Does the tallest child know they're chosen for the Ritual when they hear the bell?" I ask.

"No," Eval answers. "The chosen child knows by their palms glowing gold. It's not necessarily the tallest child currently in Krymzyn. Sash was surprisingly short when summoned for her Ritual. In fact"—Eval glances at Sash—"she was much younger than any child ever chosen."

I turn to look at Sash, but she's staring straight down the hill at the Tree. She doesn't respond to what appears to be a compliment. I return my attention to Eval.

"So the _kid_—child—just goes up to the Tree, spikes it, and drinks the sap?" I ask, remembering to instantly correct myself when a word doesn't translate.

"There's no need for a spike," she answers. "The sap of this Tree will be freely given, but only after it's been earned. The Tree won't simply let one pass without challenge."

"Are you telling me that the boy has to fight his way to

the Tree?"

"He must prove to the Tree that he has a purpose inside him," Eval answers. "If he has none, then he'll meet death at the branches of the Tree."

"What!" I exclaim loudly enough that half of the people standing on the hills look at me.

"While it's rare, it does happen. Not all who are created have a purpose."

"That seems pretty cruel," I say.

"So all on your plane are born with a purpose of value to your world?" Eval asks.

I don't reply, understanding her point, but it still seems cold and barbaric to me.

"I should mention," Eval says to my silence, "that only once in the history of Krymzyn has a child reached the trunk entirely unscathed, uninjured, and untouched by the Tree. In fact, that child was allowed to pass without challenge."

Eval's eyes swing to Sash. Sash is focused on the meadow and seems to be ignoring the conversation.

"I believe," I say to Sash, "Eval the Disciple has just praised you."

Sash turns her head to Eval, bows it slightly, and then looks back at the Tree. I guess I can add humility to the list of things to admire about her.

"When scarlet was revealed in her hair," Eval says to me, "I believe the Tree of Vision made it clear that Sash should remain as close as possible to the sustaining trees. No Murkovin has ever taken sap from a tree in the Delta since Sash became a Hunter, and we've never lacked the sap we need for our sustenance."

With her eyes still glued to the meadow, Sash replies to Eval with undeniable sincerity in her tone. "It's my honor to serve those in the grace of Krymzyn and the trees that provide for us."

"Your service has our respect," Eval says. "Now I must leave you, as I need to join the other Disciples. Please, Chase, feel free to quietly ask Sash any questions you have during the Ritual."

"Thank you. I'm truly honored to be here for this event."

She and Tork bow to us before walking down the hill to the other Disciples. Honored, I think, as long as I don't have to watch the kid get the crap beat out of him by the Tree, and I'm kind of wondering how I'm going to react if he's in trouble.

Chapter 15

"Isn't that the boy we saw on the Tall Hill?" I ask Sash.

The boy stands stoically with his back to the Tree, a Keeper at his side, and the row of Disciples in front of him.

"Yes, that's Cavu," she answers. "I believe the Tree will test his strength as well as his cunning."

My heart continues to race at the feel of her beside me. I slip my hand into hers. "Is this all right?"

She squeezes my hand. "If you're in need of nurturing, I'll provide it for you."

"I am," I say. "More than you know."

A hint of a smile appears on her face again. I want to hug her so badly that my limbs are burning, but I decide that this really isn't the time or place, especially with some kind of religious or spiritual ceremony about to begin.

I survey the hills surrounding the meadow. There can't be more than one hundred people here, and Tork said that all of Krymzyn is coming to the Ritual.

"Is this everyone in Krymzyn?" I ask.

"Everyone except for a few Watchers who remain on the walls during the Ritual," Sash says. "Those who dwell on the Mount are still arriving."

"What's the population of Krymzyn?"

"One hundred and sixty-one is the number of balance for the Delta and the Mount."

"That's it?" I exclaim.

"That's the number of balance," she replies. "If someone dies, then a new child is needed to return us to the number of balance. We don't know how many Murkovin there are, but their number is neither greater nor less than what's needed to maintain balance."

"Are there a specific number of people for each purpose?" I ask.

Sash nods her head. "There are always seven each of the Disciples, Weavers, and Travelers. We have forty-nine Watchers in the Delta and twenty-eight on the Mount. Seven Hunters dwell in the Delta and seven on the Mount, as well as seven Constructs in the Delta and seven on the Mount. We have seven Apprentices, each with the color of purpose in their hair. The number of Keepers is fourteen, as is the number of children. When that number is reduced from fourteen to thirteen, as will be the case after the Ritual, a child will be born to return the number to fourteen."

I decide that the only way the math could work out is if they had lost someone. "Did someone die recently?"

"A Watcher fell to the Murkovin," she answers.

It's a lot of information for me to absorb, and I'm still not sure which color is which purpose. I notice that every number is seven or divisible by seven.

"Is there always one Apprentice for each purpose?" I ask.

"No," she says. "If it was that way, a child would know

what their purpose would be before their Ritual. We may have several Apprentices for one purpose at any given time, and none for others."

I quickly count the people with blue hair and come up with eight. "One of the Travelers must be an Apprentice."

"You're correct," Sash confirms before pointing to a tall male Traveler.

The man looks like he's in his late forties and has medium-length black hair laced with cobalt blue. A young woman stands beside him.

"Tela," Sash continues, "who we saw with Cavu on the Tall Hill, is an apprentice Traveler. A man called Larn is her Mentor."

I recognize Tela, although she's now a curved beauty of about nineteen. She looks like she should be a bikini model, not someone known for her speed. She's around five foot six, her straight black hair highlighted with the same blue as the man's. Probably feeling my gaze, she turns her head to me. Her round face is solemn as she nods, but I see obvious recognition in her eyes. I smile at her and receive the usual head tilt at my facial expression that doesn't exist here— except in Sash now. Just as she did many years before, Tela reminds me of my sister.

"She doesn't look like she really has the right body type for speed," I say.

"Traveling speed comes more from the mind than from the body."

I'm familiar with the mental side of long-distance running, but the way Sash said "traveling speed" implies something more to me than just running fast.

As I scan the people lining the hills again, I stop on a pair of amber eyes fixed on Sash. I remember the man—the green-haired Watcher Sash argued with after she saved me from the sustaining tree. The thick muscles in his neck and arms strain like a sprinter coiled in the starting blocks before a race.

The expression on his face, although serious like everyone else's here, is different than any I've seen in Krymzyn. It's not the kind of stoic, emotionless face that I'm used to seeing. Leering at Sash might actually be how I'd describe his stare, once I really think about it.

His eyes drop to our clasped hands and then rise to my face. He narrows his eyes and sinks his eyebrows. They're not signs of curiosity like I've seen in the others looking my way. In his glare, I see a challenge.

Refusing to back down, I give him my best "what the hell are you looking at" expression, clenching my jaw so that I know my face looks as tough as I can make it. Contempt for me is what I see in his eyes.

A giant limb suddenly soars through my vision. I follow its path to watch the branch slam into the side of the bell. After a clamorous ring subsides, Cavu, still facing the Disciples, holds his hands out in front of him. Bright, golden light glitters above his palms. He raises his hands over his head for all of us standing on the hills to see.

Cavu turns towards the Tree. All the branches jump into violent motion, butchering the air above the meadow. A few boughs snake high above the ground like they're waiting for him to make a move. The boy tentatively walks around the outer perimeter of the meadow, studying the trunk. With a sudden burst, he sprints straight towards the Tree.

"Holy *shit*," I whisper when a branch slams into his midsection and hurls him twenty feet backwards.

He falls to the ground on the edge of the field, a few feet outside the range of the branches. As he gulps for breath, Sash tightly squeezes my hand, sensing my dismay.

"He must use his mind as well as his strength," she says, keeping her eyes on the boy with no change at all in her facial expression. "When he does, he'll prevail."

I remember that Sash knows these things before they happen, so I'm somewhat relieved by her statement.

The boy clenches his hands into fists as he stands. After a moment of deliberation, he dashes into the meadow. He stutter-steps and spins when the first limb sails towards him. As though it anticipated his move, a nearby branch is already cocked at the ready. It slashes across the boy's face and upper chest and again knocks him backwards to the ground. He rolls across the turf away from the Tree until stopping on his stomach.

Shaking his head with frustration, Cavu stares at the grass. Blood streams from his nostrils, drips over his lips, and trickles down his chin.

"He's learning," Sash says.

"Learning how to get his *ass* kicked," I mumble under my breath.

Her face scolds me when she turns to look into my eyes. "Cavu must know what's inside him. He must realize what he's capable of. Only challenge will reveal that."

I hold her gaze for a moment, nod my understanding, and turn back to the boy. I think about yelling a few words of encouragement, but, given the absolute silence of everyone else here, I decide I better bite my tongue.

Cavu stands, clenches his fists again, and aims his eyes straight ahead. Trotting instead of sprinting this time, he starts towards the trunk.

When a limb swoops at him, he dives to the ground and slides narrowly underneath it. A second branch slams straight down from above. Just before it hits, he rolls out of the way and springs to his feet. With his muscles bulging through the leathery black pants, he churns his legs in a determined sprint.

Another limb swings towards his midsection. With a lowered shoulder, he crushes into the branch, absorbs the impact with his legs, and spins off the blow like a fullback rolling off a tackle. A branch sails in from behind, but he ducks underneath it. After the yellow leaves graze over his body, the limb pauses in midair and then whipsaws at him again. He dips under the backlash and explodes into a final charge towards the trunk.

Cutting sharply, he veers past one last branch that passes inches from his head. With his arms spread wide, he flies into the trunk. A shroud of silence falls over the meadow and every branch, every twig and leaf, hangs frozen in the air.

Clutching the bark with his hands, he presses his lips to the Tree. A stunning spectrum of light envelops him, so blinding that I have to close my eyes and turn away. Seconds pass before the light recedes enough for me to look. As the flare fades, Cavu rests his forehead against the trunk and stands motionless, seemingly at one with the Tree. Vibrant green rips through the outer curls of his hair, illuminating the silky black.

With dried blood staining his cheeks and chin, he slowly turns away from the trunk. There's no triumphant gesture, no sign of elation, but a new and noticeable air of confidence is evident in his stance.

The Disciples and his Keeper drop to their knees. Every person watching from the hills does the same, still not a sound anywhere. Sash releases my hand and pulls my shirt when she sinks to the ground, so I lower myself to a knee beside her. Cavu humbly walks to the Disciples with his head bowed, stops in front of them, and reverently kneels.

"I'm honored to serve my purpose for the balance of Krymzyn," he loudly proclaims.

Eval rises from the ground. "And so it shall be, Cavu, Watcher of Krymzyn."

I'm disappointed that there's no applause or cheers, no smiles on the faces of the people who watch, nor any other sign of praise. Eval scans the hilltops. Her eyes pause when they reach a green-haired woman.

"Vona, will you please rise?" Eval yells up the hill.

The woman, tall with an athletic build, stands and looks down the hill.

"Cavu will be your Apprentice until he's needed as a Watcher of Krymzyn," Eval calls out.

"I'm honored to be his Mentor," the Watcher replies loudly.

Eval looks at Cavu again. "Vona will be your guide as you move forward in the ways of your purpose. When a new Watcher is needed to maintain balance, you'll then fulfill your purpose to Krymzyn."

Cavu stands, bows to Eval, and, with the Keeper he came to Sanctuary with by his side, climbs the hill to the other children. Everyone else rises and strolls away, most to the north, but a few in other directions. After Sash and I both stand, she casually takes my hand in hers. Cavu glances at me as he walks by, so I smile at him.

"Shouldn't somebody tell him, like, good _job_ or something?" I whisper in Sash's ear.

"He has no need for praise from others," she replies softly. "The Tree of Vision has already provided him with the greatest praise he can ever know."

When our eyes meet, neither of us looks away. Although six years have passed, the innate feeling of connection to her is just as intense and tangible as it had been when we sat together on the Tall Hill. Emotions that have been buried for so long are finally springing to life.

The faint smile returns to Sash's lips. She knowingly nods her head, letting me know that she feels them too.

Chapter 16

After the seven Disciples climb to the top of the hill and stop in front of us, Sash and I reluctantly turn away from each other. The five other than Tork and Eval all bow in my direction, apparently welcoming me back to Krymzyn. I let go of Sash's hand and return their gesture.

"Did you find the Ritual enlightening?" Eval asks.

"It was interesting, to say the least," I answer. "I'm really excited for Cavu."

"We're all honored by his achievement," Eval says. "We're now faced with a decision since, as we discussed, your visit presents another irregularity."

"I actually gave that a lot of thought back in my world and tried to make sense of all the anomalies."

"You have vivid memories of Krymzyn while on your plane?" Eval asks in surprise.

"Very vivid," I say.

"More than just an illusionary memory as though from a dream?"

"I remember every detail about being here when I'm on Earth. When I come back to Krymzyn, it's like I never left."

Eval drifts away in thought for several seconds before

responding. "When Tellers visit," she eventually says, "they remember their prior visits when they're here but have no real memory of being here while on their plane. I would expect you to remember Krymzyn while you're here, but your memories of this plane while in your world are quite unique."

I shrug my shoulders. "I guess I'm just lucky."

"I don't know if luck, a word introduced to our vocabulary from the Earth Teller before you, is the word I'd choose."

"What word would you choose?" I ask.

"I don't believe that's been determined yet," Eval says. "After a Ritual of Purpose, our custom is to each Commune with Krymzyn to show gratitude for balance being maintained. It's become quite evident that your purpose here is different from any Teller before you. Krymzyn appears to want you to know and understand our plane."

"It seems that way to me. I know I want to learn more."

"Based on past events, I would say Sash is meant to be your guide on this journey." Eval moves her eyes to Sash. "Rather than each of you spending Communal alone, or Chase with the Disciples, I suggest you show him the northern part of the Delta."

"I'm honored," Sash says with a hint of a smile on her face.

"That sounds perfect to me," I add. "Thank you."

Eval kneels to the ground, sinks her fingertips into the dirt, and whispers. I can just make out what she says. "Larn, please travel to us."

I glance around at the few people left walking away

from the ceremony. The male Traveler Sash pointed out to me earlier stands on the next hill with Tela by his side. A broad empty meadow separates that hill from the one we stand on. Trim with well-defined muscles, the man appears to be roughly the same height as Eval.

He and Tela start to run down the hill towards us. They quickly reach a sprint. As I watch his long, sleek stride, I think that, if I were still running competitively, I'd want to train with him. I begin to sense an immense power that resides inside him as he speeds down the slope. When they're almost to the bottom of the hill, something happens that literally takes my breath away.

Every time I've come to Krymzyn, I've noticed how fast people run. I've even thought that Sash begins to blur sometimes. I just attribute it to the atmosphere, kind of like the way my words pause and translate. What happens next leaves no doubt in my mind as to what I see.

After beams of light burst from the Traveler, brilliant streaks in the vague shape of a human blast across the meadow. The rays recede back into a human body running up the hill I'm standing on. When he coasts to a stop a few feet in front of me, I stare at him with my mouth hanging open. I didn't even have time to blink while he covered half a mile.

Trailing slightly behind, Tela does the exact same thing. In an instant, after momentary rays of light, she's standing beside the Traveler. I'm dumbfounded, speechless, and I stare at them with my eyes wide open.

"Chase," Eval says to me, "I'd like to introduce you to Larn and Tela. Larn is the tallest of our Travelers, and Tela is an Apprentice in the ways of their purpose."

They both bow to me, Larn studying my face as he does.

"I met Tela when I was here before," I babble, still stunned. "Hi, Tela. It's nice to meet you, Larn."

"And you as well," Larn says to me.

Eval looks at Larn. "Would you and Tela please ensure that Chase reaches the northern Delta as quickly as possible? We want Chase to make the most of his time here."

"Of course," Larn replies. "I'm honored to provide service to our visitor."

Eval returns her attention to me. "I bid you farewell and hope your time here is educational."

"Thank you," I say absentmindedly, still trying to wrap my head around what I just saw.

The other Disciples bow to me and then walk down the hill with Eval. I move my eyes back to Larn.

"How did you do that?" I ask.

"Do what?" he replies.

"Appear in front of me from across the field."

"I traveled to you."

"How is that accomplished is what I meant to ask."

"I blend my light," he tells me. "The principle is quite simple. As you know, our bodies consist of bonded particles of mass."

"I guess so," I say. "Science was never my thing, but I did _okay_ in it. I kind of get the concept."

"When one becomes a Traveler, we're chosen due to our mental control over our bodies as well as our physical ability. We learn to separate the particles of mass in our containment."

"What do you mean containment?" I ask.

Larn holds up one forearm and rubs his skin with the other hand.

"Oh, we call that _skin_," I say.

"Then, in your terminology, we separate the particles of our _skin_. While all in Krymzyn are able to do so to a certain extent, only Travelers have the ability to spread our containment enough to fully blend our light. We first gain speed running since that motion helps us locate beams of light moving in the same direction we want to travel. Light reflects from the particles of mass inside our bodies until the reflected light blends with the beams that flow through us. The particles adhere to the light."

"Are you telling me you can travel at the speed of light?" I ask in disbelief.

"That would be impossible," Larn answers. "Light slows dramatically as it passes through or is reflected by mass, depending on the transparency of the mass it makes contact with. Once our particles attach to the flow of energy, friction slows them even more. We're able to reach great speeds, however."

"How do you separate the mass of your organs and bones?" I ask.

"Those particles exist separated," he replies.

I'm completely confused by his answer, but I don't really want a class in Krymzyn biology. After being apart for six years, I just want as much time as possible with Sash.

"Any idea how fast you can go?" I ask.

"Whatever speed each of us can attain," he replies, with a typical Krymzyn answer that doesn't answer anything.

"Tela has yet to master her ultimate speed but will do so soon. As part of her duties as a Traveler, she must learn to carry children across the Delta and to the Mount. I suggest you ride on her back?"

I shake my head. "If you're saying she can carry me at whatever the speed you travel is, that seems physically impossible. My particles won't separate."

Larn unclips the flask from his belt and hands it to me. "Sap will allow your particles to separate enough to avoid any damage to you and not interfere with our speed."

I unscrew the top of the flask, drink the contents, and return it to Larn. Just as I felt in Sash's habitat when I was seventeen, the wave of energy from the sap is instant.

"Tela will keep enough of her mass intact for you to hold on to her," Larn continues. "While we won't be able to travel as fast as we did crossing the meadow, we'll still be moving quite fast."

I briefly study Tela and then look at Larn again. "I hate to say this, but I weigh a lot more than a child. No offense to Tela, but she doesn't look strong enough to carry me. How about I jump on your back and Sash can ride with Tela?"

"Sash has no need to be carried," Larn says. "She's the one individual in Krymzyn who's not a Traveler with the ability to fully blend her light."

I turn to Sash. She glares at me like she's a little upset, probably because of my Tela comment. She doesn't realize that I'm looking at her in awe because, as I'm learning, she seems to be the prodigy of all things Krymzyn.

"Why didn't you just offer to carry me in the first place?" I ask Sash.

"It's not my purpose," she answers. "Travelers aid others across the Delta. Hunters don't usually have the ability, so I would only do so in an emergency. You said you wanted to learn about Krymzyn, so you're learning."

"I sure am," I say and then address Larn. "When I was on the Tall Hill a long time ago, I estimated that the Delta was about twenty miles in length. Is that close?"

The words "twenty" and "miles" hang in the air a few seconds but eventually translate into a distance I assume he can understand.

"Twenty-one miles, to be exact," Larn replies.

I note that the number is, yet again, divisible by seven. "How far are we going?" I ask.

"From where we stand now to our destination, the distance is fifteen miles."

I evaluate Tela again, unable to believe that she can carry me more than twenty yards at any speed. Her face is still solemn, but there's a hint of dejection in her eyes. I assume it's from my negative assessment of her strength.

"Chase," Sash says, "did the boy look strong enough in your eyes to defeat the limbs of the Tree?"

I glance at Sash and then back at Tela, realizing how deep my foot is shoved into my mouth. "I'm sorry if I offended you, Tela," I say to her. "Let's go for a ride."

She hands her spear to Larn, offers her back to me, and I jump on. I weigh about one hundred and seventy pounds, but she doesn't even flinch from my weight.

"Please don't strangle me," she complains.

She loops her arms under my legs and holds me in a classic piggyback position. I slide my hands from around her neck to under her arms and clasp them on the center of her chest.

All three break into a sprint down the hill, and I decide to count off seconds in my head. As we run faster, I see streams of white blast out of Sash, but her spear and flask remain solid. The trails of light behind her clothing are a murky mixture of white and gray. Light seeps from Tela's skin followed by a sudden, jarring jolt of speed.

The countryside blurs by us until we're moving faster than anything I've ever experienced. I actually feel a little motion sickness, but I'm too dazed by our speed to really care.

At first, my skin stings from the wind slamming against it, so I close my eyes and bury my face in Tela's neck. Her skin feels grainy, not solid, almost like sand blowing against me on a windy day at the beach. After a few more seconds, the rushing air seems to pass through my body, tickling my insides.

I sense our motion slowing and Tela's skin gradually feels more solid against mine. When I open my eyes, the landscape comes into focus as we slow to a fast sprint. We all coast to a stop in a large meadow with my count ending at thirty.

Tela releases her hold on my legs and my feet hit the ground. As I pull my arms from around her chest, I realize I didn't take a single breath during our entire run—or travel, I guess they call it. I quickly do the math in my head.

At fifteen miles in thirty seconds, we covered a mile in about two seconds, which is thirty miles in a minute. That's over eighteen hundred miles per hour at our peak. Not anywhere near the speed of light, but almost triple the speed of sound.

"That was incredible!" I exclaim.

Tela, now panting, looks at me with the usual stoic expression on her face. She gives me a slight head nod in response to my comment. Larn and Sash both breathe heavily, but not even close to how I'd be gasping for air at the end of a three-mile race. Nobody has a single bead of sweat on their bodies, I guess due to the lack of temperature in Krymzyn.

"Tela, I want to show you something," I say. I lift one of my hands high in the air with my palm towards her. "Put your hand up like I'm doing."

She raises her hand over her head. I step forward to her and slap it with mine.

"It's called a high five," I say.

"High five?" she asks, looking up at her hand that's still floating above her head. "It seems odd."

"Five fingers," I reply, wiggling mine, "and our hands are up high. It's just something we do in my world. You can put your hand down now."

She drops it to her side, apparently not impressed.

"The customs on his plane may seem strange to us," Sash says, "but they serve a purpose to him. I believe it's his way of showing gratitude to you."

Tela bows to me. "I'm honored to serve a visitor of Krymzyn."

"That was really amazing," I say, turning to Larn and shaking my head in disbelief. "I can't believe what we just did."

"Now you understand the purpose of Travelers," he replies. "Unless you're in need of further assistance, Tela and I will begin our Communal."

"We're grateful," Sash says.

"Thank you again," I add.

Larn and Tela walk away from us. Larn begins running in one direction and Tela in another. Light spreads from their bodies and they both disappear over the tops of hills.

I look around us and, not seeing anyone in sight, step to Sash. Standing in front of her, I rest my hands on her waist. After dropping her spear to the ground, she reaches both her arms around my neck and pulls me close. Lifting her feet off the ground, I feel the bliss of our bodies pressed tightly together, a feeling I never want to end.

Chapter 17

After a long, silent embrace, I lower Sash to the ground and brush scarlet away from her face.

"It feels incredible to be with you," I say.

We slowly lean to one another until our lips meet, finally resuming the kiss that was taken away from us long ago. A vital piece of my being that's been missing for six years is flourishing inside me again. When our kiss ends, Sash rests her head on my shoulder.

"If you're here now," she hesitantly asks, "does it mean you're in pain in your world?"

"Yes," I answer, holding her to me, "but I don't care. I don't seem to think about it while I'm here, and I don't feel it at all. The only thing I care about is how excited I am to be with you."

"I feel the same, Chase."

She lifts her head off my shoulder and presses her lips to mine. Our mouths open, we caress with our tongues, and share the safety of being in each other's arms. After we finish a long kiss, she tilts her head back. Looking into my eyes, she runs her fingers through my hair. Her hand stops on the back of my neck and her fingertips gently rub my head.

"I don't want you to suffer in your world," she whispers.

"There's not a lot I can do about it. Don't you have _disease_ or _sickness_ here?"

Sash shakes her head in a way that lets me know that the words didn't translate.

"I guess not," I say. "What makes you die here?"

"One could meet death from a Murkovin. On rare occasions, someone will be killed by the branches of a sustaining tree or the Tree of Vision. For most, the height of death is reached."

"What do you mean by the height of death?"

"The height at which you've fulfilled your purpose to Krymzyn," she answers. "It's different for each who dwells here."

"And then you just die?" I ask.

"Green light appears in our palms, giving us the sign. We travel to the Mount, ascend to the peak, and lie on the Bed of Light. Krymzyn takes us."

"What if you don't feel like dying?"

"It's peaceful," she says. "We know our purpose has ended."

"I guess that beats fighting _illness_, or, I don't know, being old and worn out."

Her eyes dive inside me again and the corners of her lips curl up into a smile. "I don't want to talk about death. I feel too good being with you. _Happy_—is that the word?"

"That's the word," I answer. "I'm _happy_ you're _smiling_. You have no idea how beautiful you look when you do."

"My _smile_ only shows itself for you."

Sash pulls her arms away from me, picks up her spear

from the ground, and takes my hand in hers. She leads me into a grove of trees, a type I haven't seen before in Krymzyn. Huge, arching branches spread outward like the limbs of giant willows. The leaves of the trees are a scintillating orange and the bark a deep chocolate brown. Countless threads, some black, some white, dangle from the branches like delicate moss hanging in a swamp.

As we walk through the orchard, silky strands brush across our faces, soft and fine. With Sash by my side, I feel like I'm floating through a serene, peaceful dream. The only strange part to me is the silence—no birds chirping, no insects buzzing, and no leaves rustling in the air.

"Do these trees come to life?" I ask.

"No," Sash says. "Only sustaining trees on the Delta awaken during Darkness."

We stroll deeper into the willows and I see an older man, possibly in his sixties, sitting on the ground. His skin is free of wrinkles, as is the skin of everyone I've seen here for that matter, but there's an indefinable sense of age to his face. Splendid magenta decorates his black hair.

Leaning against the trunk of one of the trees, he looks lost in meditation. The man turns his head to us and nods as we pass by. When he looks at Sash, I see a reverence in his eyes, an appreciation that's as close to a smile as any face ever gets in Krymzyn. Tipping her head to the man, Sash returns the same look of respect.

"Who are the people with magenta hair?" I ask.

"Weavers," Sash answers. "They take thread from the trees, blend it into fabric or rope, and create the clothes we wear."

"How do they get the clothing so smooth and strong?"

"The black fabric is rubbed with pulp from vines that grow in caverns on the Mount. It makes the clothing tougher and allows the particles to be separated when we travel."

I try to digest the traveling comment. It's still a mystery of twisted physics to me, even though I've seen and experienced it firsthand.

We walk past a metallic device in the center of a clearing. I notice threads stretched between several poles of the apparatus, and realize that it's a loom made of steel.

"Who made the loom?" I ask.

"Constructs," she says. "They build our habitats, maintain the walls around the Delta and the Mount, and make all our items of steel."

"They must be the people with cyan hair," I say, determining the color by process of elimination.

"They are," Sash answers, nodding to me. "Now you know all the colors of purpose."

Hand in hand, we gradually arc around the northern point of the grove and meander down the other side. Sash asks me questions about my life since the last time we saw each other. As I explain computers, video games, and the design work I do on Earth, I'm both surprised and impressed by her ability to grasp the concepts so seemingly foreign to anything in Krymzyn.

When we reach the edge of the grove, I notice plants about my height growing in a field around the outside of the trees. It's the first time I've seen plant life of any kind in Krymzyn other than grass and trees. Large tufts of fluffy white, like softball-sized cotton balls, dangle from the ends of long yellow stalks.

"Fluffing plants," Sash says when she sees me looking at the plants. "They're used for our pillows, beds, and padding on the end of training spears for the children."

"I might have figured that one out on my own," I say, smiling at her.

She impishly jumps in front of me and blocks my path with the shaft of her spear across my chest. "Are you saying you don't need me with you."

"I would never say that," I answer, still smiling.

"Are you sure? I can take you back to the Disciples."

I quickly kiss her lips. "I'd rather stay with you if that's alright."

Lowering her spear, she returns my smile. "It's strange, Chase. Even though so much time has passed, now that we're together, I feel like you never left."

"I know," I reply. "Like part of us is always together."

"Do you remember when you asked me if I felt that we were connected?"

"On the Tall Hill," I answer, nodding.

"Do you still feel that way?"

Since the first time we spoke, I've felt that I can say anything to her. I can expose myself, share my deepest secrets or fears, and know they're safe with her. "It's never stopped for me, Sash. I missed you so much over the _years_, but I always felt like you were inside me."

"For me as well," she says. "I don't know why or how, but you're always there."

"Well, I hope we can figure it out because I really don't want to stop seeing you again."

"We'll understand when we're meant to," she says, "but I don't want to stop seeing you, either."

After another long kiss, we walk to the south with our arms around each other's waists. We cross a long, flat meadow to an enormous black canopy held up by gigantic steel poles. Sash leads me inside the open-air tent, roughly the size of a football field.

Numerous long metal tables stand in rows with neatly arranged items on their tops. Folded pants are on one and sleeveless shirts are on another. Cylindrical backpacks like the one Sash uses during Darkness, knives, and scissors each rest on their own table. One is home to metal pitchers, screw tops in place, while another has pitchers with the tops by their sides. There's a separate table for virtually every item I've seen in Krymzyn—spears included.

"This is Market," Sash says. "Everything we need can be found here. After hunting, I bring the stakes here. Constructs take care of filling the pitchers with sap and storing the rest. When I need an item, I take it from here."

"So you don't have to _buy_ anything? You don't use _money_?" None of the words I'm trying to use seem to translate. "You just take what you want?"

"We each take what we need," she replies. "No more, no less. Weavers, Constructs, and Hunters supply the items. When I need clothes, I find them here, take them to the Weavers, and they fit the clothing to my body. If I need something built in my habitat, I notify a Construct."

"How do my clothes get fitted to me?" I ask.

"A Weaver will be told through a dream of a Teller coming and the specifications for that clothing. The Weaver then creates what the Teller needs. The clothes are left here in Market and Krymzyn dresses you when you arrive." She points to a small table with nothing on top of it. "When you depart, your clothing will appear on that table."

I walk down another row of tables looking at cups, rope, pillows—the entire variety of items available—trying to think of all that's "needed" based on my comprehension of the people's existence. Everything that I can imagine they might use is here.

I stop in front of a small pile of branches on a tabletop. They're really just twigs no larger than a pencil. I pick one up and hold it out for Sash to see.

"What's this for?" I ask.

"It's called a marker. If you sharpen the end to a point, the dried sap inside leaves a mark on fabric. Hunters leave the twigs here when they're needed, ones that fall from sustaining trees during Darkness. The Weavers use them to mark fabric when they cut it to size."

"Can I use one?" I ask after thinking for a moment.

"If you need it, it's here to be used."

I look around at the tables until I find the white tank tops like the one Sash slept in. A twig in hand, I cross to that table. When I run my fingers over the fabric, it feels just like smooth cotton.

"Can I have one of these?" I ask, holding the shirt up.

"Is there a reason you need it?" she asks.

"There is. A really good reason."

"Then it's yours to use," she tells me.

With the tank top in my hand, I walk to the sheathed knives. Taking one with me, I find one of the bare, square tables like the one Sash has in her habitat. I lay the marker, knife, and fabric on top of it. From a neat row of stools, I take two, set one by the table where I left the fabric, and stand the other one about ten feet in front of the table.

"Sash, will you sit on this stool please?"

"Why?" she asks.

"Because I need you to," I reply. "Just sit for a while, but don't change your face at all. I'd really like it if you would smile while you're sitting there."

After she walks to the stool and sits, she looks up at me with a curious but smiling face. "Why do you need me to do this?"

I walk to the table and sit behind it. "I want to show you how I Commune," I say.

Chapter 18

Using the knife, I sharpen one end of the twig to a point. Wanting a pile of fine grains to dab my fingertips into for shadowing on the fabric, I shave dried sap from the other end of the marker. I neatly spread out the tank top on the table in front of me. When I draw a test stroke on one of the straps, the dried sap leaves a solid line, almost black with a hint of red.

I examine Sash for a few minutes, just to make sure I see the changes in her face compared to the hundreds of pictures I've drawn of her from memory. This sketch will have a distinct difference from every other picture I've created of her. In this one, she'll have a smile on her face.

As I begin, I quickly discover that while I can draw on the fabric, it's not as smooth as using canvas or paper. The end result won't be as refined as I'd like, but I'm happy with the progress I see when I finish the outline of her face, the angles of her nose, and the curves of her cheeks and chin. It definitely looks like Sash.

I spend a lot time on her big eyes, the dark lines around them that remind me of a wild cat, and I really focus to get the detail in her lips correct. The shadowing on her face is a little heavier than I'd usually use as I try to capture the sense of lurking danger that's part of her look.

Thirty minutes pass and I decide the head-and-shoulders portrait is as good as I can make it. I'm actually quite pleased given the circumstances. After a few final touches—a little more detail in her hair, long eyelashes, and bold eyebrows—I initial the bottom-right corner. I know it's not my best work, but it's not my worst either.

I stand and walk around to the front of the table. After carefully lifting the tank top, I gently shake the excess sap dust to the ground. I turn to Sash and hold the drawing up for her to see.

She tilts her head to the side, squints her eyes, and stares expressionless at the sketch for several seconds. She finally stands up. As she walks to me, she never takes her eyes off the drawing and has an almost befuddled look on her face.

"Is this . . . is this how I look to you?" she asks, sounding confused.

"You're beautiful to me," I say, disappointed by her reaction. "I'm sorry. I don't really have the things I need to do my—"

"This is how you see me?" she interrupts.

"That's how you look to me," I answer quietly. "I mean, it's obviously just in black and gray, and I can't really—"

"Chase," she says, interrupting again and looking into my eyes. "Your drawing is beautiful. I'm amazed you created this."

"You're more beautiful to me than anything."

"May I keep the drawing?" she asks, the word now

added to her vocabulary.

"Of course. I made it for you."

She takes the tank top from my hands and lays it on the table behind us. When she turns to me again, she wraps her arms around my waist and pulls me to her body. I instantly return her embrace, feeling a little better about my sketch.

"Thank you for sharing that with me," she says. "I can see exactly what I feel in your drawing."

"That's really the point of a picture," I reply. "It should convey emotion."

She leans back from me and smiles. "Now I want to show you something."

We quickly clean up the mess I made and return all the items to their proper places inside the neatly arranged tent. After Sash carefully folds the tank top I drew the picture on, she grips it in the hand with her spear. Holding my hand in her other one, she leads to me to the south.

As we cross over a hill and through a meadow with a lone sustaining tree in the center, I tell her about my parents, sister, and how families are structured. In response to her questions, I explain how two people meet, fall in love, and get married or live together. I also explain divorce, since it's pretty common.

The longer we're together, the more natural it feels to be with her. I know she feels the same way I do by how relaxed she seems, the almost constant smile on her face, and her displaying the same need I have to touch one another. She leans against me as we walk or playfully brushes her shoulder against mine. We hold hands and occasionally stop to hug and kiss.

We reach the top of another hill with a broad meadow below. The Keepers and children, including Cavu with his newly green hair, lie on their backs in a giant circle. Their hands rest flat on the crimson grass as they stare up at the clouds. Sash sits on top of the hill and pulls me down beside her.

"I often spend Communal watching the children," Sash says warmly. "Do you see the doorways in the base of the hills?"

I study the creases in the hills and spot three black granite doors similar to the entrance to Sash's habitat.

"I see them," I say.

"Many caverns are connected under these hills by a long tunnel. We call this area Home, where the children dwell. They each have their own small cavern to dwell in, and the Keepers sleep in caverns across the tunnel from them. A large cave is used for educating the children in things like math and science, and another is where they all drink their sap together.

"The children are also shown all of Krymzyn. They observe Weavers, Constructs, Hunters, and Watchers to learn of their purposes. Travelers take them to the Mount so they can see what goes on up there. The Disciples come here to share the history of Krymzyn with them, as well as stories of other planes."

"So the Disciples are kind of like teachers?" I ask.

"They're teachers, historians, and students of other worlds," Sash answers. "When Darkness falls, the Disciples protect the Tree of Vision with their lives. Only one Disciple, usually the second tallest, will ever leave Sanctuary during

Darkness.

"Travelers," she continues, "take the children through the Barrens so they may witness the destruction of trees there by the Murkovin. The children see how a life without balance leads to the devastation of that which sustains us. They're also taken to the Infinite Expanse so they can see and understand."

"What's the Infinite Expanse?" I ask.

"It can't be described," she says, turning her face to me. "It has to be experienced to be understood." She looks back at the children in the meadow. "Each child learns to understand every purpose in Krymzyn, every substance, everything that grows. When a child has their purpose revealed, they know the importance of their own purpose as well as the equal importance of every other. No one purpose has a greater value than the others. All are needed equally.

"They learn to take only what they need for existence and give everything they have to provide what others need. We're all responsible for the well-being of the children as they grow, and we all live as one."

I study Sash's face while she's talking, and the sublime passion in her eyes grips my heart. Watching the children in the field, her eyes fill with pride and caring. More than anything else, I sense her incredible desire to protect them. I know that Sash would sacrifice her own life before ever letting harm come to another person in Krymzyn.

The Keepers and children suddenly all stand. Seven Keepers walk to one side of the meadow with half of the children, while the other seven Keepers cross to the other side of the field with the rest of the kids. They all grasp hands, the first time I've seen anyone in Krymzyn touch another person, apart from Sash touching me, and form two, long rows.

One child runs across the field and tries to break through a pair of locked hands. When she fails, she steps to the end of the row and takes the last person's hand in hers. The game of Red Rover brings a smile to my face.

While we watch the game, I occasionally see a momentary flash in one of the taller boys as he runs across the field. It's like a split-second glitch in a monitor, probably an attempt to blend his light. The only thing missing from the scene is laughter. The faces of the children are serious and fierce. As I observed on the Empty Hill, they approach what I consider a game as a learning experience of some kind.

Sash turns her face to me, sees me smiling at the children, and gently kisses my cheek.

"Touch seems to be an important sense on your plane," she says. "You often use it to reinforce what you feel inside."

I'm momentarily taken aback by her tremendous insight into a combination of human behavior and animal instinct.

"Of the five senses, I guess it's as important as any," I reply. "But yeah, we like to touch."

"Five senses?" she asks.

"Sight, sound, touch, _smell_, and _taste_," I answer.

"_Smell_ and _taste_?" she repeats.

When the words don't translate, I unexpectedly hear Dr. Baskin's statement to me from long ago.

"Smell and taste are never present in this type of hallucination because those sensory nerves aren't affected."

I stare at Sash with a disturbing question bouncing around inside my mind. If this is a seizure-induced hallucination, did my subconscious just justify the lack of smell and taste? Or, since I believe Krymzyn is real, since I know in my heart this is real, did Sash unknowingly explain why I never smell or taste anything here?

"Are you alright?" Sash asks.

"Yeah," I answer, returning to the present. "I was trying to think of way to explain _smell_ and _taste_ to you since you've never experienced them. Think about how you see different colors with your eyes. Here you only consume sap, but in my world, we consume lots of different things. Each one has a different _taste_ in our mouth, the same way your eye recognizes different colors.

"When we breathe in through our noses, everything has a different _scent_. Like your nose recognize colors too, but in a different way that your eyes or mouth. I really can't think of a better way to describe it to you than that."

She squints at me for several moments, obviously processing the concepts. "I believe I understand," she finally replies. "In Krymzyn, we have only four senses—touch, sight, sound, and awareness."

The final word hangs in the air for almost three seconds before it finally translates for me. It seems like several other words were attempted before settling on awareness.

"Awareness isn't really a sense in our definition of senses," I say. "Feeling something with your sense of touch is being aware of it, so we're aware of all our senses."

"Awareness is a sense here that comes from inside. It allows us to feel all that's around us. Awareness is what allows us to blend our light, to feel honor, and to be fully nourished on all levels of existence."

Considering all I've seen and felt here, her explanation makes perfect sense to me. I return to watching the game of Red Rover, knowing what I want—what I need—to say to Sash, but trying to find the right words. I finally look at her again.

"I want to tell you something important," I say.

She holds my gaze. "What is it?"

"I'm in _love_ with you. I knew it the moment I saw you walking up the hill in Sanctuary."

"Explain _love_ to me again," she says.

I'd tried to give her a brief description of the emotion when I told her about my family, but I couldn't really think of a way to define it for her then.

"It's probably the hardest emotion in my world to describe. Imagine how you felt when your purpose was revealed to you. The excitement you feel when fulfilling your purpose. Then combine that with how you feel when you honor the sustaining tree, when you press your face against the trunk. How you feel when you stand on the Tall Hill and see the beauty of Krymzyn. Then add how you felt a few moments ago while watching the children.

"When you put all of those feelings together for one person and you can't stand to be without that person—it hurts you inside when you're apart—I guess that's how _love_ feels. That's what I feel for you."

She leans to me, rests her head on my shoulder, and pulls my body to hers. As I hold her in my arms, I close my eyes and drown myself in feeling her, knowing that she's it for me—the only person who can ever make me feel complete.

"If that's how you define love," she says softly, the word now added to her vocabulary, "then love is what I feel for you."

She raises her head from my shoulder and her eyes flow into mine. The amber consumes me in its brilliance. But I suddenly feel pain in my head and my body begins to shake.

"I'm about to leave," I struggle to say.

"I love you, Chase."

*   *   *

The words floated into my ears from far away. When my vision cleared, I stared into amber eyes that were made of tiny pixels of light.

"I love you, Sash," I whispered to the computer screen.

I wiped drool off my chin and let my shaking subside. After standing up, I glanced around the office.

No one seemed to have noticed my seizure. Everyone was exactly where they'd been the last time I looked. If a person had walked by my cubicle, they couldn't have missed the state I'd been in.

I glanced at a clock on the wall. Only seconds had passed since I'd checked the time right before my seizure. I must have been in Krymzyn for seven or eight hours, but almost no time had passed on Earth.

Chapter 19

"The neuroectodermal tumor is in about the same spot as before," Dr. Baskin said, pointing to the image of my brain on a computer monitor. "What concerns me more is the growth here." He slid his finger to a dark mass higher up, just above the center of my brain. "We need to do a SPECT scan to determine if it's malignant, but it appears to be a glioblastoma."

"Brain cancer," I said.

"We don't know that for sure yet, Chase."

"That's what killed Davis, isn't it?" I asked. "Glioblastoma multiforme?"

"I know how close you were to him. I remember seeing you in the hospital almost every day with Davis, so I'm sure you knew the details of his cancer. Every case is different. I've known you for eleven years. You're a fighter, a survivor. You're in tremendous physical condition and as strong mentally as any patient I've ever had. If anyone can beat this, you can."

I thought back to when I was seventeen, when part of me wanted a new tumor so I could be taken to Krymzyn. I'd never considered the ramifications of a new tumor being cancerous. Fate was playing the cruelest practical joke on me I could imagine.

"If it's malignant," I asked, "what are the survival rates?"

"If it proves to be malignant, about fifteen percent for full recovery in your age group. With treatments, two years to five years is the average. It really depends on how aggressive it is."

"Not very good odds," I said.

He smiled at me. "The odds of you making the state cross-country championship ten months after brain surgery were astronomical."

My entire body was numb, and I barely heard his words. "When can we do the biopsy?"

"As soon as possible. Tomorrow, if you can. The sooner we act on this type of tumor, the better the chances are for successful eradication."

"I'll be here tomorrow," I said. "Dr. Baskin, please don't tell my parents yet. I want to have all the facts first."

"You're an adult now, Chase. Legally, I can't inform them without your consent, and I understand if you want to be the one to tell them. But you'll need their love and support."

"I know, and I couldn't ask for more than what they give me. I'm very lucky to have my family. I just don't want to upset anyone until we know exactly what I'm up against."

"Fair enough," he replied. "Did you have a hallucination during the seizure?"

"No," I said, shaking my head. "No hallucination."

Two days later, I was back in his office. Phrases you

don't want to hear after a biopsy are "extremely aggressive" and "rapidly spreading," but those were the words spoken to me. Survival rates were suddenly cut by more than half.

"The tumor needs to come out immediately," Dr. Baskin said. "We should start radiation and chemo as soon as we can, so I'd like to schedule the surgery for early next week."

"Let's do it the week after next," I said. "We can do it on that Monday, but it has to be the week after next."

"It's in your best interest to do it sooner."

"Ally will be home for spring break next week." I paused for a moment and then spoke softly but firmly. "I just want to have a normal week with my family. It might be the last one I ever have."

He silently stared at me for several seconds. "Week after next, Chase. That'll be fine. I'll get you on the schedule for first thing that Monday."

"Thank you," I said. "Thank you for everything."

He stood from his chair, walked to my side, and rested a hand on my shoulder. "I'm so sorry, Chase, but you need to stay positive. We're going to do everything we can to beat this."

"I know we will," I said.

I left his office and rode the elevator to the lobby. I'd taken a cab to the hospital since I wasn't allowed to drive after having a seizure. Knowing I needed to get back to Sash, it had never even crossed my mind to take the anti-seizure meds I was prescribed after the initial diagnosis. I looked through the glass entrance doors for a moment, saw the row of taxis in front of the hospital, but turned the other way.

I walked to a courtyard where I used to sit with Davis,

sometimes talking for hours about his hopes and dreams for the future—the life he never had. I sat on a bench and tried to distract myself by examining the different colors of flowers in the garden. The stress of the day was almost too much to handle. I wasn't at all surprised to feel the throbbing spread through my skull. When the first convulsion struck me, I gripped the edge of the bench seat with my hands.

*   *   *

Full Darkness has already descended. Glaring crimson branches slash through the air in front of me as rain batters my skin. I instantly spot Sash at the edge of the meadow. She's locked in a savage fight with two hideous creatures, her spear a flurry in her hands.

Blood red eyes target Sash. One Murkovin lunges his spear at her, but she twists and dodges the point. Shards of light explode from his head when Sash plunges her spear through his skull. The other Murkovin jabs at her from behind. Sash ducks under the stab and spins to face the brute.

I jerk my face to a blur of white on my left. A Murkovin races through the valley straight towards Sash. The clash of metal rings through the hills as Sash battles the other creature.

"Sash!" I scream at her.

Focused on the fight in front of her, she's deaf to my call. She has no idea the other Murkovin is rushing towards her from behind.

I charge down the hill and aim at a spot in front of the Murkovin, hoping that I'm fast enough to intercept him before he reaches Sash. I drive my feet against the ground, sprinting with everything I have inside. When I reach the bottom of the hill, the Murkovin slides to a stop and whirls in my direction. I launch into him.

My shoulder slams into his gut. I clamp both of my arms around his thighs, tackle him to the wet grass, and get in one crushing blow with my fist to his nose. Black blood spews from his nostrils, but his hands clutch my shirt. He heaves me above his body and hammers me back to the ground at his side.

Rolling on top of me, he jolts upright. Trying to squirm away, I smash my palm under his chin. His claws sink into my shoulder and a fist thunders against the side of my head. Sharpened, white teeth glisten through black lips above me. His eyes suddenly dart to a flash of green above our heads.

Light glints from a point of steel inches above my face. The spear tip skewers the creature's stomach, releasing a spray of Murkovin blood onto my chest.

Another shape soars in from my side. A steel point rips into the skull of the swine, driving him off me and to the ground. I look up to see Sash, both of her hands ramming her spear through the head of the Murkovin. Standing on the other side of me is the Watcher who reached me first—Balt, the same man who glared at me before Cavu's Ritual of Purpose.

"How did so many Murkovin enter the Delta?" Tork's voice yells. He sprints to us, muscles flexed, anger seething in his eyes.

"We don't know," Balt replies.

"Are there more?" Sash calls out.

Two more green-haired Watchers, a man and a woman, run to us from behind Balt.

"No more that we know of!" the woman shouts.

Sash glances down at me. "Are you badly injured?"

"I'm fine, Sash," I say. "Go do your thing."

She grabs a stake from the pack on her back, leaps into the wildly swinging branches, and sprints to the trunk. I raise my head off the ground to watch Sash, but everything starts spinning and my head falls back to the grass. Leaning over me, Tork reaches one hand behind my head. After carefully lifting it off the ground, he holds his flask to my lips.

"Drink," he says.

I gulp down the sap. As my vision clears, Tork rests my head on the grass. He pours sap from the flask into his hand and rubs it across the gashes in my neck, shoulders, and arms. I feel the wounds beginning to heal while a soothing calm spreads through my body.

"Return to the wall and dispose of the Murkovin bodies," Tork says loudly, looking up at the Watchers. "I'll meet you at the gate when light returns."

I sit up, and Tork stands. The three Watchers each grab a dead Murkovin by their black-and-white hair. Spears in one hand, corpses held in the other, they drag the bodies to the east.

"Balt," I call out to him.

When he looks over his shoulder, his dark amber eyes

shoot straight through me.

"Thank you for helping me," I say.

He doesn't nod or acknowledge my thanks in any way. He holds my stare for a split second before turning his head and walking away. It's not contempt for me I saw at the Ritual. Those eyes clearly hate me.

The churning clouds begin to slow, the rainfall thins, and light pierces through the clouds. Tork reaches a hand down to me. After I take it in my grasp, he helps me to my feet.

"You honored Krymzyn with your actions," he says, bowing his head solemnly. "For that, we are grateful."

"I didn't do anything," I say to him. "I just got in the way."

"You put your life at risk to stop a Murkovin."

"It's my honor to serve Krymzyn in any way I can," I reply.

"That appears to be true," Tork says.

We both turn to watch Sash. She pulls the last stake from the tree and slips it into the cylinder on her back. Pressing her cheek to the bark, she rests one palm against the trunk. After several seconds of standing silently, she moves her lips, whispering something to the tree. She picks her spear up from the ground and returns to where we're waiting.

"I need to consult with the Watchers to find out how this intrusion occurred," Tork tells Sash. "Never have so many Murkovin entered the Delta during Darkness."

"I'll take care of Chase," she says. "Contaminated blood has spilled on him."

Tork returns his attention to me. "Will you forgive me if I leave you in the care of Sash?"

"Of course," I answer. "Thank you for helping me, Tork. I really appreciate what you did."

"It was my honor," he says.

Tork bows and then sprints away to the east. Smiling at her, I step to Sash.

"I'd kiss you," I say, "but I have Murkovin blood all over me."

She reaches a hand to my face and lightly runs her fingertips over my cheek. "You risked your life to stop the Murkovin."

"I did it for you, Sash. I'd do anything for you."

"I know you would," she says warmly.

"Thanks for killing the Murkovin. I didn't realize how strong they are."

She rises to the tips of her toes and kisses my lips. "Thank you for stopping him."

"You probably didn't need my help, but I couldn't do nothing and let him run up behind you."

"I should teach you to use a spear," she replies with a faint smile. "Are your wounds healing?"

"I'll be fine," I answer.

After she takes my hand, we stroll in the direction of her habitat.

"I don't think Balt cares much for me," I say as we walk.

Sash turns her face to me. "Why do you say that?"

"Just the way he looks at me."

"We grew together as children in Home," she says. "He was well focused on his education and sometimes helped the smaller children, like Tela, practice with spears. He's very skilled with a weapon. Most of the time, he was quiet and distant. As a Watcher, he's angered by the intrusion of Murkovin. Their duty is to keep them out of the Delta. But I've seen strange expressions on his face before. It's just the way he is."

"I'll try not to worry about it," I say.

I'm not at all surprised that Sash would defend someone in Krymzyn. She's the most loyal person I've ever met. But there was concern in her voice, in her explanation, and I know what I saw in his eyes.

Chapter 20

"Awaken," Sash says as she closes the door behind us.

We walk through the tunnel until we reach the softly lit cavern. The soothing sound of falling water echoes from the other cave. I immediately spot my drawing of Sash, now hanging by two hooks over her bed.

"I look at the drawing before I sleep," she says while hanging the cylinder of stakes on the wall. "It always makes me smile."

When Sash talks and when we spoke in the meadow, instead of delaying, words that never translated before now flow with the rest of our words. It's as though the words that didn't exist here, words that Sash learned from me, have been permanently added to the dictionary of Krymzyn—or maybe just to Sash's vocabulary.

"It means a lot to me that you like it," I reply.

"Sit over here," she says, crossing the quartz floor to the small table and pulling the stool out from underneath. "You need sap to finish healing."

The sap Tork applied to my cuts has already stopped the bleeding and sealed my wounds, but my back and shoulders are definitely still sore from the Murkovin slamming me to the ground. I've never felt anything that strong. My body was nothing more than a rag doll in his hands.

I walk to the stool and sit, instantly reminded of the same sequence of events happening when I was seventeen. Sash fills two cups with sap. She keeps one and hands me the other. As I slowly sip the contents, euphoria sweeps through my mind.

When we finish drinking, we both set our cups on the table. I raise my arms and Sash pulls my shirt over my head. She lays my shirt beside the cups, picks up the pitcher, and pours sap into her hands. Rejuvenation seeps into my muscles as she massages my shoulders, neck, and arms.

"I missed you," I say. "I thought about you every moment I was in my world."

"I thought about you, too," she replies, gently rubbing her hands across my back. "I felt so happy while we were together. When you left, I grew angry with myself for wanting to be with you. I know you can't come here without feeling pain in your world."

"Don't ever feel like that, Sash. I'll put up with anything I have to if it means I can keep seeing you."

"It shouldn't have to be that way," she says, "and I can't control my reaction sometimes."

I've seen her struggle to keep her anger in check. But for the first time, I realize how overwhelming it must be for her to understand the emotions she feels from my world. The range of feelings I experience on a daily basis are considered "irrational and extreme" in Krymzyn.

"Why do you think you're able to feel the things you do?" I ask.

"I don't know." Her hands stop on my shoulders. "I've discussed it with Eval. She believes the purpose will be revealed at some point in the future. I think about it often, but I have no answer."

"I'm sorry you have to go through that alone. I know how tough it can be."

"Those emotions allow me to feel the way I do about you," she says. "I would never give that up." She reaches around me to lift my shirt from the table. "Come with me. We need to cleanse."

I follow her across the main cavern to the head of her bed. After unbuckling the rope from around her waist, she loops it over a hook in the wall. Lifting her shirt, she reveals her small but perfectly-shaped breasts. The muscles in her taut, flat stomach gently ripple as she pulls the shirt over her head and hangs it beside the rope.

"Finish undressing," she says.

Oblivious to my stare, she unfastens the three metal buttons at the front of her pants, slips her thumbs into the waist, and bends over while pushing them to the ground. Her calves flex into thin but sculpted muscle when she steps out of the pants and hangs them beside her shirt.

My eyes wander up her long slender legs, over the sensuous curves of her hips, and across her narrow waist. Other than a thin triangle of short, silky black hair above the crease between her legs, the rest of the skin on her body is smooth and clean. Not a single hair grows on her legs or under her arms. Even her forearms are perfectly bare.

It occurs to me that no one I've seen here seems to have any hair except for their eyebrows, eyelashes, and what grows from the tops of their heads. The men don't have facial hair. Neither the men nor the women have arm or leg hair from what I've seen. The only hair I see on Sash, other than her eyebrows, eyelashes, and what hangs from her head, is the narrow V located above her groin.

Feeling a natural sense of comfort around Sash, I slip out of my pants. After she takes them from me, she drapes our clothing over one arm and leads me by the hand into the glistening cave. We walk through the shallow stream, soothing to my feet, until we stop under the fall. Raising our clothes up one piece at a time, Sash lets the flow of water rinse the fabric clean.

"Do you need help?" I ask.

"No, but thank you for offering," she says. "I'll be right back."

While she returns our clothing to the other room, I wash the dried blood from my neck, shoulders, and arms. Closing my eyes, I tilt my head back and let the invigorating sensation splash over my skin.

Fingertips touch my forehead. Standing behind me, Sash combs her fingers through my hair. After kissing the back of my neck, she steps into the fall by my side.

Turning to Sash, I'm mesmerized by her beauty. Aware of my gaze, she smiles at me. I lean to her and press my lips to hers. As we kiss, she reaches her hands around my waist.

Embracing me tightly, she pulls me to her body until her breasts are firm against my chest. My body has its natural reaction to being naked with a stunning woman in my arms, the only woman I'll ever love. I know she can feel my growing hardness against her stomach, but she doesn't pull away or say anything about it.

"I love you, Sash," I whisper in her ear, holding her close.

"I love you," she replies.

"I'd like to make love with you."

"What's 'make love'?" she asks, leaning her head back to study my eyes.

"It's something two people do in my world when they feel the way we feel about each other. It's like what goes on in the Ritual of Balance—mating—but it's done because we love each other, to feel close, not to reproduce. But I only want us to do it if you're sure you feel that way."

We silently stare at each other as several seconds pass.

"I want to experience with you what you would do in your world," she finally says. "That's how I feel about you."

"The only problem is," I reply, "I don't have protection."

"Protection from what?"

"Protection from getting you pregnant."

"I'm not fertile. Only when a woman has the sign of fertility can she become pregnant."

"That's convenient," I mumble.

Since there's no disease here, and I know we're both virgins, I decide that we don't have to worry about STDs.

"You've done this in your world?" she asks.

I glance down at the water flowing over my feet, knowing with every part of me that I made the right decision to wait for this moment with Sash. I'm asking her to share an experience that's never existed this way in Krymzyn. She needs to know that it's as new and meaningful to me as it must be to her. I raise my eyes to hers.

"No, I've never done it," I tell her. "You're the only person I've ever felt this way about."

She peers into my eyes me before replying. "You're the only person I want to feel this with."

I rest my forehead against hers, suddenly worrying that she has no idea what's involved. "Sash, I think it hurts a woman the first time."

"I know what to expect," she says. "When we're children, the mating process is explained to us by the Keepers."

"If it makes you uncomfortable or doesn't feel right, just say so, and we can stop. I don't want to do anything—"

She presses a finger against my lips. "I told you," she says, "I want to feel what you feel in your world. I want to feel it with you."

I take Sash's hand in mine. As we cross from the waterfall to the other room, my skin and hair instantly feel dry. When we reach her bed, we both kneel on the mattress. I watch as she stretches out on her back, knowing deep inside that she's the only person I could ever be with this way.

Lying down beside her, I prop myself up on one arm, my face inches over hers. I try to think of the perfect words to say, wanting her know how much I feel for her. She reaches a hand to the back of my head. While I hesitate, she seems to read my mind.

"You don't need to say anything," she says. "I feel what's inside you."

"I just want this to be perfect."

"It already is," she quietly replies.

I lean down to kiss her lips. As our mouths open, her

tongue searches for mine. They gently swirl together, sending a quiver through my spine.

Lifting my face over hers, I'm enchanted by her eyes. I lower one hand from her shoulder to her chest. My fingers trace the outline of her breast, gradually circling inward to her small, firm nipple.

Sash raises her head from the bed and kisses me. Her fingertips glide up and down my back. After her head sinks into the pillow again, I kiss her ear, her cheek, and softly nuzzle her neck.

My hand wanders over her stomach until I reach the soft, narrow line of fine hair. I lightly brush my palm down the top of her thigh. As I slide it back up the inside of her leg, she spreads her knees. Her smooth, moist folds reach my touch. I run my fingertips over her before tenderly slipping one finger inside. She's soft, wet, and for the first time, I feel warmth in Krymzyn.

Her fingertips graze around my side and across my chest. We nervously smile at one another as she reaches lower. Taking me in her hand with a delicate grasp, she strokes up and down.

I roll on top of her body, our eyes never parting. Still holding me in one hand, Sash presses her other against my back and guides me inside. I enter as slowly as I can, but pause when I notice a slight look of pain on her face.

"Am I hurting you?" I whisper.

She shakes her head, her eyes deep inside mine. "No. You feel right to me."

"You feel right to me, too," I say.

Both of her hands clench my hips and she pulls me

towards her. She tenses as I ease completely inside. With a deep breath and a slow exhale, she gradually relaxes. Bathed in an amber glow from overhead, we lie perfectly still, hugging each other as tight as we can.

When I start to move, her body falls in sync with mine. She breathes out and I breathe in, inhaling her, absorbing her in every way I can. We kiss each other's necks, ears, and lips. She raises her hips to my thrusts as they become faster while her hands tightly grasp the flexed muscles in my rear.

Sash throws her head back. Brilliant black and scarlet strands wisp through the air in front of me and spread across the pillow. I feel every muscle in our bodies flex together. As her stomach spasms against mine, I can't control my release inside her. We clutch each other as our bodies convulse again and again, our faces buried in each other's necks.

After our muscles calm, I lie on top of her, still inside. Her heart beats against my chest, and I feel her breath in my ear. I raise my head, look at the amber below my face, and fall further into the splendor of her eyes.

"I can't be away from you anymore," I say.

"We belong together," she whispers.

Chapter 21

"Awaken," I whisper.

Gold points of light spread through the crystal spikes overhead. I focus on the tiny creatures slowly twirling inside the clear ceiling, wondering how they know to react to only two words.

"Peace," I whisper, and the Swirls fade to black.

Sash lies on her side facing me, her head resting on the pillow and a limp arm draped over my chest. I lie flat on my back, one arm nestled between her neck and the pillow. Her breath, steady and light in slumber, caresses my cheek as I stare straight up.

"Awaken," I whisper again, kindling the golden sparks in the ceiling.

"Why don't you sleep?" Sash drowsily asks.

"I don't know," I say. "I keep thinking about everything that's happened to me in Krymzyn. None of it makes sense."

"No, it doesn't," she agrees.

"Eval told me she's not even sure if my purpose here is telling. The Disciples don't even need a Teller from my world. They've already had one."

"Maybe you were never meant to be a Teller."

I turn my face to hers. "Then what am I, Sash? Why am I here?"

"I think you have to answer those questions."

"The only answers I have right now are that I love you and I can't stop seeing you again."

"I feel empty when you leave," she says.

"How would you feel if I stayed in Krymzyn all the time?" I ask hypothetically.

Sash takes my hand in hers before she answers. "When we sat on the Tall Hill long ago and you left, you took a part of me with you. I only feel whole again when you're here. I feel complete with you, Chase. I want us to be together always. But I would never ask that of you."

The emotions she expresses are an exact replication of everything I felt after I left her when I was seventeen, and how I feel with her beside me now. The message contained in her final sentence suddenly hits me.

"There's a way I can stay here, isn't there?"

"There's a way," she confirms.

"What is it?"

"Chase, what if you stay here and I die?" she asks, almost pleading. "What if I'm killed by a Murkovin? Would you still want to be here if I met death? If you stay here, you can't ever return to your world."

"If it meant never having to leave you again, I'd be thankful for whatever time we have together."

"I don't want be the cause of you feeling like you made a mistake," she says firmly. "I care too much for you."

I sit upright and look down at her face. "I might die in my world, Sash. There's a much better chance of this tumor killing me than there is of my living. I've seen death firsthand, just like you. It doesn't scare me. I feel like my life is here with you. But if you die for some reason, I'll still be content living in Krymzyn."

Her facial expression never changes while she studies my eyes. "Would you be willing to risk your life to stay here?" she finally asks.

"I think I proved that a little while ago."

She nods her head but doesn't say anything.

"There's something I can take in my world," I explain to her silence, "that stops me from coming. I took it when we were younger, after the first time we met. It made me stop coming to Krymzyn until they removed the tumor from my head. I'm not taking it now. I keep coming here because I want to, because I want to be with you. But if I die in my world, I won't ever come back. If I'm healed, I won't ever come back. The only way we can be together is if I stay here."

Sash slowly sits up, pulls her knees to her chest, and wraps her arms around her legs. "When we're children," she says, "the Disciples tell us the story of the second plane. Krymzyn was the first plane. It was created at The Beginning, existing before all else.

"During a period of Darkness, a brilliant light appeared in each of the four primary directions of the Infinite Expanse. A new plane of existence rose from the light—the second plane—but it traveled to a dimension outside of Krymzyn.

"The first Teller to ever come to Krymzyn visited from the second plane. His world, the Teller told the Disciples, consisted of four distinct quadrants, each vastly different than the others. Only one inhabitant lived in each quadrant. Those inhabitants were called North, South, East, and West.

"The Teller who came to Krymzyn, North, told the Disciples that each of those who dwelled on his plane possessed great physical power, mental awareness, and immortality if physically unharmed. But they each had a unique philosophy regarding how their plane should be shared.

"North wished to rule the other three, believing his intellect and strength were superior. East wanted them to share their quadrants evenly, dwelling in harmony. South wanted each of them to ignore the other three and live isolated in their own quadrants. West desired that they all trade items from their quadrants for items from the others.

"North, believing he was superior to all who existed, wanted Krymzyn to serve him when he visited this plane. The seven Disciples of that Era refused his demands. North was infuriated and tried to kill the Disciples. Due to North's tremendous power, it required all of Krymzyn to destroy him.

"Several Darknesses passed, and a new Teller arrived in Krymzyn, South, from the same plane as North. He told the Disciples of an event he and the others on his plane couldn't understand. North had ceased to exist. The Disciples knew the only possible cause of North's death on the second plane was his death in Krymzyn."

"So if I die here, I die in my world?" I ask.

"Yes. You'll be dead in both worlds," she says. "The Teller South told the Disciples that after East and West realized North was dead, East and West reached a compromise to share their plane without South. They attacked South, who then went into hiding in his quadrant. While in hiding, South returned to Krymzyn.

"Darkness never fell while South was here, so sap never flowed in the sustaining trees. Time passed, people grew taller, and the supply of sap was almost depleted.

"The Disciples traveled to the Mount of Krymzyn to look into the Reflecting Pool deep inside the mountain. Questions are often answered for us in the Pool. When they asked why South remained in Krymzyn, they were shown his death on his plane. East and West had found South while he slept in his hiding place and killed him. They learned that when he died in his world, because he was in Krymzyn when it occurred, he continued to live in Krymzyn."

"What happened to South after that?" I ask.

"When the Disciples returned from the Mount, golden light appeared in South's hands, giving him the sign for the Ritual of Purpose. He faced the Tree of Vision to determine if he had a purpose here."

"And did he?" I ask.

"No," Sash answers quietly, shaking her head. "The Tree killed him. After his death, Darkness immediately fell, providing sap for the people."

"That means I could have a Ritual of Purpose," I say.

"Only if you're given the sign," Sash replies.

"How do I get the sign?"

"Krymzyn will give it to you if that's what you truly want. But if you don't have a purpose here, you'll meet death at the branches of the Tree."

"I understand that," I say. "Darkness never fell while

South was here. It's like Krymzyn didn't want him here. I've been here three times during Darkness."

"That doesn't mean you have a purpose here."

"There's only one way to find out," I say. "Let's go see the Disciples."

Chapter 22

We hurriedly dress, and since it's only about two miles to Sanctuary from her habitat, Sash and I run there side by side. We reach the top of a hill overlooking the Tree of Vision, the same hill we stood on to watch Cavu's ritual. Eval and Tork are sitting at the edge of the meadow, branches gently waving in the air over their heads. When Sash and I walk down the hill, the two Disciples notice us and both stand.

"Tork has informed me of your encounter with the Murkovin," Eval says to me when we reach them. She drops to one knee and bows her head. "You've shown great honor by risking your own safety to protect Krymzyn. For that, we are grateful."

"I'll do anything to protect Krymzyn," I say, dipping a knee to the grass and then returning to upright.

Eval stands. "I believe you mean that, and in more ways than you know."

"Have you discovered how the Murkovin entered the Delta?" Sash asks Eval, obvious anger in her voice. It's not anger directed towards Eval—just that Murkovin were anywhere near the trees that are so precious to her.

"We haven't yet," Eval answers. "They must have found

a way to cross the river and enter the Delta at some place the Watchers can't see."

Sash looks away in thought.

"Maybe they just swam across the river," I say. "The Watchers on the wall are far apart from each other a lot of the time and can't see the entire river. After they're across, the Murkovin could hoist someone over the top of the wall and he could a throw a rope to the others."

"Only Serquatine swim in Krymzyn," Eval tells me. "The river belongs to them. Neither Murkovin nor those in the grace of Krymzyn ever enter the water."

"What are Serquatine?" I ask.

"Creatures who dwell at the source of the river. They're Guardians of the Infinite Expanse."

Although intrigued by her answer, I worry that I might return to Earth at any time and want to get to my questions. "May I ask you a few things?"

"Of course," Eval replies. "We're always honored to share our ways with you."

"When I'm here, almost no time passes on Earth, regardless of how long I'm in Krymzyn. But we all seem to age the same when I'm not here, like the same amount of time passes in my world and Krymzyn. How can that be?"

"When Krymzyn brings a Teller here," Eval answers, "time is suspended for them on their plane. Only moments pass in your world, but Krymzyn keeps a Teller here for as long as is needed for us to learn of balance on their plane. It would be unfair to deprive a Teller of time in their world, and as I told you before, Tellers are typically asleep or in a state of meditation when they depart their world. When you're not here, the amount of time that passes on all planes, although methods of measurement may be different, is the same."

"So Krymzyn can just alter time in my world?" I ask.

"Krymzyn created time, so it can manipulate it as it chooses."

I have to let that sink in for a few seconds before deciding that it makes enough sense to move on to questions that are more important to me. "What exactly is sap?" I ask, looking back and forth between Eval and Tork.

"That which sustains us," Eval answers.

"I'd like a more detailed answer, please," I say.

Eval and I maintain eye contact, neither of us blinking or looking away. She seems to be prying into my mind, attempting to assess where this conversation is headed.

"Sap is energy," she finally says, the word "energy" taking a long time to translate. "Energy in its purest form. Without sap, nothing exists."

I actually scratch the back of my head in a cliché reaction, not sure I grasp her meaning. "What do you mean 'nothing'?"

"The word means what the word means," Eval says sternly.

"You mean nothing in Krymzyn?"

"I mean nothing," Eval states firmly, "anywhere. Sap is the energy that allows all other forms of energy to exist."

I nod, slowly accepting her answer, and phrasing my next statement in my mind. "I have something in my world called a _tumor_," I say, noticing that when I talk to someone other than Sash, certain words don't translate again. "It grows on my brain and will probably kill me soon. If I'm wounded in Krymzyn, sap heals me and the wounds aren't there when I go back to Earth. While I'm in Krymzyn, I don't feel any of the effects of my _tumor_. As soon as I'm back on Earth, I feel them again."

"Sap has great healing power," Eval explains. "It can't return you from death, but as long your brain is functioning, sap will revive your body. It's far too powerful to exist on any other plane where perfect balance isn't a constant, so its effects are only evident on this plane."

"So when I drink sap, it has no effect on me anywhere but here?" I ask.

"You'll only feel the effects of sap while in Krymzyn, and any injuries from your plane won't travel here with you."

"But if I die in my world while I'm in Krymzyn, I'll still live here, won't I?" I ask.

Eval glances at Sash then back at me. "Sash must have told you the story of the Teller South."

"She did," I say.

"As was the case with South, you'll still be alive in Krymzyn if you're here when you meet death on your plane."

I slowly look up at the sky, at the motionless gray clouds and stunning beams of light. I feel more aware here, more alive, than I've ever felt on Earth. When I'm with Sash, the part of me that I always felt was missing in my world is instantly found. Maybe fate isn't executing a vicious practical joke on me. Maybe I'm being given an opportunity to live in the way I was meant to.

I'll miss my family more than I can ever imagine, and I know I'll feel terrible loneliness at times without their love and support in my life. I doubt I can replace my close friends, especially Connor, with anyone in Krymzyn. And I don't want to hurt the people I care about.

But if I go out the way Davis did, none of that will matter anyway, and the suffering of people I love will be prolonged. My one chance to be with Sash, to feel complete, is in front of me now. The people who truly care about me would want me to seize that opportunity.

Every event in my life since I was twelve has brought me to this moment. Everything that's happened to me, that I've experienced, has evolved in a way to help me freely make the decision I'm about to make. I lower my face from the sky and stare directly at Eval's eyes.

"I want to live in Krymzyn," I say. "I want to find out if I have a purpose here."

"Why do you want this?" Eval asks.

I quickly try to construct some Krymzyn response in my head full of words like balance, honor, and gratitude. Instead, I say exactly what I feel inside.

"I belong with Sash. If I belong with Sash, then I must belong in Krymzyn."

"Do you fear your own death on your plane?" Eval asks softly. "Is that the reason you want to stay here? Just to save your own life?"

"My _tumor_ will probably kill me in my world," I answer, "but it might not. Either way, I won't return to Krymzyn. If I'm healed, I'll have to live the rest of my life on Earth wondering what might have been. I think that would be worse than death."

I see the strangest thing I've ever seen in Krymzyn—and I've seen more than my share of strange things. The corners of Eval's lips curl up slightly into an approving smile.

"You've gained an understanding of balance," she says. Her expression returns to stoic as she turns to Sash. "How do you respond to the statement by Chase?"

"I belong with Chase," Sash says, her voice rich with passion.

For the second time I've noticed—the first was when I was seventeen—Sash and Eval share an unspoken communication for several seconds. Eval finally breaks their gaze and looks at me.

"I don't believe," Eval says, "that you were ever meant to be a Teller. But to dwell permanently on this plane, a person must have a purpose in Krymzyn. If you enter the Ritual of Purpose and have none, you'll meet death here and on your plane."

I nod my head. "I understand. I don't think I was meant to be a Teller either, so I must have another purpose here. I hope so anyway, but I'll take that chance."

Eval's eyes glaze over for a moment in faraway thought, like she's remembering something from long ago. She refocuses them on me before she speaks. "Prior to a child of Krymzyn reaching the height of purpose, they each stand in the Reflecting Pool inside the Mount. Questions are answered for them as they look into the waters of the Pool, questions they may not even know exist.

"I would suggest, prior to making your final decision, you travel to the Mount and visit the Pool. If, after doing so, you still wish to seek a purpose, then you may ask Krymzyn for the sign."

"I'll do whatever I have to do," I say.

"Upon your next arrival, a Traveler will take you to the Mount." Eval moves her eyes to Sash. "Since you and Chase are in this journey together, you'll also accompany Chase to the Mount. You should be with him when he looks in the Pool."

Sash lowers her face to the ground. A sudden, unmistakable look of sadness washes over her. I can't figure out why she's reacting this way.

"I will," Sash quietly replies, her eyes never leaving the grass.

Before I can say anything else, all of my muscles involuntarily clench at once. As dizziness spins my vision, I stagger to my side. Sash steps to me and reaches out a hand, but I fall backwards to the ground.

*   *   *

I fell hard onto the wooden bench. The seizure convulsions must have been powerful enough to lift me out of my seat. When the shaking ended, I tried to relax my muscles and looked around the empty courtyard.

Why had the talk of the Reflecting Pool upset Sash so much? The more I thought about it, the more I couldn't understand why her expression had changed so dramatically.

I rubbed my temples and sat quietly on the bench. I'd made my decision and it was final. Sitting for an hour in the courtyard, I planned the steps I'd need to take on Earth to turn that decision into reality.

Chapter 23

"Hi, Mom," I said when she answered the phone that night.

"Chase, how are you?" she replied.

"I'm good, Mom. I want to let you know that I'm finishing up a big project at work this week and can take next week off. I may have to make a few design changes during the week, but I can use my laptop. I was thinking that since Ally will be in town, I'll stay there for the week."

"Oh, that'll be great!" Mom exclaimed. "Your dad and I are both taking a few days off, so maybe we could all go to the beach one day."

"I'd really like that," I said. "Mom, can I ask you something kind of personal?"

"Of course," she said.

"You know, a lot of my friends' parents got divorced over the years, but you and Dad always managed to stay together. How'd you guys do it?"

"A lot of hard work, Chase," my mom laughed.

"Seriously, Mom. How'd you know Dad was the one for you?"

After a brief pause, she spoke in a voice filled with warm

affection. "I knew I belonged with him, and he knew he belonged with me very early in our relationship. We were just lucky that way. Not everyone feels that, Chase, but it's important to recognize the difference between belonging *with* someone and belonging *to* someone. Does that make sense?"

"Yeah, it does," I said. "Like Jess wanted me to fit her vision for who I should be, not just let me be who I am."

"Exactly," Mom replied. "When I met your dad, I felt complete. I felt better with him than without him. It's an overused term, but I felt a connection with him that I didn't feel with anyone else. We just bring each other, I don't know . . . I guess you'd call it balance."

"Interesting word choice," I mumbled under my breath.

"It doesn't mean it's not a lot of hard work, because it is. You always have to try to make time for each other and not so much remember how you felt when it was all new and exciting, but make sure you still feel those things as you move forward in life. People change, Chase, and you have to evolve with your partner. You have to support their changes. That's what your dad and I do, anyway."

"You know what, Mom? You're pretty smart sometimes."

"Thanks for finally recognizing that," she said sarcastically. "Did you meet somebody new?"

"Yeah, I did. Well, I've kind of known her for a while. But it's a long-distance thing, so we'll see what happens."

"I can't wait to hear about her."

"Let me ask you one more thing," I said. "Would you have moved halfway around the world to be with Dad?"

I listened to silence on the phone for a few seconds before I heard her voice again. "Yes, I would have. Is that question related to the long-distance thing?"

"I don't know yet. I just wanted to ask what you would've done."

"If you leave Los Angeles, we'll miss you," Mom said without hesitation. "But I'd be much more upset if you missed your chance for happiness with someone."

"Thanks, Mom. That means a lot to me. I'll be over Saturday night. Plan on me being there all week."

"I'll get your room ready, and your studio is still out back if there's any work you need to do."

"There's actually a painting I'm working on. Kind of a fantasy thing, but I'm doing it on canvas, not digitally."

"I can't wait to see it," she said.

"Not until it's done," I replied, for two reasons.

I didn't like anyone to see a painting I was working on until it was finished, especially this one. But I also wanted a private escape if a severe headache came on during the week. Headaches didn't always result in seizures, but seizures never started without a headache first. I didn't want my family to know what was going on with me.

"Yeah, I know how you are about those things," Mom chuckled.

"Love you, Mom."

"Love you too, Chase. See you Saturday."

I hung up the phone, picked up the electronic pen, and returned to painting at my digital tablet. The company I worked for, needless to say, understood my need for a medical leave of absence. Before starting the time off, I wanted to finish the video game designs I was almost finished with. I decided to work from my apartment for the remainder of the week since I couldn't drive.

As each day passed, at least half of my waking hours were spent painting the picture I'd mentioned to Mom. It was something deeply personal to me that I wanted to leave for my family if I ended up in Krymzyn. Or, if for a number of reasons, my life suddenly ended.

When Friday night came, a half-eaten pizza by my side, I finished the last video game composite. After uploading it to our company server, the dull headache I'd felt for several hours abruptly sizzled through the veins in my head. I frantically clicked "record" on the camera built into my laptop and slid my chair back, wanting to know what I looked like during a seizure.

*   *   *

Sash, a spear slung over her shoulder, stands halfway up the hill, looking in my direction when I arrive. The shirt she's wearing has long sleeves and a crew neck, but is made of the same black material as all the other clothing here. A peek down at my arms reveals that I'm wearing a long-sleeved shirt as well.

"Good timing," I say.

I walk down the hill and stop in front of her.

"I've stayed near the Empty Hill to be here when you arrive," she replies evenly.

The melancholy haze that showed up as soon as the Reflecting Pool was mentioned still surrounds her face. Every moment since my last visit, the possible reason for that expression had been gnawing at me.

"Why are you so upset about me going to the Reflecting Pool?" I ask.

Sash lowers her eyes to the ground and silently stares at the grass. No one is capable of lying in Krymzyn. Maybe the Murkovin, but not the others here. They simply don't answer when they don't want to lie to you or spit out an answer that isn't really an answer, just a rearrangement of the words in your question.

I reach out my hands and rest them on her waist. "Sash, I love you no matter what. Are you sure you want me here?"

She looks up at my eyes. "More than anything," she says, "but you may not understand the questions asked in the Pool or want the answers given."

"Then why does Eval want me to go?" I ask.

"She protects all of Krymzyn, including me."

"Protects you from what?"

"Answers you may not understand," she says.

I'm more confused now than when the conversation started. "Sash, I don't really know what you're talking about. What are these questions?"

"They're different for each person who stands in the Pool," she replies.

I quickly realize that she's not going to give me a more specific answer. "Then I guess we should get going and see what happens."

Sash drops her spear to the ground, slips her arms

around my waist, and pulls me close.

I whisper in her ear. "Nothing can change the way I feel about you."

"Nor I," she says in return, holding me in her arms.

"The necessity for physical contact in your greeting customs is quite strange," Tork says from behind me.

After Sash and I release our grasp on one another, I turn to Tork. He holds out a black rope belt with steel clasps on the ends and a metal flask hanging from the center.

"Is that for me?" I ask.

"I've brought you sustenance to take with you on your journey," he answers.

After taking the rope from him, I fasten it around my waist. He unclips his own flask and hands it to me.

"You should consume the contents of this flask now for your travel," Tork says.

"Thank you, Tork," I reply. "I really appreciate this."

I drink the sap, instantly feeling the surge of strength spread through my muscles. When I hand the flask back to him, he focuses on something over my shoulder. I turn my head to see what grabbed his attention.

Three bodies of light sail over the top of the next hill, cross the valley, and stop in front of us. Larn, Tela, and another female Traveler all nod to me. The woman I haven't met before is about my height with a black-and-blue braid falling down her back. She's trim but muscular with beautifully sharp features cast in a slender face. All three hold spears in their hands and are wearing black long-sleeved shirts.

"Larn, Tela, and Miel will aid you in your journey," Tork

says.

Miel and I bow to one another.

"What's up with the long sleeves?" I ask the group around me.

"Protection, should Darkness occur while you're on the Mount," Tork answers.

"Protection from what?"

"Awakened steel trees," he says.

I decide not to pursue that line of questioning for now. I'll wait until we're on the Mount to learn what I need to about steel trees.

"I'll transport you," Larn says to me. "We'll be traveling much faster than we did crossing the Delta."

"I can't wait to travel again," I excitedly reply.

"You should know," Larn says grimly, "we're always at risk of Murkovin attacking us in the Barrens, especially if Darkness falls. They can reach great speeds, although rarely can they keep pace with Travelers."

"They can blend their light?" I ask, surprised by what he told me.

"Some are able to," Larn answers. "But the decrease of available light during Darkness greatly slows our traveling speed."

"What do we do if they attack?"

"We'll try to outrun them, but we'll fight if there's no other option," Larn says.

"You have sap in your blood now," Tork adds with a grave expression on his face. "As Eval once told you, they sometimes try to drink our blood for the sap inside. Do whatever you must to defend yourself."

I'm sure my face shows obvious concern at Tork's warning. I involuntarily clench my muscles as I remember the phenomenal strength of the Murkovin I fought. Sash, probably seeing my reaction, rests a hand on my shoulder.

"We'll be safe," she says softly.

I turn my face to her and, once again, sense her presence surround me. As I've so often felt, I know I'm safe with her—in every way.

"Have a safe journey," Tork says.

He bows to us before sprinting away towards Sanctuary.

"We should get going," I say to Larn. "I never know how long I'll be here."

After Larn offers his back to me, I climb on, he loops his arms under my legs, and we all sprint to the east. Just as I experienced when Tela took me across the Delta, we burst into exhilarating, mind-blowing speed.

200

Chapter 24

When we slow to a stop seconds later, the black marble wall of Krymzyn towers in front of us. Light from overhead reflects from two enormous steel doors hinged into an arch in the wall. One Watcher, green ever present in his hair, stands on top of the wall by the doors. I glance to the south to see another Watcher, also on top of the wall, walking towards the gate from about half a mile away.

The Watcher standing over the gate descends a ladder and waits for us beside a rack of leathery black shoes, more like ankle-high boots. After Larn drops me to the ground, we all walk to the gate. As the Watcher intently studies my face, I nod to him in the manner of Krymzyn.

The Travelers and Sash each take a pair of shoes from the rack and slip them on their feet. Sash picks up a second pair and hands them to me.

"These were made for you," she says.

I sit on the red grass and slide my feet into the shoes. They're made of the same material as the clothes we wear, but the fabric is thicker and seems tougher. Once I tie the straps around my ankles and stand up, the fit is snug, like low-cut, soft leather boots hugging my skin.

The Watcher, his brawny arms straining, lifts a steel peg from the ground at the base of one door. He slides a long metal beam from across the seam in the doors out of the way and swings one door open. An almost deafening sound of raging water bursts through the gate.

We walk through the opening and across a small span of grass. What appear to be the heads of enormous spikes secure the end of a bridge into the ground. We step onto the edge of the steel bridge that's the width of a two-lane road and spans the entire quarter-mile-wide river. After walking up a gentle slope to the arch in the center of the bridge, I stop near the edge.

I kneel by a six-inch-high lip that runs along the side, no other railings of any kind on the bridge. Looking down, I see the turbulent rapids thirty feet below. Waves as tall as ten feet high surge out of the river and crash back down to the silvery-blue water. Farther downstream, a few huge slabs of black granite jut upward and out of the swells. Like fireworks blooming against a stormy sky, giant splashes explode off the rocks and glint scarlet light in the air. Sash drops to one knee by my side.

"I see why no one swims in this water," I say.

"The rapids run through the entire river," she replies. "We don't need to swim. Only Serquatine swim in the river."

I lean over to study the underside of the bridge, an intricate array of horizontal and angled steel poles. They provide the only support to the bridge, no legs extending down into the water. I bounce up and down on the twenty-inch-thick steel, but there's no movement at all in the structure.

As Sash and I stand, I glance down at the steel under our feet. A diffused blur of our shapes reflects in the scratchy metal, no detail showing in our faces. I turn back to the black marble wall with its dull satin sheen. I suddenly understand why Sash seemed so shocked by the picture I drew of her, so confused by her own appearance.

I don't think anyone in Krymzyn has any idea what they look like. There's no standing water on the Delta to see a reflection in, no mirror, and no glass. The deep blue-gray quartz of the cavern walls reflects only ambiguous shapes of light. The crystal ceilings are too jagged for a recognizable image to appear. It somehow seems to fit their complete lack of ego, their sense of everything being one.

"Is something wrong?" Sash asks me as I stare at the wall.

"No, I'm just amazed by it all," I answer.

The three Travelers walk down the slight slope in the bridge towards the far side of the river. I give Sash a quick kiss on her lips. She smiles at me, just a hint of a smile on her face, before kissing me again. Despite the smile, her eyes are still filled with unexplained sadness.

Focusing my attention on the gate, I see the Watcher who opened the door for us slowly swing it shut. The clang of a bolt locking in place is muffled by the rapids. Standing directly over the doors, eyes trained on Sash, is the Watcher who walked to the gate from the south.

I recognize Balt from my encounter with the Murkovin, the same man I stared down during Cavu's Ritual of Purpose. The same man who ignored my thanks and fired blistering hatred in my direction after the fight with the Murkovin.

Balt's eyes shift from Sash to me. His expression changes after his eyes move. Neither of the looks, either at me or at Sash, is the kind you want to see aimed in your direction.

What was it I saw in his stare at Sash, a facial expression that clearly looks so different from any I've seen in Krymzyn? There's definite hatred directed at me, but there's something else as well.

"Chase!" Larn calls out from the end of the bridge, startling me. "We need to go."

"Sorry!" I yell to him. "I was just admiring the view."

Sash and I walk over the rest of the bridge to where the Travelers stand. I glance over my shoulder at Balt again, but he saunters away from us along the top of the wall to the south. When we reach the end of the bridge, I finally see more detail in the Barrens stretched out in front of us.

A black dirt road begins at the edge of the bridge and winds through the dreary wasteland. The path gradually rises to the colossal Mount in the distance, its black slopes washed in forest-green light. I lean down to touch the compressed dirt surface of the road and find that it's firm and solid under my fingertips. When I return to upright, I scan the Barrens and river to the north of the Delta and spot light glistening off steel.

"Is that another bridge?" I ask Sash.

"Above the fork in the river is the bridge leading to the western Barrens," she answers.

"Is there a gate on the other side of Krymzyn?"

"No," she says. "There's only one entrance to the Delta."

We all walk on the road into the Barrens. The light

overhead fades from orange and scarlet to pale white and gray.

Grass on either side of the road thins until the ground is just loose dirt, almost like coarse black sand. Occasional sustaining trees sprout from the hilly tundra, but their bark is black and crumbly. A few have gangly branches growing outward with sparse, gray leaves. Many of the trees are branchless, their rotting limbs strewn on the ground around them.

Sash veers off the road and walks to a tree. All the limbs have been ripped off the trunk, so all that's left is a giant, black stump rising out of the ground. Standing by the tree, she turns and motions for me to join her.

When I reach her side, she slips an arm around my waist and pulls me to the trunk. She presses a cheek against the bark, so I do the same. Her face is right in front of mine.

"This tree was alive the last time I was in the Barrens," Sash says solemnly. "Murkovin have killed that which sustains them."

The look of agony that crosses her face is as great as any I've ever seen, as though her own arms and legs had been torn off. She closes her eyes, but I continue to stare at her. Her caring, respect, and anguish resonate through the bark. I'm reminded of lying next to her when I was seventeen and Sash resting a hand on mine, a show of compassion and nurturing to a frightened stranger. If I've ever had a question as to why I love her the way I do, it's answered for me in this moment.

As we return to the road, I take her hand in mine. The three Travelers stand with their heads bowed. I don't know if it's a show of reverence for the recently destroyed sustaining tree or for Sash. After we step onto the road, Sash looks up at the sky.

"Is Darkness near?" Larn asks.

"No," Sash answers, shaking her head. "We should have light for our journey."

"How far is it to the Mount?" I ask.

"Seventy-seven miles," Larn replies, the atmosphere translating the distance for me.

Tela and Miel scan the Barrens around us with keen, alert eyes. After Larn turns away from me and crouches, I jump on his back. I slip my arms around his shoulders and clamp my hands over his chest. With his spear in one hand, the other hand looped under my leg, he begins to jog towards the Mount.

We gradually build to a sprint and then I feel the whiplash. Sash, Tela, and Miel all race in front of us, rays of light trailing the vague shapes of their bodies. I'm in absolute awe of the speed we reach and have to squeeze my eyes shut from the sting of air slamming into them. I soon feel the air rushing through me as the sap I drank separates my particles.

I try to open my eyes to a narrow squint as we speed through the Barrens. The road steepens while the huge black Mount zooms towards us. After maybe a minute at full speed, our motion slows, and a forest of evergreens comes into focus by the side of the road. The beams around the shapes of Sash, Tela, and Miel recede and all three slow to a sprint.

What I assume are steel trees spike at least two hundred

feet into the air, but I was mistaken to think of them as evergreens. Although shaped like pines, dark blue needles shine against rich purple bark. Gigantic black marble boulders lie scattered across the forest. There's no grass in the ebony dirt, but a thin blanket of blue needles covers the ground below the trees.

Larn comes to a stop, releases his grasp on my legs, and my feet drop to the road. The others stand in front of us, all of them breathing heavily. In my mind, they should collapse from exhaustion, not casually stand like they just finished a slow jog. We covered seventy-seven miles in roughly one minute, which equates to almost five thousand miles per hour.

"That was incredible!" I say to Larn, shaking my head. "Unreal!"

"I'm pleased traveling speed didn't bother you," Larn replies, nodding with a stoic expression.

"I can't tell you how _jealous_ I am that you can do that," I say.

I start to laugh, but the smile leaves my face. I wince when I close my eyes.

Chapter 25

Sash grips my arm in her hand. "Have you been injured?"

I don't answer at first, finally recognizing what I saw in Balt's eyes. It's as obvious to me as looking at photographs of people's faces with the names of emotions written underneath them. I open my eyes and focus them on Sash.

"I'm fine," I say. "I just realized something. Do Watchers ever go into the Barrens?"

Sash sighs with relief before answering. "They often go. They look for signs of Murkovin near the edge of the river."

"Do people ever get *jealous* here?" I ask.

Sash shakes her head, letting me know that the word didn't translate for her.

The expressions I saw on Balt's face, in his eyes, shouldn't exist here. There's only one way Balt could have those "extreme" emotions according to what I've learned about Krymzyn.

"I think Balt's been drinking sap from the trees in the Barrens," I say.

All four stare at me with stern expressions. Miel hasn't said a word to me since we met, but she steps forward and glares at me.

"That's a serious accusation," she says firmly. "One that's not taken lightly in Krymzyn."

"The Disciples told me contaminated sap creates extreme and irrational emotions," I explain. "When we left the Delta, Balt was looking at Sash and then at me with expressions on his face that I've never seen in Krymzyn. I see them all the time in my world. Extreme emotions are common there, and you can see them on the faces of people."

"What did you see?" Larn asks.

"He looked at Sash with something we call _jealousy_," I reply, "an overwhelming desire to have something that somebody else has, but you can't have it. I think he's _jealous_ of Sash's gifts . . . wants to have them for himself. But _jealousy_ can grow inside people until it takes over their minds and makes them do terrible things.

"Then, when he looked at me, I saw pure hatred," I continue, surprised that hatred translates. "It's like he doesn't want me here. These are common emotions in my world, and they're as extreme as it gets. I promise you, I know what they look like on someone's face."

With his eyes locked on mine, Larn briefly deliberates his response. "Perhaps you misinterpret his expression," he finally says.

I turn to Sash. "Do you remember the _picture_ I _drew_ of you? When you look at it, can you tell how you felt while I was _drawing_ it?"

She thinks for a moment and then nods her head. "When I look at the _picture_, I see what I felt at the time."

"That's what I do in my world," I say to Larn. "I'm what

we call an _artist_, and the most important aspect of what I _draw_—create—is that people's faces show exactly what they're thinking and how they feel. I know what I see in people's faces."

"He speaks the truth," Sash says emphatically. "He understands what he sees, and I've seen strange expressions on Balt's face many times. They've become more severe recently, similar to what I see on the faces of Murkovin."

Miel takes a step back and relaxes her stance.

"We'll address this with the Disciples when we return to the Delta," Larn says.

"Thank you," I reply. "The only reason I'm telling you this is to warn you. I don't have any other reason to make it up."

Miel bows to me. "I apologize if I offended you."

"Don't worry about it," I say, returning her bow. "I'm just trying to help."

I'm not surprised they can't recognize what I see on Balt's face. Those emotions—extreme or irrational, they call them—simply don't exist here. Well, they do exist, but only in the Murkovin, which probably explains why "hatred" is a word in their vocabulary.

We all walk towards a high marble wall that curves in a semicircle from the face of the Mount. Sash looks at me and nods her head as if to say, "You're absolutely right about what you saw in Balt."

Spaced a mile apart, six Watchers stand guard on top of the black wall. The two closest to the gate in the center disappear behind the ledge as we approach. A few seconds later, a steel door swings open.

I glance over my shoulder at the road descending from the Mount to the Barrens and try to guess our altitude. We're at least ten thousand feet higher than the Delta based on my experiences hiking in Mammoth and Yosemite. Through the clear, sharp air, a scarlet ambience radiates around the faraway Delta.

We pass through the gate and stop by the side of the entrance. After the Watchers close and secure the doors, a thick, muscular woman walks to a steel rack near the gate. When she turns to us, she hands each of us a pair of leathery black gloves and a metal helmet.

"What are these for?" I ask Sash.

"If Darkness descends, they're needed on the Mount," she tells me. "If the light begins to dim, put these on before the trees become aware. The needles are extremely sharp."

Curious about the trees, I step off the road and walk into the forest of blue and purple that spreads across the mile-long flat area between the wall and the Mount. Sash trails slightly behind me, and we both stop at the nearest tree. I reach out my hand to touch a low branch. Almost as if they were injected into me, the needles prick my skin. After I jerk my hand away, speckles of blood appear on my fingertips.

"You could have warned me," I playfully complain, smiling at Sash and not actually mad.

"Doing is a more effective method of learning than hearing," she says with a faint smile.

I have to silently chuckle at the closest thing to a joke I've heard in Krymzyn, even if it was at the expense of my fingertips. Sash and I return to the trail.

"We need to prepare items for our return journey," Larn

says to Sash when we reach him. "We'll meet you after your visit to the Pool has been completed."

Larn, Tela, and Miel disappear into the forest on the far side of the road. Sash and I stroll along the path towards the steep Mount. I estimate that the glossy black slopes rise another fifteen or twenty thousand feet over us. With the peak hidden in the clouds, it's hard to tell. But it's taller than any mountain I've ever seen—maybe even taller than Everest.

A clearing opens in the forest on one side of us, a few hundred yards long and half as wide. Slabs of marble, like picnic tables, stand on rectangular marble legs. Smaller marble shapes, some no larger than a shoebox, sit on top of several of the slabs.

Three men and four women, all with cyan in their black hair, work around the tables. A few are working with chisels and hammers, slowly etching shapes in the marble. Others use black pumice rock the size of a sponge to sand items made of steel.

"What are they doing over there?" I ask.

"This is where the Constructs of the Mount work," Sash answers, "creating all that's made of steel."

"The steel is the sap of these trees?"

She nods her head. "Hunters on the Mount take the sap during Darkness. The Constructs mix in powder they grind from the black crystals in the dirt, and the powder hardens the sap into steel. They use molds carved into marble to shape the steel, then brush the items smooth with stone."

"So they don't use _fire_ at all?" I ask but realize that "fire" never translates. "How do they _weld_—attach—the legs of the stools?"

Sash points to the side of the Mount. "Binding made from the juice of berries."

Growing out of cracks in the rocky face just above the forest are holly-like bushes with bright yellow berries clustered inside purple leaves.

"Binding from those berries," Sash continues, "seals the parts as though they were one solid piece."

I think about the huge marble wall in the Delta and the one I just saw here on the Mount. Their sides are seamless and smooth, as though they're one continuous slab.

"I guess you don't want to get binding on your fingers," I comment.

"Binding connects steel to steel or marble to marble," Sash replies. "It has no effect on any other material."

I shake my head, my usual acceptance of a seemingly impossible explanation. "I've wanted to ask you something else for while."

"Go ahead," Sash says.

"When you kneel to the ground and whisper, other people can hear you, right?"

"The person's name I say is aware of my words."

"Any idea how?"

"The roots of the grass carry our words across the Delta. The person whose name we say hears the words through their sense of awareness."

"Does it work here on the Mount?" I ask.

"The needles on the ground do the same," she answers. "The Barrens are the only place it doesn't occur."

A moment of enlightenment arrives. Every substance in

Krymzyn synthesizes perfectly with everything else that exists here. Each has a distinct purpose designed to complement some materials but not interfere with others.

Steel cuts marble. Marble molds steel. Pumice sands steel but also softens in water. Binding only works with marble and steel, nothing else. Crystal dirt hardens steel. Pulp from vines on the Mount blends threads grown on the Delta into smooth leathery fabric.

One type of tree on the Mount, two types of plants. Two types of trees on the Delta, excluding the Tree of Vision, and one type of plant. Telepathic grass and needles cover the ground. Seven botanical wonders supply everything the people need. Every substance in Krymzyn, every form of life, creates a labyrinth of flawless unison. Never more than they need, never less. It's an existence of eternal—there's only one word I can use—balance.

We reach the end of the road at the base of the steep Mount. After we both stop, Sash turns to me. When she smiles, it takes effort on her part. The gloom on her face is deepening, and as hard as I try, I can't figure out why.

"You should consume your sap," she says.

"Why?" I ask.

"For the sign of entrance to appear."

I remove the flask from my belt, twist off the top, and drink half the contents. I don't really feel the need for sustenance because I'm still energized from the sap Tork gave me. If I had to guess, based on what I've seen, each person only drinks four or five cups a day, and that seems to be all they need. Sash takes the flask from her belt and drinks as well.

After I return the flask to my side, we start up a narrow trail carved into the side of the Mount. The path is just wide enough for us to walk beside each other. Snaking back and forth along the face, we climb about a mile until we reach a flat ledge.

A single Watcher guards a granite door, steel spear at his side.

"Greetings, Sash," he says, bowing with a solemn face.

"Greetings, Inda," Sash replies, handing her spear to the Watcher. "The Teller Chase and I are here to view the Reflecting Pool."

"Do you have the sign for entry?" Inda asks.

Sash holds out her hand. As she turns it up to the sky, aqua light rises from her skin.

Even though I expect what I see, I'm still stunned when I extend my hand. The same blue-green rays dance over my palm.

The Watcher swings open the black door. "No one else will enter while you visit the Reflecting Pool."

"We're grateful," Sash says.

After we step inside a dark tunnel, the stone door slams shut behind us.

Chapter 26

Side by side, we walk through the passage. Cool aqua light leads us to an oval opening at the tunnel's end. The sound of trickling water, calm and soothing, echoes around us as we walk.

When we reach the end of the corridor, an immense round cavern opens in front of us. Cyan vines dangle from the domed black marble ceiling of the cave, emitting a soft blue luminescence. Tiny starbursts of golden light, like fireflies on a summer night, weave in and out of the vines. I start to step through the opening, but Sash grabs my arm and pulls me back into the tunnel.

"We must remove our clothing before we enter," she says softly. "Only your containment may touch the water."

We set our helmets on the ground, take off our clothing and boots, and hang our clothes on hooks in the wall. After Sash takes my hand in hers, she leads me into the cavern.

A circular pumice walkway surrounds the enormous Reflecting Pool. Light sparkles in the water that trickles down the ebony walls, gently flows across the black stone path, and spills over a smooth edge into the Pool. At my first few steps, the stone is scratchy against my feet. As we walk around the outside of the cave through the water that dampens the rock, the path softens into a firm spongy texture.

Aqua light and moving points of amber gleam in the Pool's glassy surface. The air around us is still, not warm, not cold—a perfect feeling of nothingness against my bare skin.

We continue until we're a quarter of the way around the Pool. I stop to glance up again at the floating points of golden light.

"What are those?" I ask Sash.

"Flits," she replies. "They dwell in the caverns on the Mount. The creatures never rest. They're always in motion."

I gaze into the familiar amber of Sash's eyes, her face splashed in blue. I lean to her and kiss her full, red lips.

"Walk to the center of the Pool and look down at the water," she says quietly after we kiss.

"Are you coming with me?" I ask.

She shakes her head. "This portion of the journey is only for you."

I turn away and step into the Pool. My feet are immersed in an invigorating wetness, no feeling of temperature at all, but still refreshing to my skin. As I slowly tread through the water, it's ankle deep at first, but gradually rises up my legs.

When I reach the center of the Pool, I stand still with the water just above my knees. The tranquil sounds inside the cavern serenade my mind. I remain motionless while the shallow swells created by my movement disappear. I glance up at the Flits circling overhead and then look down at the mirror of water.

My reflection stares back at me. An unexplained circular ripple spreads from the center of my face, seeming to wash away my skin. I lean closer to my reflection, trying to perceive the changes in my appearance as the water calms.

A deathly white skull, blurry around the edges, replaces my face. Deep, hollow eye sockets, empty black with circles of blue, pierce into my mind. A colored spectrum of light undulates in the center of my skull. Murky brown waves fall from the outline of my head, while dull red lines frown at me.

My eyes drift down the skeletal frame of my body—luminescent bones encased in a web of three-dimensional blue veins. A crimson-red glob pulses in the center of my ribcage.

I lift my hand to my chest, watching bony fingers move across my shape. Each throb of red in the center of my chest matches the beat of my heart. It's like staring at one of the scans I'm all too familiar with in the hospital, stripped bare of skin, showing only my organs and bones.

When I raise my eyes to the ceiling of the cavern, the vines electrify like sinuous fiber-optic strands. The tiny floating points of gold momentarily flash halos of green when they intersect with the aqua light. Above the semi-opaque surface that defines the ceiling of the cavern, tangled midnight blue roots spread upwards, candescent inside the black void.

I tilt my face down to the pool, returning my focus to my own terrifying eyes. The sunken, shadowy sockets with rings of blue in the center send a shiver through my spine. I try to grasp what I see, try to comprehend this vision. Everything I've ever seen, heard, and experienced in Krymzyn strobes through my mind, including the words Eval spoke to me when I was seventeen.

"Although you may believe all things everywhere to be as they are in your world, that belief is simply not a truth of existence."

My pulse soars with revelation. I know why Sash was so confused by my sketch of her. She knows exactly what she looks like, but I don't.

Nothing in Krymzyn exists as I see it. Everything has been shaped, molded, given a texture and a surface that I can grasp within my understanding of reality. The obscure shapes of light I saw in the metal bridge and in the quartz walls of Sash's habitat—those are what I look like here. What I see in Krymzyn isn't what this world really is. They're fabricated images for my eyes.

I slowly turn to Sash.

A specter stands at the edge of the pool—Sash stripped bare and naked to the core, as she actually exists. Tiny gray particles swirl in her glowing white skeleton while a maze of glimmering veins hovers around her bones. Pulsing organs cast red light, molecules moving within. A brilliant spectrum of color oscillates in her skull, neon scarlet tendrils growing out of it and weaving through the black that hangs from her head. A thin, translucent film contains the light, shaping it into a human form.

The hideous apparition momentarily stings me to my marrow.

"This is how I look to you?" I ask.

She lowers her eyes to the water. A single glistening orb of amber light falls from her face. Suddenly, in slow motion, my eyes follow the sphere as it floats down the front of her ghostly form. Crimson bursts around the tear when it splashes into the water at her feet.

"You're beautiful to me," Sash cries.

I return my eyes to Sash's face. Krymzyn wants me to see this world as it truly is. A dimension of light and energy, spiraling molecules of matter, all molded into eerie shapes. Krymzyn is putting a question before me. *Can you accept this world for what it is?* What Krymzyn doesn't know is that every question was answered in my mind before I ever stepped into this Pool.

I can design fantasy worlds for video games, or I can live in one that's real. I can struggle to stay alive on Earth, probably die after a painful fight with cancer, or thrive in Krymzyn if I have a purpose here. More than anything else, I can stay in my world knowing that there's no woman there I'll ever love. In Krymzyn, I can be with the only person I belong with.

The answer to the question given to me by the Pool was never meant for me. This answer has to come from me. This answer is for Sash.

"Not as beautiful as you are to me," I say.

Amber points rise from the water and flow across the cavern into my eyes. Skeletal fingers veined in blue rise in the air, reaching out to me. I run through the water to Sash, hold out my hand, and take hers in mine.

A flood of amber blinds me. I close my eyes, open them when the light recedes, and see Sash standing in front of me—my perception of her once again. Porcelain skin glazed in aqua light, long black hair shining with scarlet, and tears falling from amber eyes.

When she pulls me to her, I step out of the pool. We engulf each other in our arms. Sash burrows her face in my neck, presses her breasts to my chest, and holds me against her body.

"I do belong with you," she whispers.

"I know," I say. "And I belong with you."

I kiss her neck while her fingertips trace up my spine. Our lips find each other's, and we kiss while absorbing each other in our arms. I crave her in all of my senses, wish I could smell her and taste her, long to be filled by her in every way I can.

We drop to our knees on the spongy stone. Facing one another, our hands tenderly explore each other's bodies. As we kiss, passion burns through her skin and into my veins. Sash gently pushes me to my back, the shallow water tingling against my shoulders and legs.

She climbs onto me and crouches over my body, her face directly over mine. After reaching one hand between her legs, she slowly strokes me with her smooth, slender hands. I skim my fingertips down the length of her hair as she guides me inside. Amber beams dazzle my eyes when she slowly slides down on top of me, lowering her hips until I'm completely within.

Thousands of sparks erupt in my nerves. Brilliant blue streams out of my eyes and intersects with an amber flare. The water around me seems to seep into my skin, blending with my blood and flowing through my body. I hear the beat of Sash's heart reverberating through the rock beneath me while the Flits circle inside my mind.

"Sash!" my voice echoes through the cavern.

"Be calm," Sash whispers, looking down at me with a knowing smile. "Your sense of awareness is awakening inside you."

Her fingers gently slip through my hair. Wet, soft warmth grips me inside her. She leans her head down, scarlet brushing across my face, and kisses my lips. I feel everything inside her, around us, my new consciousness leaping to life.

Sash raises her hips, sinks them again, and then moves up and down on top of me. I lift my hips to meet her then lower them as she glides back up. Her hands hold the back of my head, clutching my hair. I run my fingers along her shoulders, lower them to circle her nipples, and finally rest my hands on the curves of her hips. Time stops inside the aqua cavern while we make love, everything inside us exposed and shared with the other.

Our rhythm quickens and our breathing grows heavier. I feel her tense and arch my back when our bodies both spasm. Waves of orgasm surge through us until she collapses into my arms.

As our muscles relax, she stretches out on top of me, legs on legs, chest on chest, keeping me inside her. Intertwined with my hair, her fingers gently massage my head. Minutes pass, maybe hours—I have no idea. We lie silently with our heartbeats pulsing against each other, her eyes never leaving mine.

"Was this why you've seemed so sad?" I finally ask. "Were you afraid of how I'd react to what I saw?"

"I didn't know what the Pool would show you," she

whispers.

"It showed me what I already know," I say. "That I love you."

Sash smiles the most beautiful smile that ever was.

Chapter 27

When we step into the pale green light outside the tunnel, I suddenly worry that the Watcher might have heard what happened inside the cavern. I have to assume that it was a first for Krymzyn. His face appears as solemn as it did when we entered, so I decide that everything's fine.

"Thank you," I say to him.

"If your experience was enlightening, I'm honored," he replies.

After bowing to the Watcher, Sash takes her spear from him. We walk down the trail hand in hand. As I look out over the forest below, I see a few scarlet-haired Hunters strolling through the woods. Constructs work at marble slabs in the clearing. Watchers stand guard on the distant wall. They all feel the world around them, deep inside every part of them, every moment of their lives.

They don't need to show feelings of fulfillment with a facial expression, Sash once told me. If I don't see smiles or hear laughter in Krymzyn, it doesn't mean the people lack emotion. If they don't have immediate family as I know it, it's because they have the entire world around them, including every living being in this world. They seem to have transcended beyond emotions as I understand them. They feel a perpetual sense of fulfillment, honor to serve the whole, and share those feelings with everything around them.

"The first time I came to Krymzyn," I say to Sash, "I was in awe of you, fascinated from the moment I saw you. Now, I feel that way about everything here. I mean, it really is a world of balance."

"When you feel that balance," she says, "you understand Krymzyn."

I stop walking and pull her by the hand to me. "I do understand Krymzyn. I want to be here with you."

When Sash looks at my eyes, her face is darkened again by overwhelming sorrow. "If you seek a purpose in Krymzyn, you should do so because you want to be in Krymzyn, not because you want to be with me."

"Why are you saying that, Sash?"

"I want you to live the life that's best for you," she answers, "because I care about you."

"I belong here . . . with you," I say.

"We belong together, but that doesn't mean we'll be together."

"Sash, what are you talking about?" I ask, more confused now than by anything I've ever seen or heard in Krymzyn.

"Make decisions that are best for your life, Chase. That's all I want for you."

"My life is with you," I say.

She whisks by me and walks down the path. I know this discussion is over. She's the most determined person alive—

which is a polite way of saying stubborn—and I'm not sure how to react. With frustration growing inside me, I trot to catch up to her. As I walk beside her, she takes my hand firmly in hers but doesn't say a word. Larn, his face stoic, waits for us where the trail meets the road.

"Have you successfully completed your visit to the Reflecting Pool?" Larn asks when we reach him.

"I saw what I came to see," I answer, still distracted by the conversation with Sash.

The three of us walk down the road towards the gate. Sash is quiet, withdrawn, but she keeps my hand grasped in hers as we walk. Larn breaks the silence.

"We have items to transport to the Delta on our return journey. Our travel will be slowed, but I'll carry you as we did coming to the Mount."

"Larn," I say, "I never know when I'm going to leave, so if I'm suddenly gone, I want you to know that the only reason I said what I did about Balt earlier is because I care about what happens to all of you here."

"I believe your intentions are sincere," Larn replies. "I'll discuss this issue with the Disciples immediately upon our return."

"Thank you. It means a lot to me."

As we near the gate, I see two large metallic objects by the side of the road that look like they belong in the Smithsonian. One reminds me of a fuel tank from a fighter jet, a twelve-foot-long tube, maybe two feet tall, with rounded points on both ends. The rear stands on forks connected to a single wheel, a foot-high thin orb of solid steel. Like wheelbarrow handles, two metal arms extend from the front.

The other is a football-shaped wagon the same length as the aerodynamic tube. Inside the wagon stand a few stools with their feet in the air, four table legs sticking straight up, and an assortment of spears, stakes, pitchers, and knives. A black mesh net stretched over the wagon and tied to the sides holds the steel items in place. Two metal handles are attached to the front of the cart, while a single wheel holds up the rear. Both of the vehicles have small angled wings seamlessly adhered to their sides.

"Travelers transport items the Constructs make on the Mount to the Delta," Sash tells me as I study the vehicles. "The tube is empty but will be filled with sap from the sustaining trees and returned to the Mount."

"Why didn't you just have me ride in a wagon on the way up here?" I ask Larn.

"If Murkovin attack during our journey," he answers, "they often target our transports, either for the items we create, such as spears and rope, or for sap when the tube is full. Since we can't travel as fast with the transports behind us, we never use them to carry people."

I recall how quickly the people from the Mount reached the Delta for Cavu's Ritual, and wonder if I can get a sense of their running speed. "How much faster are travelers than other people in Krymzyn?"

Larn ponders for a moment. "At the speed we traveled coming to the Mount, I can make twenty trips while someone who isn't a Traveler, excluding Sash, does so only once. My top traveling speed is more than double what it was on the way up here."

If we peaked at five-thousand miles per hour coming to the Mount, that means Larn can reach about ten thousand miles per hour. The average person in Krymzyn can run at a speed of over two hundred miles per hour. I know I won't win any cross-country races in Krymzyn if I have a purpose here.

"How fast will we travel on the way back?" I ask.

"Our speed will be cut in half," he says. "We're not able to blend the light of steel, so the drag of the vehicles reduces our speed."

I nod to him with the whole traveling concept making much more sense to me after what I saw in the Pool. Sash takes my helmet and gloves from me and, with hers, returns them to the rack by the gate. We all walk to where Miel and Tela stand waiting for us.

"Drink more sap to ensure you're safe while traveling," Larn says to me.

I unclip the flask from my belt, drink all of the remaining sap, and return the flask to my side.

"We're ready to depart," Larn calls out to the Watcher standing above the arch.

The green-haired man descends the ladder, unlatches the bolts, and swings both doors open. Miel's arms flex with creases of toned muscle when she lifts the handles of the large steel cart. Tela takes the arms extending from the long tube in her hands. With the transports rolling behind them, they both pass through the gate.

I turn to Sash, rest my hands on her shoulders, and look into her eyes. "I don't know how much longer I'll be here, but I'll be back soon. I want to have my Ritual. I believe I have a purpose here, and part of that purpose is being with you."

Sash struggles to smile, her face again veiled by sadness. "I love you, Chase," she says. "Don't do anything on your plane that would risk your life there."

She kisses my lips before I can say anything, turns, and sprints away.

Larn crouches for me to leap on his back. After I'm in place and secure, he begins to jog behind Tela and Miel. Once we all start down the steep road towards the Barrens, the human shapes ignite.

A wake of light from Sash leading her way, Miel rockets down the road in front of us with her transport in tow. Tela trails behind the wagon, her aerodynamic tube lifting a few feet off the ground when she blends her light. Two minutes from the time we left the Mount should put us at the edge of the bridge.

I vow to keep my eyes open on the journey since, according to Larn, we'll be traveling at about half the speed we reached when we came to the Mount. The air is perfectly clear, clean, and absent of any dust or particles, so I decide that I'm not really risking abrasion to my eyeballs. I also know, as they told me, that the sap I've consumed should prevent any damage.

A little over halfway through our travel, the rays I know are Sash slow until she's beside us.

"Darkness!" Sash shouts.

The sound warps past my ears and dissolves into the air behind us. Sash races to the front of Tela and Miel. Thirty seconds later, the light around the clouds begins to flicker. The billows animate, drops of rain slam against our faces, and Darkness descends. Our motion slows with a stutter as the light fades. When we rise over a hill, I see the metallic bridge a couple of miles in the distance.

As the rain pounds down, human shapes of blurred white appear from the Barrens in front of us—four streaking to the road from the north, and four speeding directly into our path from the south.

Chapter 28

We're within one hundred yards of the bridge when two black-veined beasts slam into the transport behind Miel. Metallic thuds resonate through the Barrens. The cart flips high in the air before crashing into the wet dirt beside the road.

Miel spins from the impact, no weapon in hand. Another Murkovin flies into her, drives her off the road, and tackles her to the ground. Claws rake across her face while the two grapple in the mud.

Sash flashes in behind the creature with every muscle in her body coiled. A wrath is unleashed when the tip of her spear splits open the Murkovin skull. We jolt to a stop after we pass them, and Larn drops my feet to the road.

"Tela!" Larn shouts. "Get Chase to the Delta!"

Sliding to a halt, Tela drops the handles of the tube. As she darts towards us, Larn shoves me in the direction of the bridge.

Red eyes flaming through the tempest of rain, four Murkovin descend upon Sash. Larn bursts straight towards them. Miel struggles on the ground at Sash's feet with blood smeared across her face. Clangs of steel shrill through the storm while Sash defends Miel from the onslaught.

Sash impales a gruesome head on her spear, releasing a spray of blood-soaked beams. Another brute leaps past her towards Miel. Soaring into the fight, Larn smashes him to the ground. Miel staggers to her feet and wobbles towards the bridge. When she stumbles, a fifth Murkovin blasts out of the dark.

I start towards Miel, but a hand grabs my shirt and jerks me in the other direction.

"Run!" Tela hollers. "We don't have spears!"

She points to the two Murkovin who crashed into the cart. With weapons clutched in their hands, they charge at us from fifty feet away. Tela yanks me into a sprint towards the bridge.

I look over my shoulder at Miel as we run. A creature stabs his spear down at her. She tries to deflect the blow with her hands, but the point rips open the side of her head. He throws himself on top of her. They wrestle on the ground with his face at the gash, her blood streaming to the dirt.

In one fluid motion, Larn springs to Miel's side, rams a spear through the head of the beast, and grabs Miel by the shirt. Bolting towards the river, he drags Miel by his side. The two Murkovin chasing Tela and me cut towards Larn and Miel.

Hard metal pounds against my feet when Tela and I reach the bridge. She pulls me by the shirt as I desperately try to keep pace. Straining my head to the side, I spot Larn running towards us with Miel's limp body still in the grip of one hand. Sash sprints at his heels, four corpses on the ground behind her, four Murkovin alive and in pursuit.

Tela and I cross over the crest of the bridge and stop

halfway down the other side. The gates in the wall swing open.

"Get inside!" Tela yells at me.

She turns away and races back towards the center of the bridge. Balt explodes through the gate doors in front of me. On the ground behind him, a Watcher lies face down in a pool of blood. Balt's eyes aren't amber. Points of burning red scorch the air between us. Tensing my muscles, I crouch and ball my hands into fists.

He slows as he nears me, taking aim with malevolent eyes. He suddenly thrusts his spear at my chest. I twist, dodge the tip, and hammer my elbow into his gut. His fist batters the side of my head, knocking me to my knees.

"Balt!" Tork's voice screams.

Ignoring the voice, Balt cocks his weapon and jabs at me again. I hurl a fist against the steel pole, knocking the tip away from my face. Tork and five Watchers storm through the gate. Balt glances at them and then dashes up the bridge towards the arch.

I try to stand to my feet but feel dizzy from the blows to my head. After I fall to my knees, my eyes follow Balt through the scathing rain. He runs up the bridge towards Sash and Larn. They're still locked in a vicious fight with four Murkovin at the center of the bridge. Miel lies motionless on the steel behind them.

Tela reaches the arch, leans down, and scoops Miel in her arms. She speeds back down the slope with the Traveler's body held tightly against her chest. Balt races past her and aims at Sash. When Tork and the Watchers reach me, I jump to my feet, fight the dizziness, and churn my legs towards the arch.

"Sash!" I shout as Balt closes in on her.

Sash spikes one Murkovin in the chest, but another creature stabs at her from the side. Larn swings his spear over the top of his head, knocking the Murkovin weapon away from Sash. A third beast gouges Larn's shoulder. Larn turns, swings his spear with one hand, and crushes the creature's nose.

"Sash!" I yell again.

As she spins to the sound of my voice, Balt lunges his spear at her stomach. With her feet at the edge of the bridge, Sash jerks her hips back and shoulders forward. The point arrows past her torso, the metal of the shaft sliding against her black shirt.

Balt lurches to a stop in front of Sash. With both hands grasping the steel, he slams the shaft against her chin. When her feet lift off the bridge, she tries to catch the narrow ridge with her toes.

Larn twists and fires a clenched fist at Balt. After Balt ducks under the punch, he flees towards the Barrens. The other Murkovin retreat as Tork and the Watchers arrive.

Teetering on the lip of the bridge, Sash's arms flail wildly in the air. Larn, off-balance and falling to the metal surface, stretches a blood-stained arm to her. Their fingertips just graze before Sash plummets to the rapids below.

"We don't need to swim. Only Serquatine swim in the river," shouts inside my head.

I suck in a huge breath as I sprint, angle to the side of the bridge, and leap into a dive.

Chapter 29

Pounding waves flip me when I hit the water. The savage rapids suck me into the depths until I lose all sense of direction. Completely disoriented, I spin around, searching for Sash. Through the torrent of murky silvery-blue, I spot streaks of red.

I stroke with a fury in my arms, kick with a frenzy in my legs, straight towards Sash. Her listless body is caught in a relentless current deep under the rapids. Rushing water sweeps us down the river with Sash thirty feet in front of me. I close the distance between us. Twenty feet. Ten feet. Five feet. I surge forward.

A tornado of bubbles whirls around us. Long, slender fingers with webs up to the middle of the knuckles snatch Sash by the hair. Like entering an underwater vacuum, a stagnant pool inside the deluge of water, we float perfectly still.

I'm shocked by the woman in front of me. She appears to be roughly my age, with snow-white skin and a face crafted in timeless, stunning beauty. Bleach-blond hair floats around a smooth, thin face while bubbles of air rise from sparkling golden lips. Her emerald green eyes pierce through the dark water. I reach out to grab Sash by the arm, but the woman wrenches her body away from me.

Keeping a firm grip on Sash's hair with one hand, the woman studies my face. Her other hand is concealed behind her back. A noose of black rope cuts into the skin of her long, narrow neck. I look down her nude body to sleek legs, but in place of feet, fins grow straight down from her shins. Long and broad at the tips, they struggle to tread water because of rope tightly binding her calves.

Through the static pocket of water, the woman stares at me with anger, pain, and distrust. When she writhes and strains to move the arm behind her back, I arch my neck to see rope cinched around her wrist. The hand is stretched to the center of her shoulder blades and secured to the noose around her throat.

I extend one hand out towards the knot, but she flinches away and glares at me. Limp in the creature's hand, Sash floats with her eyes closed and no air bubbles leaving her nose or mouth. Using my hands, I mime untying a rope from my neck.

The woman slowly turns to the side with her emerald eyes locked on my hands. Fighting to keep the air inside my lungs, I reach to the noose and loosen the knot. I pull the rope from around her neck, untie her wrist, and free her hand. Pushing against her hips, I lower myself to her legs and release them from the rope.

As I float back up in front of the woman's face, her expression changes from suspicion to curiosity. After lifting a hand to my cheek, she tilts her head to the side and, with one finger, touches the corner of my eye.

She suddenly shoves Sash to me. I grab Sash by her shirt and pull her body close to mine. The blond-haired woman wraps both of her arms around our waists. Without warning, she powerfully kicks her feet and torpedoes us up through the turbulent rapids.

We're launched through the river's surface and into the air. I gasp for a breath before a wave slams us against a rock. With one hand, I cling to an edge, Sash still held tightly in my other arm. Straining every muscle in my body, I throw Sash up to the face of the slab and safely out of the rapids. The blond woman is nowhere to be seen.

Clawing my way up the granite, I clutch Sash by the shirt and drag her to the top of the rock. Waves splash high off the edges of the black stone while rain continues to pour. As I lower my cheek to her face, I dig deep in my mind for memories of the CPR classes I took with my family. I don't feel any breath against my skin from her nose or mouth. When I press my ear to her chest, I don't hear a heartbeat.

I pull her mouth open with my fingers but don't see any blockage. Trying to remain methodical and calm, I pinch her nostrils, inhale deeply, and lower my lips over hers. My breath steadily pours into her lungs. I lift my face away, suck in more air, and exhale again into her mouth. Two breaths, I remember.

Crossing my hands, I center my palms on her chest and sharply pump thirty times. When I listen for a heartbeat, her body is silent. I feed two more breaths inside her before thrusting my hands against her chest again and again.

"Breathe, Sash!" I yell.

There's not a hint of breath or heartbeat when I finish

the compressions, so I frantically repeat the steps one more time. Silver drops fall from the sky and splatter on the lifeless face in front of me. I listen to her chest, but the only sound is rage from the rapids around us. I need to shock her heart, use a defibrillator, but there's nothing like that in Krymzyn.

"It can't return you from death, but as long your brain is functioning, sap will revive you," I hear inside my head.

Sap, pure energy, should shock her heart. Her brain is still alive and can live for thirty minutes with CPR. Blood circulates through the veins during compressions and will carry the sap to her heart. I know my flask is empty, so I rip hers from her belt, open it, but find that it's dry inside.

"You have sap in your blood now," Tork had said. *"As Eval told you, they sometimes try to drink our blood for the sap inside."*

An unconscious person can't swallow, and I doubt her digestive system is functioning anyway. I know that some drugs on Earth will absorb directly into the blood from under the tongue or around the gums. I reach to the edge of the rock and slide my wrist over it, but it's smooth from countless waves crashing over its sides.

I lean over Sash. First closing my eyes, I hold my wrist to my mouth, clamp my teeth as hard as I can, and tear a small chunk of skin away. I dab my fingertips into the crimson flow and reach them inside her mouth. Spreading my blood under her tongue and around her gums, I hope—pray—that her veins will absorb it.

I pinch her nostrils and fill her lungs with air. My shoulders strain while I desperately pump with my hands.

"You have to come back!" I shout.

My count reaches thirty. No breath. No heartbeat. No sign of life.

I soak my fingertips in blood again. While coating the inside of her mouth, I scratch into her veins so I'm certain my blood mixes with hers. I quickly give her two more breaths, tenderly grasp her head in my hands, and slide my lips from her mouth to her ear.

"Sash," I whisper, tears burning my eyes, "please live."

Beads of rain race down the ridges in my arms as I flex them against her body. I shout the count out loud, trying to deafen the despair sweltering inside my mind. The volume of my voice increases with each passing number until I shriek twenty-eight. Her body convulses under my hands, and water spouts from her mouth. When I hear gurgling in her throat, I roll her on her side. She finally gasps for air.

Sash coughs several times, spitting out more water. I fall to the rock beside her. Amber is revealed as her eyelids open, and she gulps another breath.

"Breathe slow and deep," I tell her.

She fights to suck in air, exhales, and then breathes again. I place my hand on her chest to feel the beat of her heart, steady and strong. I sit up and gently raise her, supporting her in my arms.

"Can you breathe?" I ask.

She nods and coughs again, but her breathing gradually returns to normal. I stand and look towards the bridge. Tork and the others crouch at the edge, watching us from two hundred yards away. I cup my hands around my mouth.

"Get a pillow and rope!" I yell. "Use the pillow to guide

the rope down the river to us!"

Larn sprints across the bridge until beams disappear through the gate. I sit on the rock beside Sash, rain still falling from above, and slip my arm around her shoulder. She stares at the rock below our feet.

My body starts to tremble when the image of her dead face flashes in front of my eyes. I gently rest my lips against her forehead.

"I thought I'd lost you," I whisper.

She leans back from me, her eyes red and filled with tears, and gazes straight into my eyes. "Not now," she says. "Not ever."

"How are you feeling?" I ask.

"I'm better," she replies quietly. "You saved my life."

"I think I might have owed you at least one."

She shakes her head. "You never owe me anything."

"I owe you everything," I say. "No matter what, Sash, you've given me a life I never knew I could have."

Her eyes reach deep into mine. "How did you bring me back?"

"I did something called _CPR_. I blew air into your lungs and pumped your heart to make the blood circulate. I had to put my blood in your mouth to get sap in your veins."

"Now I know what I saw," she murmurs to herself. "My Vision of the Future came to pass."

"What do you mean?" I ask.

"When we sat on the Tall Hill, I told you that you were in my Vision of the Future. My Vision was my body on this rock, dead, with you leaning over me."

I'm stunned by her words. "Why didn't you tell me?"

"I didn't know if it would happen while you're here now," she replies. "It could have been on your next visit. I only knew it would happen before your Ritual of Purpose. In my Vision, there was no color of purpose in your hair."

"That doesn't explain why you didn't tell me."

"The last time you were here, you said you could take something to make your visits stop. If I'd told you I would die when you're here in Krymzyn, you never would have returned. Even if it meant you had to die in your world, you wouldn't have come back so that I could live."

I listen to her answer again in my mind. "You're right," I say. "I would've done whatever I had to so I wouldn't come back if I thought it would keep you from dying, even if they can't heal me in my world. You really know me, don't you?"

"I do," she says softly, "just as you know me."

As I study her eyes, her logic for never telling me sinks in. "You were going to let yourself die without saying anything so I could stay in my world if they could heal me, but come back here to live if I thought I would die on Earth?"

She nods her head. "That was my hope. I wanted you to have the choice."

"That's what you meant on the Mount when you said to make decisions that are best for my life?"

"Yes," she answers. "I just wanted you to have a chance for life no matter what happened to me."

Her explanation is the exact selflessness I would expect from her. Sash thought she would die in this river but still fought on top of the bridge so that others could get to safety. The idea of running to save herself would never enter her mind, even when believing that the end of her life was moments away.

I lean my forehead against hers. "Now that this is behind us, do you think we can be together?"

"That's what I want," she says, finally smiling, "and I believe we will."

We gently kiss and hold each other in our arms. The swirling inside the billows overhead slows. As the rain stops falling, the first rays of scarlet cut through the edges of the clouds. Out of the corner of my eye, I see bright light by the bridge. Larn seeps from the light and runs to the top of the arch.

Tork securely ties the pillow to the end of a rope and throws it into the river. After waves toss the pillow high in the air, it falls back to the water. Tork slowly feeds more rope while steering the pillow through the rapids to the edge of the rock. As I guessed it might be, when I pull the pillow from the water, it's perfectly dry. I untie it from the end of the rope and kneel in front of Sash.

She helps me wrap the rope behind her back and under her arms. I tie a knot in front of her chest and check it several times to make sure it's secure. Enough spare rope still dangles from the knot for me to attach the pillow in front of her.

"Hold the rope tightly with both hands," I say, "and use the pillow to keep your head above water. Kick your feet to stay upright. If you see a wave about to crash over you or feel yourself going under, take a huge breath and hold it in."

Sash nods her understanding.

"Are you ready to do this, or do you need more rest?" I ask.

"I'm ready," she says.

I help Sash to her feet, face the bridge, and make a megaphone around my mouth with my hands. "Pull fast when she's in the water!" I shout.

Tork waves a hand over his head, acknowledging that he heard me.

I look at Sash again. "Hold your breath when I tell you. I'll throw you as far as I can out into the water so you're clear of the rock. Once you're on the bridge, have them send the pillow back to me. You won't have any problem doing this."

"Chase," she says. "I love you."

"I love you, too," I reply. "Always. But right now, let's get us both to safety." I grip her waist with both hands. "Take a big breath."

After she inhales, I fling her as far as I can into the rapids at the side of the rock. A wave immediately washes over her. I glance at the bridge to see Tork, Larn, and a Watcher furiously pulling the rope. My eyes follow the black line from the bridge back to the rapids, finding where it disappears under the water. Sash surfaces, kicks her way up and over a wave, and then gulps a new breath. Another wave surges over her, but she comes back up behind it, still clutching the rope in her hands.

Time doesn't seem to move as they drag her through the rapids. I finally see her body emerge from the water under the bridge. Glittering scarlet swings in the air as they pull her up to the edge. Tork grasps her arm, lifts her onto the bridge, and rests her on the steel surface.

When I see Sash cough a few times, I know she's conscious and breathing. Tork hands her his flask and she drinks from it. Sash finally waves to me to let me know she's safe.

Tork and Larn untie the rope from Sash, reattach the pillow to the end, and throw it back into the river. While they guide it down the rapids, I take several long, deep breaths, allowing myself to finally feel relief.

My head starts spinning and my knees feel weak. As my muscles convulse, I fall backwards to the rock. Bracing myself with one hand on the granite, I try to wave good-bye to Sash. She'll know what's happening to me.

A giant wave splashes off the side of the rock and high into the air in front of me. Silver foam fills my vision.

*   *   *

"Sash," I whispered to my computer screen.

As soon as I stopped shaking and strength returned to my hands, I slid the chair up to my laptop. I watched the recording of my seizure over and over, frame by frame, amazed by what I saw.

Chapter 30

I dove for the Frisbee, slid on my knees across the soft, warm sand, and whipped the disc back to my dad. After snagging it one-handed from the air, Dad jogged across the beach to me.

"That's all, Chase. I'm worn out," Dad laughed.

I stood up and gave him a sweat-soaked grin. The planets had aligned, the weather gods had smiled, and we had a beautiful, warm, sunny Friday at Zuma Beach. I turned to my mom and sister, who were sitting on a blanket spread out on the sand.

"Ally, come for a walk with me," I called out, motioning to her with my hand.

"Not now, Chase. Mom and I are chillin'," she replied, wrinkling her face.

"Come on," I said.

I walked to the blanket and lifted Ally by the arm to her feet. As she stood, a feigned frown on her face, I was instantly reminded of Tela. Maybe I just wanted to see a resemblance between them, comforting my mind that I could find a surrogate in Krymzyn to replace my sister.

We strolled along the edge of the water while calm

waves broke onto the shore and white foam lapped at our feet. I'd started taking the anti-seizure medication as soon as I'd returned from the trip to the Mount. I'd had a lot to take care of over the past week and wanted everything in place before my Ritual in Krymzyn, just in case the outcome wasn't what I hoped for.

I'd spent late nights in my studio working on the painting to leave for my family, only sleeping an hour or two each night. Since the cancer was still in a relatively early stage, the only symptoms I'd experienced were headaches, mild nausea, and occasional blurry vision. I'd been able to hide them all from my family, despite how tired I'd felt.

Every moment of the day, every second I could, I'd spent with Mom, Dad, and Ally. When feelings of sadness and anxiety would hit me, panic at times, I'd ease my mind by telling myself that I didn't have to go through with it. But I knew I would.

Mom had said that she'd be more upset if I missed my chance for happiness than she would be if I moved away. She hadn't known that moving away meant never seeing each other again, but that didn't lessen the meaning of her words. My chance for happiness was with Sash.

For a few minutes on a slab of black granite in the center of a violent river, I'd had that chance taken away from me. When the breath of life had returned to Sash, I'd vowed that I would do everything I could for as long as I lived to make sure that chance never slipped away again. Those minutes on the rock, a scene from her own Vision of the Future, had been meant for me—final, absolute confirmation that my life belonged in Krymzyn.

As Ally and I walked down the beach, she filled me in on her junior year at Berkeley. I steered her to an area where no other people were nearby. After I sat on the sand, Ally plopped down beside me. We both watched the sun descend towards the horizon.

"You know, we're lucky we grew up the way we did," I said. "We have, like, a perfect family."

She smiled at me. "Yeah, we are lucky. It's funny to hear you say that, considering all you had to go through."

"That didn't matter," I said, looking out over the waves, splashes of sunlight on their crests. "Shit happens, you know. But the important stuff has always been there for us. I mean, I hope they know how much I love them, and I hope they know that you and I appreciate everything they've done for us."

"They do," Ally replied, still smiling.

"Ally," I said softly. "I want you to know that I love you. I mean, I know I was a jerk sometimes. That's just how big brothers are. But you're the best sister a guy could ever have."

She hesitated before saying anything. "Why are you saying this stuff, Chase?" She reached one arm around my shoulder and her voice cracked. "It's back, isn't it?"

"Two tumors," I told her. "They're both malignant."

Her hands shook as she reached her other arm around me and smothered me in a hug. Tears dripped from her face onto my shoulder.

"What did they say?" she sobbed in my ear.

"Six months to two years. Who knows? There's always a chance for full recovery. The surgery is in a few weeks," I lied, wanting her to return to school. "I haven't told Mom and Dad yet. Please, Ally, I don't want you to say anything. I'll tell them after you go back to school. I just wanted us to have this week together."

She couldn't control the flow of tears from her eyes. "I won't say anything. This really sucks. I love you so much, Chase. You don't deserve this."

"I'll let you know the exact date of the surgery so you can come back if you want to," I said, continuing my string of lies.

"Of course I want to be with you," she murmured.

Sitting on the sand, we held each other for several minutes. I eventually leaned back and looked at her eyes.

"Ally, I have to tell you something, and you have to listen to me. You're going to think I'm crazy, but you have to listen."

She nodded, never taking her eyes off mine, and bit her bottom lip.

"I'm sure you know all those pictures I've drawn over the years, and you've heard me describe what the doctor called a hallucination when I was younger."

"I remember," she said. "Mom thought you obsessed over it so much to escape reality."

"It *is* reality. I go there, like to another dimension or universe or something, and I know for a fact it's real. If I die on Earth, there's a way I'll still live in that world."

She smiled at me, but it was a sad, patronizing smile, as if to say, *"If that helps you get through this, it's okay to believe that, and I won't say anything to dispel your fantasy."*

"Ally," I said firmly, "come to my studio late tonight after Mom and Dad are asleep. I'll prove to you it's real."

Curiosity momentarily lit up her eyes. I pulled her close to me for a hug but didn't saying anything else. With our arms around each other, we both looked at the ocean and watched the sun until it touched the water. When I was sure her emotions were completely in check, we walked back to our parents.

Late that night, Ally knocked on my locked studio door. She was leaving the next afternoon to go back to school. This was my only chance to convince her it was all real. I opened the door, walked her around my easel, and stood her in front of the four-foot-by-three-foot canvas I'd been working on all week.

I watched Ally's pensive reaction as she studied the oil painting of Sash and me on top of the Tall Hill. In the painting, our hands were clasped tightly together, spears dangled from our other hands, and our feet were surrounded by crimson blades of grass. Under billowing clouds, brilliant streaks of scarlet and orange high above our heads, we both had peaceful smiles on our faces. I'd added a huge sustaining tree to the side of the hill in the foreground that wasn't accurate as far as its location, but no one on Earth would know the difference. The Mount of Krymzyn rose behind us in the distance, majestic in its forest-green glow.

"Geez, Chase," Ally remarked. "You've been drawing that girl since you were twelve."

"Her name is Sash," I said, "and the love we share, the way I feel about her, is more real than anything I've ever felt with anyone here."

She slowly turned her face to me and frowned. "Do you realize how incredibly insane that sounds?"

"Yeah, I know, but listen. Have you ever had a recurring dream, but the exact same amount of time passes in between your dreams and in real life? Like, when you wake up from your dream on a Tuesday morning, in the dream it was Tuesday morning as well? Two days later, Thursday night, you reenter the same dream and it's Thursday night in the dream? Like the dream and real life are in perfect sync, and it happens over and over?"

"No, of course not," she replied.

"Well, that's what happens when I go there. Hallucinations don't work that way, Ally. Everything is sequential when I go. People age the same amount as I do between visits. I mean, I first went when I was twelve, then seventeen, and now twenty-three. Everyone there has aged the exact same amount as I have. If I make a plan for something while I'm there, it happens the next time I go. My seizures are only seconds here, but I can be there for hours during them."

She spent a few seconds digesting my words. "That is kind of weird," she said.

"I want to show you something else."

After we stepped to my desk, I turned my laptop towards Ally. The video was already queued, so I clicked play and showed her the recording of my seizure. In the video, my body suddenly convulsed, legs stiffened, and hands jerked away from my body. I shook in my chair with drool dripping from my lower lip. Right before the seizure ended, my entire body jolted again like I'd been hit by an electric shock.

"I've seen your seizures in person," Ally said quietly. "I don't need to see them again."

"But you never saw this."

I scrolled back to the beginning of the seizure and zoomed in on my face. Stepping through the video frame by frame, I showed her the first convulsion. I went back and forth through the frames, making sure she saw them over and over. In only one frame, dull beams of amber light streamed out of my eyes straight towards the camera.

"What is that?" Ally asked.

"Watch," I said.

I scrolled to the end of the video, to the last flex of my body before my muscles relaxed, and stopped on a frame. The same amber light flared from my eyes.

"Where I go," I said, "they do something called 'blending their light.' They merge their own bodies with rays of light. It's complicated. The amber light you see is what takes me there."

Ally stared at the screen for a few seconds then turned to look at the painting again. For a brief moment, I saw belief in her eyes, but she quickly returned to her perception of reality.

"This isn't proof of anything, Chase," she said, shaking her head. "That could be a computer glitch, or maybe you even painted those on there."

"I didn't touch the video," I told her.

"It still isn't proof of anything," she argued.

"If the cancer kills me," I said, knowing that it wouldn't be cancer that killed me, "I want you to know I'm alive there. I have pages and pages of all that's happened to me in a journal. You can also look at my drawings. I have hundreds of them you haven't seen. You'll know, Ally. You'll know I'm there, and you have to convince Mom and Dad it's all real so they know I'm safe."

Ally looked down at the floor and started to cry. After I stepped to her, we hugged tightly.

"Just keep an open mind, Ally," I said in her ear. "You know I'm not a psycho. Besides, maybe I can beat it." The last words were said only to calm her down.

"It's sure a beautiful painting," she whispered. "The best you've ever done."

"Thank you, Ally. Anyway, you'll come back before the surgery, so we can talk more about it then," I said, lying to her yet again. "I just wanted you to see this before you left."

I hated deceiving her, but it was the only way she would return to school without saying anything to our parents. She spent another few minutes studying the painting and then went to bed.

I'd stopped taking the anti-seizure meds the day before, wanting to get them out of my system as soon as I was ready to return for my Ritual. A headache had started that afternoon, but I didn't think much of it at the time. They were gradually getting more frequent as the cancer spread through my brain.

As the headache amplified, shooting from the back of my neck to my temples, I knew what it was. I had just enough time to sit in the chair and hit record on my laptop before the seizure started.

Chapter 3 |

When I arrive in Krymzyn, Sash is seated ten feet down the Empty Hill with her back to me. I know she knows I'm here, but she doesn't turn to me. I walk to her and sit on the grass beside her. After slipping one arm around her waist, I pull her close to me. She nuzzles my neck with her nose.

"I would have come sooner," I say, "not that I can really control it, but I had a lot to take care of in my world."

"I understand," she says with her head resting on my shoulder. "When I last slept, I saw you return in a dream, so I've been waiting for you."

"Have you recovered?" I ask.

She raises her head and looks at my eyes. "Yes, I've healed. Thank you again for what you did."

"It's just what we do for each other," I say. "What happened to Miel?"

"She's still part of Krymzyn. Her body was taken to the Bed of Light on top of the Mount, and she'll always be with us."

"I'm really sorry, Sash. You did everything you could to save her. I should have done more to help."

She shakes her head. "Tela did the right thing. Neither

of you had weapons. The Murkovin would have killed you both."

I lower my eyes to the grass between my feet. "I feel like it was my fault Miel died."

"You can't blame yourself for events you don't control," she says firmly. "Apprentices are taught to always get to safety in the face of confrontation. They're not ready to fight Murkovin. If you and Tela had joined the fight, Larn and I might have been killed trying to help you."

We silently sit side by side for several minutes. I try to accept Sash's reasoning but can't help feeling as though I should have done more.

"Tela's no longer an Apprentice and is now serving her purpose," Sash says to break the silence.

"Good for her. She deserves it."

"Two Darknesses have passed since you departed. After each, a man and a woman were chosen for the Ritual of Balance. Two children will be born, one to replace Balt and one to replace the Watcher who died at his hands. Another child is still needed to take the place of Miel."

"You weren't chosen for the Ritual, were you?" I nervously ask.

"I told you before," she says softly. "Hunters are never chosen."

I let out a slow sigh of relief. "Any sign of Balt?"

"None," she replies with a look of disgust on her face. "He'll soon be a Murkovin."

"I want to talk more about Balt. I gave him a lot of thought back in my world, but let's wait until we see the Disciples."

She nods her head, takes her flask from the rope around her waist, and hands it to me. "Drink the sap. You should have all of it."

I drain the contents of her flask, instantly feeling the energy pulse through me, and then hand it back to Sash.

"Sink your fingers into the ground," she instructs, "and whisper what you want most from Krymzyn."

I dig the fingertips of one hand into the dirt below the red blades. "I want to know if I have a purpose in Krymzyn," I whisper.

Sash takes my hand in hers and holds it up for me to see. Golden light sparkles from my palm. In the distance, I hear a single ring of the bell.

"The first bell," Sash says with a smile. "You've finally reached the height of purpose."

I have to smile as well. I honestly think she's learned to make a joke. She swings a leg over me, lays her hands on my shoulders, and kneels on my lap. I slip my hands around her waist. We kiss and then hold each other tight.

"You seem to know what the children's purposes are before they're revealed," I say. "Any idea what mine is?"

As she leans her head back, the smile leaves her face. "With you, it's different. I haven't been shown anything. But I believe the Tree will see what I see inside you."

"What's that?"

"Balance," she answers. "Maybe instead of a third child being born, you'll be the one to return Krymzyn to the number of balance."

"I love you, Sash," I say. "You're the only person who can ever make me feel this way. No matter what happens during my Ritual, I wouldn't trade what I've felt with you for anything."

"I love you, Chase. As long as I live."

Another ring of the bell crosses over the hills. I remember that Tork told me the second bell summons the people of Krymzyn to the Ritual.

"I guess that's for me," I say. "How do the people on the Mount know it's time for a Ritual?"

"They can hear the bell on the Mount."

Her answer doesn't really surprise me. If the atmosphere can translate our languages, I'm sure it can carry sound waves where they need to go.

After another tight embrace, we both stand. We hold hands as we casually stroll to Sanctuary. I estimate that if they run at their top speed, it will take about twenty minutes for the people from the Mount to reach the Delta, so I don't feel the need to rush to the Ritual.

I study Sash's face as we walk, inhaling the beauty in her eyes, face, and scarlet-laced hair. Occasionally, I stop to hold her close to me, feeling the sudden need for her body pressed against mine. She describes amazing places in Krymzyn she wants to show me, and experiences she wants us to share. I try to imagine our lives together in a world so different from mine, but with the person I know I belong with.

We eventually cross over the Telling Hill, walk through the last meadow, and climb to the top of the hill overlooking the Tree of Vision. A few people are already standing on the hilltops, looking down at the crimson field. The dark red limbs of the Tree, a stark contrast to the brilliant yellow leaves, gently sway in a breeze that isn't there. The Disciples stand beside the bell in a semicircle with their backs to us.

After we descend the hill, Sash leads me to the front of the Disciples. My back faces the Tree of Vision, and the bell pole stands at my side. All seven Disciples drop to one knee and bow their heads.

"With gratitude, Chase," Eval says, "we honor you for risking your own life to protect those in the grace of Krymzyn. You'll always be remembered as the one person from another plane who truly understands our balance."

I kneel in front of them. "It's my honor to do what I can for Krymzyn."

"I know that to be true," Eval says as we all stand.

"Someone here told me once," I reply, "that if words are spoken in Krymzyn, they're the truth. I've learned to live by that statement."

For the second time since knowing her, I see a hint of a smile appear on Eval's face—for my benefit—and a look of warm appreciation in her eyes. I glance at Tork, and he nods, knowing my reference.

"Before we start this thing," I say, "I need to tell you something important. I think I know how the Murkovin are getting into the Delta."

"Please share your thoughts," Eval replies.

"When I dove in the river after Sash, I saw a woman with blond hair, webbed fingers, and fins instead of feet."

"A Serquatine!" Eval exclaims.

"She grabbed Sash when I was swimming after her and then she helped us to the surface."

I glance at Sash. She's staring at me in absolute disbelief.

"If you'd come into contact with a Serquatine," Eval says, "she would have ended your life. They consider our blood a great delicacy."

"Well, this one didn't end my life," I tell Eval. "She had rope around her neck, one hand tied behind her back, and her legs were bound together. I untied the rope and freed her. I don't think she could've done it with only one hand and those webbed fingers. After I helped her, she swam us up to the surface, and we made it to the rock."

"That's very strange," Eval remarks.

"I gave it some thought and what I came up with is this. If the Murkovin captured her and tied her up, maybe they used her to cross the river, rode on her, or had her take rope across the bottom or something. Then they could cross the river during Darkness and scale the wall. I think it's safe to assume that Balt was helping them."

"That's an interesting theory," Eval says.

"I also think Balt's trying to kill Sash and using the Murkovin to do it. I think he's organizing them."

"Why do you believe that?" Eval asks.

"He's feels threatened by how powerful Sash is," I answer. "In my world, we have people called _sociopaths_—extremely bad people who don't care at all about other people or society. I think Balt fits that description. When I was here and three Murkovin came into the Delta, they all went straight to where Sash hunts. If they wanted sap, it seems to me they would have gone to a tree closer to the wall. They were here to kill Sash, and I think Balt helped them get inside the Delta."

I look at Tork, Sash, and then at Eval again. They all

have their eyes trained on me, but they're in distant thought. Even as intelligent and intuitive as they are, a premeditated attack on someone here is a concept almost beyond their grasp. The people are pure, honest, and trusting. They battle the Murkovin, but the conflict is on a primal level. There's no hatred involved. They accept the Murkovin as part of their balance. While I'm sure they've heard stories of evil from other planes, the thought of betrayal from one of their own is almost beyond their comprehension.

"When you and I were in the Barrens recently," Sash says to Eval, "I chased after a Murkovin."

"I remember," Eval replies.

"There was a trap waiting for me. I saw a vision and was able to stop before entering it. Balt was in the Barrens with us when it happened. He could have secretly alerted them that I was there."

"He also saw us leaving for the Mount," I say to Sash.

She nods her head. "You're right. He was on the wall when we departed. He could have entered the Barrens after we left and organized the attack. Murkovin don't usually attack so close to the bridge."

"As much as I dislike admitting it's a possibility," Eval says to me, "everything you say makes sense, Chase. We're thankful for your insights."

I smile at Eval. "I hope it helps. I'd check the edge of the river all around the Delta for any signs of where they come out of the water. Maybe there's a rope secured along the rocks that leads to the other side."

"And so we shall," Eval says. "Your help in this matter is yet another first."

"Well, let's hope for one more first. By the way, just out of curiosity, are there seven Serquatine?"

"Seven is correct," Eval answers. "There are four Gateways to the Infinite Expanse. Each Gateway has seven Guardians. The Serquatine protect the northern Gateway."

"Who are the other Guardians?" I ask.

"The Schorachnia to the west, the Reptalients to the east, and the Aerodyne to the south. All of the Guardians are eternal beings, but they're not considered to be among those in the grace of Krymzyn. While they serve an important purpose to our plane, they belong to the Infinite Expanse."

Before I can ask more about the Guardians, I jump from the earsplitting clang of the bell beside me.

Chapter 32

"Why do you stand before us?" Eval asks loudly.

Sash walks to the end of the row of Disciples and stands facing me.

"To seek my purpose in Krymzyn," I answer.

"Do you have the sign?" she asks.

I extend my hands in front of me, revealing the golden glow from my palms.

"Show Krymzyn you've been chosen," Eval commands.

I hold my hands up high over my head and scan the many faces on the hilltops surrounding the meadow. Larn and Tela are standing side by side, exactly where Sash and I stood for Cavu's Ritual. As my eyes roam over the people of Krymzyn, I have to wonder if they'll have any reaction if I'm killed by the Tree. And will they accept me as one of their own if I'm not?

Lowering my hands to my side, I return my attention to Eval, and for the first time, it really strikes me that I might die in a few minutes. The morbid realization floods my mind with sudden fear and doubt.

"Since you're not a child of Krymzyn and have no Keeper," Eval says to me, "Sash will stand in support of you."

Sash steps forward with fierce determination in her eyes. I actually see pride in her gaze, the same way she looked at the children when we watched them play Red Rover in the meadow. The passion in her eyes, the caring I see, calms my nerves, revives my confidence, and reminds me why I've made this choice. But I still know that these may be the last words I ever speak to her.

"Sash, in case something happens," I say, "just know—"

"Believe in yourself," she interrupts, pounding a fist against her chest. "Believe."

The inspiration is so immediate and unexpected that my pulse soars. Does she somehow know the meaning that word has to me from my world? No other word could have as much impact on me as that one does right now. I silently nod to her and then turn to face the Tree.

Giant branches swing wildly through the air. Loud swooshing sounds fill my ears as the limbs pass in front of me. Remembering Cavu's Ritual, I quickly review my plan. I gave it a full week of thought back on Earth, even making diagrams of my path to the trunk.

Walking around the edge of the meadow, I examine the Tree. The branches abruptly rise in the air and hang motionless, leaving a clear path to the trunk. Maybe the Tree will just let me pass. It let Sash go by without challenge, Eval told me. Maybe the Tree will do the same for me. It kind of makes sense, so I jog straight towards the trunk.

Of all the decisions I've made in my life, this is the worst. A limb soars across the meadow straight at me. I duck as the branch sails over my head, just a few leaves scraping the back of my neck. I jerk my head up just in time to watch another limb hammer against my stomach. The blow instantly knocks the wind out of me, and the branch catapults me backwards. I land on my rear twenty feet away, sucking for air, just inches out of the limbs' reach.

When I finally get my breath back, I stand and slowly circle again. The Tree set me up, toyed with me. I need to be more physical.

Hunched low to the ground, I charge at the Tree, dip my shoulder into the first limb that smashes into me, and spin off of it. My face slams directly into another branch lying in wait, spawning a gush of blood from my nose and lips.

Momentarily dazed, I stagger while a third limb swings into my hips. The branch wraps around my midsection, clenches me in a tight grasp, and hurls me through the air. I land on the ground at the base of the hill and roll to a stop. I'm getting the crap beat out of me, and there doesn't appear to be much I can do about it.

I wipe the blood from around my mouth with the back of my hand, stand, and look at the crowd on the hilltops. No one's expression has changed, every face stoic. Their unwavering eyes focus on the meadow. I turn my head to Sash.

"Don't try to do what you've seen," Sash calls out to me, clenching both of her hands into fists. "Only do what's inside you. That's what the Tree wants to see."

"Do what's inside me."

What am I good at? What's inside me? Long-distance running? That's pretty useless right now. Drawing? I don't think sketching a quickie of the Tree will do much to impress it. I guess I notice things others don't, details from an artist's perspective. But what do I feel inside me?

Most of the time, I feel different here. Not around Sash. I feel perfect when I'm with her, as though we're one. But everything about my visits to Krymzyn has been different than those before me—a first for Krymzyn—and Krymzyn knew it would be that way. I have to do something unique, original, something the Tree hasn't seen before. That's what it wants to see inside me.

What do I know about trees? All I've ever done is paint them, sit under them, and climb them when I was a kid. A childhood memory pops into my mind.

My family was on a hike in Franklin Canyon when I was twelve. It was the weekend before the first time I went to Krymzyn. We came across an enormous old oak tree on the side of the trail. A few branches grew outward and fell to the ground. Others extended into the air over our heads. I climbed up to the highest branch and crawled out to the end.

"Don't go so far out on the limb," Mom yelled at me. "You'll break your neck."

"He's fine," Dad said. "He's like a monkey up there."

"Not a monkey," I hollered, hanging from the branch by my hands and legs. "I'm a sloth."

"Well, you better go as slow as a sloth," Mom said. "And do it now."

Casey excitedly barked at me while prancing back and forth underneath the limb. Ally plopped on the ground, shook her head, and rolled her eyes at the entire scene.

I pulled myself back to the trunk hand over hand, foot over foot, hanging upside down by all fours.

When I crossed that branch, I could've gone much faster than I did.

I jump up and down a few times, shake my arms, and slowly walk around the perimeter of the meadow again. Exactly like I'd do before the first stroke of a painting, I scrutinize the branches and angles I'll need. After finally settling on the limb I'll use, I glance at Sash.

She nods encouragement, a knowing, confident look in her eyes. I flash her a quick smile and then sprint towards the trunk.

A giant limb speeds directly towards me. I dive to the grass and slide on my stomach just under the leaves. The branch I want flies down from straight overhead. I roll away from it, crouch as it roars into the ground, and leap onto the limb.

With my arms and legs locked around the bough, I cling to it as it whips back up in the air. When it slows high over the meadow, I nimbly pull myself towards the trunk. Hand over hand and pushing with my feet, I slide as fast as I can. The limb abruptly swoops down, so I firmly clutch it again with my arms and legs around the wood.

After it hits the ground, trying to knock me off, it rises into the air again. Suspended underneath, I pull with my arms and drive with my feet to the feel of burning in my muscles. Another giant branch flies towards me from the side. I hug the limb with all my might and press my face against the bark.

I flex in response to the other branch pounding into me. A bolt of pain shrieks through my body on impact. As soon as the branch pulls away, I ignore the pain and furiously scoot farther along the limb, closer and closer to the trunk.

One last branch slashes at me, but I swing to the ground a split second before it hits. As soon as my bare feet feel the grass beneath them, I launch into a sprint.

With my arms spread wide, I slam into the blazing red trunk. My lips clamp to the bark, and thick sap flows onto my tongue. When I swallow, I'm instantly blinded by pure, perfect light.

*   *   *

I stand in a void of white. Silence encompasses me. I look to my sides, behind me, but all I see is brilliant emptiness. I turn forward again. I stand in front of me.

"Where am I?" I ask.

"The Beginning," I answer.

"The Beginning of what?"

"The Beginning of time and the center of all that exists."

Staring at my own face, I try to comprehend the answer. "Do I have a purpose?" I ask.

"You have to find the answer to that question."

"How do I find the answer?"

"Choose a direction," I reply. "There are seven directions to choose from, but only one will reveal the answer."

"What are the seven directions?"

"If you don't know what they are by now, you don't belong here."

I know the four primary directions in Krymzyn. East, west, north, and south. I look to my left, to my right, and behind me. All I see is static light. I turn to face me again, but I'm gone. I stand alone in the radiant void.

Everything in Krymzyn is in sevens. Seven directions to choose from. What are the other three?

"A new plane of existence rose from the light—the second plane."

I look up. I only see distant light. I look down. I stand on nothing. North, south, east, west, up, down. Six directions. Sash's voice wisps through my mind.

"In Krymzyn, we always look to the inside."

"Your sense of awareness is awakening inside you."

"Only do what's inside you."

I close my eyes and race in the seventh direction.

When I open my eyes, I stand on the black marble wall of Krymzyn looking over the rapids to the west. A Serquatine emerges from the water, the same woman who helped me in the river, a black scar around her neck. Her long blond hair reflects the glow of red and orange from overhead while her emerald green eyes pierce into mine. Her face of pale beauty smiles at me, but it's a sinister smile. She turns to look over her shoulder to the west and then dives under the rapids. I follow the path her eyes took across the colorless Barrens.

Two glowing points of red appear far, far away in the wasteland. Like laser beams traveling through the sky, trails of red streak over my head—the Murkovin eyes looking over me, not at me. The eyes belong to Balt. I feel their hatred boiling in every part of me.

I spin to see where the red streaks lead. My eyes zoom

to the top of the Tall Hill. There, on the grass-lined crest where I first kissed Sash, where I first tasted balance, my Vision of the Future is revealed.

Tears fill my eyes as I gaze upon the hilltop. One single drop falls from my cheek to the marble at my feet. I lower my eyes to a splash of crimson blood glistening against the black stone.

Closing my eyes, I sink to my knees. My palms slide down the sculpted bark of the Tree. With humble devotion, I rest a cheek against the trunk.

"Thank you," I whisper. "I pledge my life in service to Krymzyn."

I stand, grab a handful of hair from the side of my head, and stretch it in front of my eyes. Strands of shimmering blue now define the brown.

Under peaceful branches, I turn away from the trunk and walk towards the Disciples. The seven, and all of Krymzyn, drop to one knee. When I reach the Disciples, I kneel while scanning their faces. At the end of the row, Sash has her head bowed to me and a virtuous smile on her face.

"I'm honored to serve my purpose for the balance of Krymzyn," I proclaim.

Eval stands. "And so it shall be, Chase, Traveler of Krymzyn." Eval turns to the hill behind her, points to the top, and speaks loudly. "Larn will be your Mentor while you're an Apprentice in the ways of your purpose."

"It will be my honor!" Larn shouts down the hill as he stands.

Tela rises beside him. She raises a hand in the air over her head. After I smile at her and lift one of my hands, we both mimic a high five. All of Krymzyn stands when I return to my feet.

"When you next come to Krymzyn," Eval says to me, "if you're certain you'll be here permanently, you'll be given a habitat of your own."

"No!" Sash interrupts in a loud voice filled with unyielding conviction. "He'll share mine, and it will be ours."

If the volume can be turned up on silence, it goes to full blast. Every face in Krymzyn, including Eval's, turns towards Sash. When Sash glances at me, I nod my agreement to her. She returns her attention to the Disciples.

"Chase hasn't had the benefit of living at Home with the Keepers," Sash says, "or learning the ways of Krymzyn from them. Due to his maturity, he wouldn't be comfortable living with the children. Alone, he'll lack the education he needs to properly understand the ways of our plane. While Larn can Mentor him as a Traveler, there's more to understanding Krymzyn than just fulfilling one's purpose. I've been his guide throughout his journey here, so I should continue to be that for him."

Eval takes a step forward speaks to Sash in a deadly serious tone. "You understand that Chase must adhere to the customs of our world if he's to dwell here, do you not?"

Focusing intently on Eval, Sash replies with what can only be described as a commanding voice. "He's proven his loyalty to Krymzyn at the risk of his life. On his plane, it's customary for people to dwell together and necessary for their balance. We should welcome him with the same loyalty to his needs as he's shown for protecting ours."

After a moment of silent communication, Eval nods to

Sash and then turns to me.

"Chase, is this an acceptable arrangement to you?" Eval asks.

"I understand Krymzyn through Sash," I say. "And she's right. There's still a lot more I need to learn. The better I understand Krymzyn, the better I can fulfill my purpose. But my balance here comes from being with Sash."

Eval's face softens with understanding. "While not customary on our plane to dwell with another, I do recognize the benefit to you."

"Thank you," I say, bowing my head to her.

I begin to shake, feel dizzy, and collapse to my knees. When I look up at Sash, she crosses her hands over chest and embraces me in her eyes.

"Sash," I call out to her, "when I return, I won't ever leave again."

Chapter 33

Ally left on Saturday afternoon, both of us maintaining brave faces as we said good-bye. I felt like my guts were being ripped out of me, knowing this was probably the last time I'd ever see her. I promised to call her after I told Mom and Dad about the surgery. She wanted to schedule a flight home to be with me during a procedure that would never happen. The truth was, I wasn't going to my surgery on Monday, and I would never say a word to my parents.

After Mom, Dad, and I spent a quiet evening together, I stayed up almost all night making a few important revisions to the painting for them. Casey kept me company in my studio, although he snored most of the night. Early Sunday morning, I took him for the last walk we'd ever share together.

Back at our house, I covered the framed canvas with a sheet before loading it into my car. I had to spend thirty minutes alone in my room to muster enough courage for the most difficult moment of my life. When I said good-bye to my parents, I struggled to avoid a breakdown in front of them.

Even though I wasn't supposed to drive, I'd taken my

care to my parents' house so they wouldn't suspect anything. Severe headaches rarely came in the morning, which is why I'd chosen early Sunday to drive back to my apartment. I made it about a block before I had to pull over, but not from fear of a seizure. I couldn't see because of the tears that filled my eyes. Maybe how Davis had left was better—not having to say good-bye, not knowing that, when he fell asleep one night, he'd seen his family for the last time.

I'd given almost two weeks of thought to what Davis's family had gone through during the months and months of his fight, the toll it had taken on them. My family had been through enough. A sudden shock would be easier for them to recover from than months, or even years, of prolonged agony.

I spent Sunday afternoon adding the most recent events in Krymzyn to my journals. When evening came, it took me a while to gather the strength for the last phone call I had to make. Connor had been working long hours in production on a documentary. He'd only had time to stop by my family's house once during the prior week. I'd invited him to go to the beach with us, but he hadn't been able to get out of work that day. When I felt like my emotions were reined in, I dialed Connor's number.

"Hey, Chase. What's going on?" he answered.

"Not much," I said. "Are you finally getting a break?"

"Yeah, I am. We're done with the shoot for now. I'm sorry I couldn't spend more time with you guys last week."

"No problem. I know what it's like, but we were all glad you stopped by."

"Ally looked great!" he exclaimed. "I really enjoyed

seeing her."

I paused for several seconds, momentarily confused by the tone of his voice. It instantly made me forget about the real purpose of this call.

"You have a thing for my sister," I finally said.

"I don't know," he replied. "She's really cute, Chase. I mean, she's grown up now, and she's always been smart. We're into a lot of the same things and . . . I just feel good when I'm around her."

I didn't really hear the individual words, but I understood their meaning. "You have a thing for my sister," I absentmindedly repeated.

A feeling of warm comfort spread through me as I tried to digest my own words. Connor was the most honorable, loyal, and respectful guy I'd ever known. He would never do anything to hurt Ally. Connor broke the silence.

"Look, if it makes you uncomfortable, or you're not cool with it, I'll just—"

"No!" I interrupted loudly. "I think it's awesome."

"Thanks, Chase. I've been wanting to talk to you about it. She and I have been texting for a while. Maybe we can hook up for a beer one night this week and talk more about it."

The reality of the phone call hit me again. I clenched my jaw, took a deep breath, and tried to speak in a normal voice.

"I'm really crazed at work the next few days," I lied, "but later in the week should work."

"Perfect," he said.

"Listen, in a couple of days, I'm going to send you a picture of a painting I did and something I want to you read."

"What is it?" Connor asked.

"Just something I've been working on for a while, but it's important to me. More important than anything I've ever done."

"I'll look at it the second you send it."

"Connor, I want to tell you something." I had to pause again and use everything inside me to say the words without my voice betraying me. "No matter what, you always stood by me. I want you to know that always I knew that. You're the best friend anyone ever had."

A few seconds of silence passed before he spoke. "What's going on Chase?" he asked.

"Nothing bad. I promise. I was just thinking about old times last week, being at home and all, and wanted to tell you that."

"Are you sure everything's okay?"

"Absolutely," I said. "I just don't think I ever told you how much it meant to me that you were always there for me."

"It goes both ways," he replied.

I had to end the phone call. My voice was starting to get hoarse, and I didn't know how much longer I could suppress the swelling in my throat and chest.

"I have a lot of work to finish for tomorrow," I said quietly. "Love you."

"Love you too, Chase," he said. "Are you sure everything's cool?"

"Couldn't be better. I'll see you later this week, and keep your eyes open for an e-mail from me."

"You got it."

"Connor, I'm really happy about you and Ally. I hope it works out."

"Thanks, Chase. That means everything to me."

"Take care," I said.

"You too."

After we hung up, it took a few minutes before the numbness subsided enough for me to move. I scheduled an e-mail to automatically send to him two days from that night. I attached a digital photo of the painting I'd made for my family and a copy of my journals. I typed one word in the body of the e-mail.

"Believe."

*   *   *

An hour later, when I looked at the painting for my family one last time, I was again amazed at how closely my Vision of the Future had matched what I'd already put on the canvas. I didn't know if it was coincidence, serendipity, or fate. The painting I'd shown Ally had depicted Sash and me standing on the Tall Hill, holding hands. Each of us had held a spear in our other hand.

In my revisions, I'd had to remove the spears. To my side, I'd added a beautiful little girl, her hand tightly grasped in mine. She looked exactly how I'd imagined Sash would've looked at the age of six or seven, with brilliant black waves flowing over the shoulders of her lean frame.

I'd also added a little boy standing beside Sash with his

hand in hers. He looked remarkably like I did when I was five—if my hair had been black. Both of the children, as I'd seen in my Vision of the Future, had blue eyes the exact same shade as mine. I guessed that boys looking exactly like their fathers and girls looking like their mothers just ran in my family's blood.

I stored my journals on a flash drive for my family to read and put it inside an envelope with a note that simply read: "Please read the manuscript carefully. I love you." I guess you could say it was my farewell suicide note—for my life on Earth, anyway.

My hope was that after Mom, Dad, Ally, and Connor had read everything I'd written over the years, combined with the conversation I'd had with Ally, they'd realize that everything that had happened to me in Krymzyn since I was twelve had been real. The same amber light had shown up the second time I'd recorded my seizure, so they'd see those videos as well.

When they sensed the realism in my painting for them, the passion I'd put into it, and the unconditional love displayed in the eyes of Sash, me, and our children, that's the moment I hoped it would sink in for them. That's the moment I hoped they'd know as an absolute truth, hoped they'd feel deep inside exactly what I'd known and felt when I'd sat with Sash watching the children of Krymzyn play a game of Red Rover.

In Krymzyn, I'd be alive in a way I could never have been in this world. I'd be free of cancer and tumors and pain. But I'd be more than just alive, because I'd be happy, healthy, and fulfilling my purpose in life. And more than anything else, I'd be completely, totally, and perfectly in love with the only woman I'd ever belonged with. I'd found my balance in Krymzyn.

The amber rays weren't my only discovery from the recordings of my seizures. I'd learned that they always lasted exactly seven seconds on Earth. From amber burst to amber burst, exactly seven seconds. Imagine that.

I'd also discovered that, every time a seizure started, immediately after the light in my eyes showed up, my hands jerked away from my body with tremendous force. Certainly enough force to pull a trigger after I was already taken to Krymzyn.

A dull headache had started after the phone call with Connor. The pain gradually grew as the evening wore on. Everything was already in place for what I'd have to do, so I sat at my desk and waited. When my next seizure started, my life here would end. But in that world, an infinite plane of existence called Krymzyn, my new life would begin.

Chapter 34

The young woman with scarlet in her hair sits alone on the Empty Hill. Her spear rests by her side on the ground, a sap-filled pitcher in her hands. She stares at the motionless sustaining tree in the meadow below her.

A woman, the tallest of the Disciples, strolls from the north into the meadow. Following a long talk with the children, telling them wondrous stories of other planes, she's returning to Sanctuary. The Disciple sees the young woman, walks almost to the crest of the Empty Hill, and stops in front of where the young woman sits.

"You wait for him," the Disciple says.

"He'll need sap when he arrives," the young woman tells the Disciple, her eyes never leaving the tree.

"Why?" the Disciple asks.

"I was shown his arrival in a dream," the young woman answers. "He'll be injured from what he must do in his world to stay here."

"Any physical injuries from his world shouldn't travel with him."

The young woman looks up at the Disciple. "They will this time. His spectrum will still be in transition when the damage occurs, partially in both planes."

The Disciple nods her understanding. "Your Vision of the Future came to pass in the river. Do the events all make sense to you now?"

"They do," the young woman says. "Thank you for your insights in the past."

"If you had known the eventual outcome of the events on the rock, that knowledge may have influenced your decision to stay close to him. As it turned out, the feelings you share with him evolved despite believing he would be with you at your death. Nothing could be more genuine than what you feel for him."

"I understand that now," the young woman says.

"I never doubted he would have a purpose here. He stood up to face every challenge Krymzyn put in front of him. Instead of turning away in fear, he embraced the opportunity. The two of you truly belong together."

"We do belong together," the young woman says, "because we want to be together, not because we should be or have to be. We _love_ each other, to use the word from his plane."

"It must be strange to feel so much for one person, in addition to the whole," the Disciple comments.

"It doesn't lessen our dedication to Krymzyn," the young woman says. "I believe we're both stronger because of our _love_."

"I believe so as well. He's a very strong young man in many ways, intelligent, resourceful, and loyal. The Tree of Vision saw that in him."

"I saw a strange vision during his Ritual," the young

woman says, "when the Tree took his mind to the future."

"Do you want to share with me what you saw?" the Disciple asks.

The young woman looks directly into Disciple's eyes. "When the light surrounded him, instead of his body, I saw myself kneeling at the Tree. My face looked as I did when I reached the height of purpose. My own image turned to me, but my eyes were blue. The same color as his."

"How do you interpret the vision?" the Disciple asks.

"I'm not sure. Maybe it means that we should both feel as though we're one now, which we do. I'm confused by it."

The Disciple glances around the empty meadow and hills, steps to the top of the hill, and sits beside the young woman.

"Before my Ritual of Purpose," the Disciple says with a thoughtful expression, "I hoped blue would be revealed in my hair, just as it was revealed in his hair. I know it's wrong for a child to hope for one color over another, but I wanted to be a Traveler of Krymzyn."

"Why did you want that?" the young woman asks.

"I wanted to feel my light crossing our plane as only the Travelers can. I wanted to travel south to the Great Falls, north to the Springs where the Serquatine dwell, to the west to stand at the edge of the Eternal Canyon, and to the Desert east of the Mount. I wanted to travel through the Infinite Expanse to see it stretch out in front of me."

"Your wisdom as a Disciple is unsurpassed," the young woman remarks. "All in Krymzyn appreciate and honor your service."

"Don't misunderstand me. I'm honored to serve as a

Disciple. In retrospect, I was wrong to hope for anything else."

"I feel privileged to live during your Era," the young woman replies.

"And I," the Disciple says, gazing deeply into the young woman's eyes, "to witness the exceptional person you are and the events in your life. I know you never fully understood your Vision of the Future until it came to pass. Only recently have I understood mine. I believe I'm meant to share with you what I was shown in my Vision."

"Why would you tell me of your Vision?"

"So you understand what you saw at his Ritual of Purpose. Your Vision of the Future weighed on your mind since your own Ritual. You've lived a brave, selfless life with the image of your death constantly in your eyes. I believe you deserve peace as you move forward with your life, and now that I understand my own Vision, I can give that to you.

"In my Vision," the Disciple continues, "I was shown several events that have never occurred in Krymzyn. I saw a female Hunter holding a little girl in her arms. The Hunter had been chosen for the Ritual of Balance and given birth to that child. The Hunter was you, and the girl in your arms looked exactly as you did when you were a small child. I have such vivid memories of the way your face looked.

"But the girl you were holding had blue eyes passed on from the man who will be chosen to join you in the Ritual of Balance. Your relationship with that child will be different than any other in Krymzyn. As she grows, she'll know you're the woman who gave birth to her. I believe what you saw during his Ritual was a glimpse of her."

A serene, peaceful smile slowly spreads across the young woman's face. "Thank you," she says warmly to the Disciple. "What I saw makes sense now."

The Disciple stands and looks down at the young woman. "Do you know if he'll arrive soon?"

"The next time I sleep, he'll be beside me," the young woman answers.

"The two of you should spend some time alone together before he begins his journey here. He may find his transition into our world and leaving his own difficult at first. When you're both ready, he can begin his Apprenticeship."

"Thank you," the young woman says with deep appreciation in her eyes.

The Disciple walks down the hill towards Sanctuary. As the young woman watches the Disciple, she tightens her grasp on the steel pitcher in her hands, curls her bare toes in the crimson blades of grass, and slowly inhales a long, deep breath.

"Were you ever chosen for the Ritual of Balance?" the young woman calls out to the Disciple.

The Disciple stops walking. Another decisive moment is before her, a break with ways that have existed in Krymzyn since the beginning of time. She turns to face the young woman.

"I was chosen for the Ritual once. I was later in life than when most are chosen."

"Before I was born?"

"Yes," the Disciple answers. "Before you were born."

"But after the child born before me?" the young woman asks, already knowing the answer.

"I should say no more," the Disciple replies. "You and I seem to often break with our ways, and change must come slowly."

"Changing our ways," the young woman says, "appears to be in our blood."

"I believe you're correct," the Disciple agrees. "Change is in our blood. But I warn you. Turmoil can often accompany change."

The young woman glances off to her side and then returns her eyes to the Disciple. "Turmoil is coming."

"Have you seen a vision?"

"No," the young woman answers. "As much as anything I've ever felt, I feel it inside me."

The Disciple nods her head. "Based on recent events, I'm afraid that I must agree with you. I trust you'll be ready to do what's needed."

The young woman clenches her jaw. "My spear is always at the ready. Spilling the blood of our enemies is part of who I am."

"Although I would prefer that wasn't your path," the Disciple says, "I know that to be true. For now, enjoy peace while you can."

Author's Note

The author and publisher of this fictional work do not condone suicide. If you ever have thoughts of suicide for any reason, please seek qualified counseling.

The Journals of Krymzyn

Krymzyn

The Infinite Expanse

A Traveler's Fate

Barrens Rising (Publication Date TBA)

The War of Origin (Publication Date TBA)

The 8th Purpose (Publication Date TBA)

Light of Krymyzn (Publication Date TBA)